DESERT GOLD

DESERT GOLD

E. ROY HECTOR

iUniverse LLC
Bloomington

Desert Gold

This is a work of fiction. All of the characters, names, incidents, organizations, and dialogue in this novel are either the products of the author's imagination or are used fictitiously.

iUniverse books may be ordered through booksellers or by contacting:

iUniverse LLC
1663 Liberty Drive
Bloomington, IN 47403
www.iuniverse.com
1-800-Authors (1-800-288-4677)

Because of the dynamic nature of the Internet, any web addresses or links contained in this book may have changed since publication and may no longer be valid. The views expressed in this work are solely those of the author and do not necessarily reflect the views of the publisher, and the publisher hereby disclaims any responsibility for them.

Any people depicted in stock imagery provided by Thinkstock are models, and such images are being used for illustrative purposes only.
Certain stock imagery © Thinkstock.

ISBN: 978-1-4917-0618-3 (sc)
ISBN: 978-1-4917-0620-6 (hc)
ISBN: 978-1-4917-0619-0 (ebk)

Library of Congress Control Number: 2013916521

Printed in the United States of America

iUniverse rev. date: 09/06/2013

Other titles by E. Roy Hector

Escape from Hell's Corner

Gangs of bloodthirsty and ruthless outlaws terrorized the American Southwest before and after Mexico ceded the land now called Texas. One such pack of thirty or forty cutthroats had what they thought was a perfectly impregnable hideout until a trio of U.S. Marshals was given the mission of bringing them to justice. These marshals were no barroom toughs they'd been brought up church-going citizens, and all three had been schooled in the art of self-defense and survival. The outlaw leader made a fatal mistake when he ordered his killers to kidnap a rancher's beautiful daughter.

Return to Hell's Corner

In the exciting, fast-paced western adventure sequel to *Escape from Hell's Corner*, crazed killer Amos Clarke (aka Amos Watson) will stop at nothing to avenge the death of his outlaw father. Set in the picturesque Texas Mountains, *Return to Hell's Corner* combines danger, romance, bravery, and good old-fashioned western justice to provide an exhilarating ride through the lawless wasteland of the Old West.

Vengeance Was Hers

When outlaw Chet Brode rapes, tortures, and nearly murders *Susan "Sue" Boatwright*, the daughter of a rancher in southwest Texas, the peace-loving and law-abiding citizens of Deadman Falls suddenly realize the stark reality of the harsh land they call home. But none realizes this cruel reality more than Sue: she survives the degrading abuse and mental anguish inflicted by the rapist and his attempt to murder her. She vows to avenge the crime against her body. At times, she thinks the devil himself is driving her down a path of self-destruction. Yet she stays on the trail, determined to one-day track down her tormentor and bring him to justice one day.

"This is a well-told, exciting and fast-moving story of how the strong-willed settlers in our Southwest disregarded warnings of lawlessness because of an unquenchable thirst for land they could call their own.

Undeterred by reports of outlaws, violence, and hardship, many died. "Vengeance Was Hers" tells how some survived." The Oklahoman

Brazos River Marauders

Colt Horn was born on a pioneer trail to Scottish parents seeking new land they could call their own. But at the age of fifteen, he finds his parents murdered and is set adrift on a dangerous mission of vengeance. He grows to manhood surviving battles, hardships, and struggles, eventually becoming the owner of a large ranch. When he meets Liz Hanes, he wants to marry her and settle down. Nevertheless, none of his dreams can be realized until his parents' murderers are brought to justice.

Colt learns that the man who'd killed his parents and is now leader of the Brazos River Marauders wants him, dead or alive, and has posted a large bounty on his head. The attacks on neighboring ranches and on his life provoke him to leave his ranch and work full-time in an effort to eliminate the lawlessness in his valley. He will, at last, bring the leader of the Brazos River Marauders to justice or die trying. Plenty of action brings the Old West to life in this tale filled with cowboys, love, revenge, and ultimate redemption.

Range Fury

Known for his tenacity in pursuing lawbreakers, U.S. Marshal Frank Marlin follows a dangerous mission to quell a brewing range war on the western frontier. He's told that Cottonwood Valley, a rich fertile land in the State of Texas, is the target of the trouble. The valley's large-ranch owners blame each other for the cattle rustling, ambush killings, and other acts of lawlessness. They threaten to wipe each other out; fury on the range seems unavoidable. During his mission, Marlin learns that a wily outlaw boss, who strikes ranches and towns from his hideouts in the badlands, perpetrates the trouble in Cottonwood Valley. When the outlaw boss hears Marlin is on his way, he offers his henchmen a large cash bounty to anyone who kills the feared marshal. Marlin must always be on the lookout for those who want him dead. Encountering life-threatening situations and suffering serious wounds, Marlin never loses sight of his intense desire to stop the killing and cattle rustling.

CONTENTS

PROLOGUE

The quest of the brave and adventurous pioneers who settled America's Western lands was not much different, if at all, from that of early humankind. The Bible tells of Eve eating fruit from the forbidden tree. Was that the beginning of mankind's insatiable need to seek adventure, with its rewards and sins, to explore the unknown reaches of human life and the wonders of the universe?

Throughout the ages, humankind has sought to experience the unknown and discover new environs. That unrestrained and boundless spirit lives on today. And in the Old West, some sought wealth; adventure, virgin fertile lands, excitement, love, and greener pastures over the next mountain. Those courageous men and women who settled the western frontiers were driven in large part by their burning desire to experience the unknown and to release suppressed curiosity as they sought new beginnings. Among the frontier settlers were poor, rich, old, young; believer and nonbeliever, God fearing, secular, law abiding and lawless representing almost every human race. They came by foot, horseback, and covered wagons drawn by oxen, mules, or horses.

Contrary to popular belief, frontier settlements were not tamed by a lone hero going from one confrontation to another beating the bad guys to the draw, and riding off into the sunset with the beautiful maiden. Nor was the settlers' dialogue limited to such utterances as *'What's ya'll gonna do with them there ropes?'* In fact, most settlers spoke plain whole words and phrases prevalent throughout the country at that time.

This novel chronicles a search for stolen government gold and the lawlessness that reigned in part of the Southwest as the frontier crept ever-westward toward the Pacific Ocean. In those early years settlers had to provide their own protection from outlaw gangs that attacked farms, ranches, and towns. Marauders were ruthless and did not value human life—except, perhaps their own. In parts of the frontier anarchy prevailed; outlaws roamed unchallenged until law and order finally reached the isolated areas with the help of the brave citizenry. These pioneers never thought of themselves as heroes, although their lives often depended on undaunted courage and firearms skills. An outlaw dying from bullet wounds stashed eighty thousand dollars in gold coins, in the desert wanting to make amends for his lawlessness. Knowing that he was dying, he double-crossed his murderous gang leader and absconded with the stolen gold. Then he died after writing a letter giving his brother, a U.S. Marshal, clues as to where to find the gold, pleading forgiveness and beseeching him to return, the gold to the government.

U.S. Marshal Tom Leach, the outlaw's brother, tries to unravel the confusing, painful, and quickly—concocted clues that shielded the desert hiding place of the gold. He soon discovers that murderer Quirt Evans and his bloodthirsty gang wants to kill him and find the stolen gold. During all the ensuing battles, he never loses his desire for a peaceful life; yet his sense of duty and responsibility creates a weighty confliction that's difficult to resolve. To quell the anarchy and return the gold to the government, Tom Leach needed the help of brave lawmen and honest citizens. He even accepted help from an outlaw who wanted to end his life of crime and walk on the side of the law. Tom Leach's bullet scarred body was a stark reminder that the mission ahead was live or die. He chose to live. Imposing law and order on the frontier would be costly, but he was willing to face the odds to quell the lawlessness and bring peace and tranquility to the frontier.

CHAPTER 1

OUTLAW GANG

The outlaw boss signaled a halt. His gang members reined their mounts in close to his; they were surprised at the sudden stop as the posse was closing in fast. He rarely stopped in such situations except to change plans or to vent his wrath on one or more of the unsuspecting outlaws. The gang had learned to close in around him in such situations. The boss disliked speaking in a loud voice as he was still bothered by an old bullet wound to his throat. The gang members waited patiently for the boss to speak; he took his time, then he removed his sombrero, wiped his brow, scowled, and stared back down the trail. The outlaws were anxious to put more distance between them and the posse, but none dared to question why he called the halt. Most of them feared the boss more than they feared the posse.

His animal like steel gray eyes and prominent nose, with flared nostrils, had struck stark fear in many victims. His long unkempt coal-black hair fell almost to his broad shoulders, his barrel chest and muscular arms suggested strength while his scarred face, covered with a scraggly beard, told of the many scrapes and fights he survived on his climb to his present unchallenged status of gang leader. He seldom smiled, and then when he attempted to his rotten and blackened teeth were bared and it was more a snarl than a smile. His followers knew that he did not value life except perhaps his own.

They had witnessed him shoot and kill other members of his gang for questioning his orders or failing to meet his expectations. He possessed a hair-trigger finger and temper. They knew he was fearless and would fight as long as he could draw air into his lungs. He did his own dirty work, never asked anyone to use the blacksnake or do the killings. He seemed to enjoy inflicting pain and destroying those he considered his enemies. Evans often defined 'enemies' as pilgrims that need killing. Most of those who rode with him secretly hated him; but they stayed on because they shunned work and wanted excitement, money, whiskey, and women that Quirt provided.

His reputation as a ruthless killer was known throughout the Southwest and as far north as the Indian Territory. The name *Quirt Evans* struck fear in the hearts of ranchers, settlers and other law abiding citizens. They lived under constant worry of the Evans gang. Some had arranged to stand twenty-four hour guard shifts to protect their families and property.

Outlaws following the Owl Hoot Trail vied to join his killer gang. He and his gang were infamously recognized as the greatest threat to peace and tranquility in the settlements. Evans picked his targets carefully, raiding the weakest with the greatest promise of loot and women to abuse. Leaving death and destruction behind was his trademark.

Now on the run, Quirt and his cutthroat gang had robbed a train up near Fort Worth and had since struggled to stay ahead of a large posse of lawmen. The outlaw's horses were blowing hard from the long arduous hours on the run in the hot sand. The chase had started several days before and the posse was relentless in its pursuit. Neither the gang nor the posse had much chance to rest. They were all exhausted. The outlaws wanted to cross the Rio Grande before the posse caught up with them. Quirt and the gang used Mexico as their safe haven.

Evans shifted his weight to one side of his saddle, staring hard at one of the outlaws, who had gunshots wounds on his left shoulder and lower right arm. Blood oozed from his shoulder. Evans spoke quietly, "Jake, you'll not make the border, and you know it. Your only chance to get well is to hole up and wait for me to return in a week. Look around, do you recognize where we are?" Jake Leach slowly raised his chin and looked around at the rising hills and mountain tops to the west. The great loss of blood was sapping his strength and will power.

Jake, a handsome fellow with cropped blond hair and blues eyes that had attracted the attention of many females was aware that Quirt Evans and most of the other outlaws resented him; but they did not dare draw on him. He had earned his reputation as a lightning fast gunslinger during battles which discouraged challenges. On the trail he chose to bring up the rear to avoid a bullet in his back. At the moment death did not seem too bad a choice. He once again, struggled to answer Evans' question. His vision was still blurred. He closed his eyes a couple of times trying to focus on Quirt. Then he managed to speak in a weak voice, "Quirt, we seem to be close to Bat Cave. Why stop now?" A question like that could get him killed. The gang waited.

Quirt Evans did not reply right away; he tried to control his temper as he had made a decision. He wanted all the gold for himself. He'd use wounded Jake Leach to make sure the gold was not divided among the gang. Jake Leach had not been with him as long as the others, but he was convinced that Jake would do as he was told. He'd be no good dead.

He replied in a half friendly tone, "Jake you can't make it unless you stop bleeding. You'll die on the trail if you don't take care of yourself."

Jake asked, "What do you want to do, stand and fight the posse?"

Quirt's temper flared again, yet he managed to say, "No, that's not to our advantage. I'm going to trust you; the penalty for disappointing me is death. We'll not make the river with the gold and you bleeding to death. The only way is for you to take the gold and hide it in the cave. The posse is getting too damn close."

The other outlaws waited restlessly, not believing what they were hearing, but too fearful to object to Quirt's plan. They wanted their share of the gold and disliked Quirt's plan.

Quirt continued, "Our only chance to escape the posse is to split up and go in different directions to the border. We'll lose too much time if we stop now to divide the gold. The posse will catch us for sure."

Jake tried not to show his pain. He said, "I don't understand how this is going to work."

The outlaw leader stared at Jake and said sharply, "It will work as I've planned. You will take the gold and hide it in the cave; wait there for me to return. Then we'll take the gold to Mexico and divide it with the gang."

Jake looked around at the hostile faces and through his dim vision asked, "Is this what the others here want?" Jake didn't care at this point if Quirt shot him. It would be a relief from his pain. Waiting for a bullet he braced his weak body.

Quirt Evans surprised all of them and smiled. He said, "Jake, I know how you got those bullet holes. You lagged behind, giving us a chance to get away. I still don't know how you got in the saddle shot up like that. Everyone trusts you and agree this is our only chance to save you and the gold." Quirt acted real friendly toward the wounded outlaw.

He paused and stared at the other outlaws. A couple of them didn't flinch. They stared back while others looked down or out to the Southwest. None wanted to die here in the desert.

Quirt continued, "Jake, we've wasted too much time talking. To save time we'll take your horse, and you get on the packhorse and take the gold to Bat Cave; it's just over that ridge to the west. You can make it. When you get to the cave, dig a hole, and bury the gold. I know you can make it, tend your wounds, and stop the bleeding." Then Quirt looked at the outlaw next to Jake and ordered, "Help him with the saddle and gear."

Jake slowly dismounted and watched while the outlaw removed his bedroll and saddle bags and placed them on the packhorse. Then the fellow without comment helped Jake mount. He was in so much pain that he barely heard Quirt when he continued, "I'll be back with one of these no-goods when we get the posse off our tails. As I said, it may be a while. We'll give you food and there's water close to the cave. Stay right there while, the boy's give you whatever they have to eat and then pad the feet of the packhorse. I don't want the posse trackers to notice that one of our horses left the trail. They will think we stopped to rest our mounts."

Quirt then looked around at the group and said in a gruff voice, "Well you heard me, get at it. Time is a wasting. I can feel that damn posse breathing down my collar." Less than three minutes later, the gang continued toward the border.

Jake Leach watched Quirt and the others until they went over a small hill and then he urged the packhorse toward the cool cave where he was told to bury the gold. As he rode toward the cave, his pain increased and he began to think he should not go to the cave; if he waited in the cave he could die before Quirt returned, and who would probably kill him on sight. That did not seem to be a good choice. No, he had to find help. Then his mind turned to years on the Owl Hoot Trail. He had made many mistakes in his life and now facing what he thought was sure death he felt remorse. He began to worry about the hereafter; he had realized for the last several years that he was living a godless life, but never felt a need to change his ways.

His life of crime had started when he left home; but now that he could see the dark side, it scared him. His troubled mind wondered why he had not thought more about all his crimes and misdeeds before now. He reasoned that since hitting the Owl Hoot Trail he had been on the run and never took the time to reflect much on his childhood, his family, nor the reasons for his life of crime. He stared out to the distant horizon and decided it was time to make amends for his crimes.

He had watched other wounded outlaws try to justify their crimes at the last moment and he had joined in poking fun and scoffing at their fears of dying. Now he thought of his only living relative that he had wrongly blamed for being forced to leave home.

He continued to meander along, still thinking about his past and remembered when he learned that his brother Tom had joined the U.S. Marshal Service he was proud of him. On hearing that Tom was a Marshal, he fervently hoped Tom would never have to face him in a final showdown. His present condition reminded him that such a meeting was highly unlikely. But had it ever happened he knew Tom would have acted to defend the law; he could never draw on Tom, he'd rather take a fatal bullet. Since Tom had joined the Marshals Service, Jake had tried to stay out of Tom's territory, sometimes playing sick and saying he was unable to ride when he knew that Quirt intended to pull off raids that might be in Tom's territory. But he'd never changed his name, as he was still proud of his family.

He could not shake the idea that it was time to do something to show Tom he was not all bad. He had to let Tom know that he was sorry that he had tarnished the reputation of the Leach family. Although he had not seen Tom in years, he felt sure he would still consider him his brother. He rode on undecided how to find help and contact Tom.

Jake had yet another reason for wanting to change his ways; he had known that the outlaw leader had planned to double-cross his gang. Jake had quietly carried the knowledge that Quirt was planning to take all the money and go to Portugal with a woman named Silvia One night last month, she came to Jake's room drunk as Quirt had decided he needed a change of female companionship and had gone to the Cantina. She was in a rage and knew he was looking for another girl. She also knew he would not be back before sunrise. She was very talkative and threatened not to go with him to Portugal. Jake was smart enough to hold his tongue and not comment. He helped her back to her room, hoping that she would not remember saying anything about going to Portugal. Before he closed her door, she was sprawled on top of the sheets, legs spread, snoring.

Jake remembered that Quirt was planning to cheat him and all the other outlaws of their fair share of the gold. It made him angry and regretted not telling the other gang members of Quirt's intention to cheat them. He had already decided that if Quirt found him alive at the cave, he'd take the gold and kill him immediately.

Then his mind flashed back to the train robbery; he recalled that the guard on the train told Quirt that there was more than eighty thousand dollars of government gold coins in the safe. That was seconds before Quirt shot the guard between his eyes. Well to hell with him, Quirt would not find this eighty thousand. Jake looked at his back trail searching for signs of the posse. He was now on the west side of the hill and decided to find a place where he could see the posse if it passed the spot where Quirt had called a halt. He noticed that since he had not been riding so fast, his bleeding had stopped, but the pain had increased. He took a small sip of water. His senses seemed to be clearing up.

He could not shake the vision of Tom, his older brother. Jake again felt that his time on this good earth was severely limited. Now he did not really think that getting medical help would save him, but he grasped at the hope it would. He suddenly decided he must live to get word to his brother Tom about the gold and try to set the record straight. Now was the only time he might have to do something that would relieve his deep sense of guilt. He reasoned that he had not been pushed into a life of crime. He said to himself, *'hell, it's all my own doing; I've always had a wild streak; but I'm finished with the Owl Hoot Trail. If the good Lord lets me live, I'll go west and work with the settlers.'* It then flashed through his mind, that it might be too late to go west or make amends with Tom. He decided, live or die, he had to get a letter to Tom. He was now desperate.

He remembered that horrible morning when he arrived home to face his pa after several days of drunkenness. He had spent the twenty-one dollars that he took from the fruit jar his family kept to get thorough unexpected hardships. He knew at the time it was wrong and that his pa had worked hard to put away a few dollars that not even he would touch unless someone's life depended on spending it. His pa met him in the yard and ordered him to leave and never come back. Tom had tried to talk his pa into letting him stay. But Jake could see the controlled rage his pa carried and knew then that he had to leave.

In the beginning, on the Owl Hoot Trail, he had tried to justify taking the family money, but he always came back to the realization that it was pure selfishness and lack of love and respect for his family. Then after awhile and a few gunfights, the feeling of deep guilt disappeared. He began to enjoy riding the Owl Hoot Trail with rustlers and other bad hombres and having enough money to enjoy being with the saloon girls.

Jake wanted to conserve his strength so that he could improve his chances of making it to Tincup. He found a clump of mesquite bushes where he could see the posse if it showed up. He then tried again to stop the bleeding by using dirt to cover the wound that was bleeding the most. It helped somewhat. Jake decided to write a letter to Tom and tell him about the gold. He searched his saddle bags and found a stub-pencil and some wrinkled paper. He settled down in the partial shade of the small bushes to rest. Jake then painfully started the letter to Tom.

A little while later he was roused from a short nap by one of those miracles that appear in the deserts; a thunder and lightning storm was forming right over the area. The rain fell in great drops and brought a cool wind that helped to revive his strength and will power. Jake scrambled to protect the letter he had started to Tom. He swiftly placed it in his leather saddle bag. The cool rain made him feel much better.

He was about to start out again when he saw the posse. The riders were going slow and did not seem to even look at the ground where the gang had stopped briefly. Riding with their heads covered with slickers trying to avoid the rain, they were not looking for tracks, but going in the direction they thought the outlaws had taken. As they passed, he waited several minutes to make sure there were no stragglers and then he crawled most of the way back to his horse tied to small cactus. It seemed the storm was gone in minutes, leaving the steaming sand and the searing heat from the returning sun. He was careful not to do anything that might cause his wounds to start bleeding again.

During the wait for the posse to pass, among other mixed thoughts, his mind continued to search for a way to make sure his letter reached Tom. He decided his only chance was to make it to Tincup and mail his letter. He was not sure where to send the letter, as all he knew was from a fragment of a newspaper that had a story about Tom. The Abilene Newspaper had high praise for the brave and fearless actions of Marshal Tom Leach. The article allowed that only a dedicated lawman could breakup the outlaw gangs and bring the killers to justice. They said Laredo citizens could walk the streets and sleep better at night because of the Marshal's bravery. A letter would be his only hope of telling Tom where to find the gold.

Well, Pa would have been pleased with at least one of his sons. He tried to think back when he heard that his pa had died of the fever. More than three years he guessed.

He decided not to waste any more time and set a course for Tincup, which he guessed was at least thirty miles across the desert. It was getting late in the day and the sun was still hot; he and his horse had about reached the end of their endurance. He slowed the horse down and for a few minutes considered getting off and trying to walk. But his continued blurred vision and weak feelings discouraged that idea.

As the hot searing sun sank behind the mountains to the west he became aware that the horse was struggling to walk, he was wobbly and staggering. Jake overcome the pain somewhat and dismounted. The horse was his lifeline out here, as his legs would not carry him very far. Death would be certain and the letter to Tom would never be mailed. He let the horse rest for a few minutes. The saddle would have to be left behind. Riding bareback might cause his wounds to start bleeding again. He would just have to take that chance. He removed the saddle and placed the gold and food in his bedroll. He managed to get the bedroll across the horse's shoulders and then mounted belly first, pulling his right leg over the back of the horse. It took him a few moments to let the pain subside and then he urged the animal on toward Tincup. After the sun dropped out of sight the air became much cooler and Jake made dry camp in a clump of rocks and cactuses. His bleeding had stopped. That renewed his hopes to make it to Tincup.

He sparingly took a few sips of water and again gave the horse about the same amount from his hand. The water was about gone. He ate some of the dried hardtacks and chewed on a large piece of jerky. Then he fell asleep. When he awoke the full moon was rising in the east. His horse seemed to be recovering and showed signs of strength. He felt cold and stiff. Moving on toward Tincup was better than dying here in the rocks. He mounted and walked the horse toward Tincup. The need to find a landmark that he could describe easily to hide the gold was now heavy on his troubled mind. He knew that he could not go into town with the gold. Hide it, he must. He would look for a good hiding place.

Toward dawn he came on what at first he thought was a large cactus; closer examination revealed that it was actually a clump of three or four cactuses, weirdly twisted together by the desert winds as if some giant hand had braided them from the top down, leaving a den like space below. He had never seen such a sight. This then was a good place to hide the gold. It took all his remaining strength to slowly dig out a shallow hole between the trunks of the cactuses. In his weak condition he got to his feet without thinking about the cactus thorns; they inflicted more pain.

He wrapped the gold in a piece of the horse blanket and placed it in the hole, then covered it over very carefully. When he finished the ground where the gold now rested looked like all the other space around it. He felt his work had been worth the energy he spent. He took the time to rest a little more and finish the letter to his brother. Then it struck him that all he knew was that his brother was a U.S. Marshal and according to a newspaper item he was in Abilene. Jake addressed the envelope with a shaky hand, which read: To U.S. Marshal Tom Leach, Abilene, Texas. He did not show a return name or address. He folded the letter and placed it in his pocket and then he headed for Tincup. He told himself that he must live to see the letter mailed.

*   *   *

On the way to the Rio Grande, Quirt took the lead and mused, *'Jake will make it to the cave and die there. All the gold will be mine and with the money I have hidden across the river it will be enough for a good life in Portugal.'* He almost smiled at the thought of Silvia and a life in Portugal. He found out that she had money hidden, but he had not been able to discover its location. He'd make up his mind what to do with her after they got to Portugal. She could not be trusted, so he would get a replacement for her. The good part of the plan, He'd escape the hangman's noose.

He glanced around and motioned the others to split up and head for the border at different crossings. He wanted to make it difficult for the posse to follow; most of all he wanted to return to Bat Cave for his gold.

Quirt Evans and three of his killers crossed the Rio Grande to Mexico. On reaching the far riverbank, Quirt reined in and waited. The outlaws urged their mounts in close to his. Quirt said, "We can breathe easy now. The nooses are all on the other side of the river. Ben will go with me and you two will go on to our hangout. You can stop in the village and buy what you need and take some of the girls who want to go along. When you get there tell the others to start recruiting new members. I want gunslingers not afraid to die. If Jake is dead we'll bury him in the cave. You don't have to worry anymore about the posse they will rest up and make camp near the river, then start back tomorrow. They will never come into Mexico. I know a crossing up river about three miles and we'll take the rustler's old trail through the hills back to the cave. We'll find fresh mounts or rest the horses tonight, and tomorrow we'll cross the river. We should be back in about two days. Now get on your way."

The outlaw called Ben was almost a carbon copy of his boss; he was sunburned, had stained and broken teeth and almost always has an evil snarl on his ugly warty face.

Quirt did not expect anymore discussion, but one of the outlaws, known by the moniker Burk, was brave enough to look at Quirt and say in a hostile voice, "I'm coming with you and Ben."

Quirt's anger flared and he had his revolver about half out of its holster when he suddenly changed his mind. He said in a friendly voice, "Burk, I guess that is good idea. We may run into trouble and need your guns." He looked at the other outlaw and continued, "Are you going or coming along also?"

They all could see the rage Quirt was struggling to control. The scared and rattled outlaw reined his horse around and said over his should, "I'll go back and find some more gunslingers like you said." He did not wait for a reply as he rode away.

A half hour later Quirt reined in close Burk and without saying a word shot him twice; Burk fell out of the saddle. Quirt said to Ben, "Search him and his saddlebags, and then turn the nag loose. That poor bastard couldn't wait to get killed." Ben did as he was told.

Quirt and Ben rode on toward Bat Cave. After a few miles Quirt said to Ben, "You keep what you found on Burk; he won't be getting his share of the gold." Ben smiled and continued to lead the way to the cave.

As they at arrived at the hideaway cave entrance and all hell broke loose; Quirt turned to Ben and raised his voice, which he only did when extremely angry. He mixed Spanish and English, calling Jake by the vilest names ever heard on the Owl Hoot Trail. He threatened lynching, drawing, and quartering, being staked to a cactus and then buried alive in the hot sand. He knew without getting out of the saddle that Jake had not come close to the cave, and that left only one possibility in his mind—a double-cross and theft of the gold.

Ben tried to offer other possibilities, that the posse may have captured Jake; and then Quirt flew in another rage and threatened to kill Ben on the spot. Ben held up both arms to show he was not thinking about drawing his pistols, and said, "I'm sure you are right. I don't know why I could not see it your way immediately. Let's go find the traitor and get the gold."

That put Quirt back on his train of thought and he offered in a low dangerous voice, "I'll let it pass this time, but if we don't find him and the gold, I'll send you to hell after him. Now let's go."

Quirt knew the area surrounding his hideaway better than some of the settlers living within a hundred miles of his cave. He was smart enough to know that Jake, in his condition, had only one of two choices; set out for Tincup where there might be a doctor who could help him, or go to Moss Singletary's Lazy S Ranch which was harder to reach over the mountains.

The Singletary's were known to help all strangers stopping by their ranch as they had sufficient number of gunslingers to ensure their safety, but Jake needed medical attention and he would not find it at the Lazy S spread. The other choice was the small town of Tincup. Quirt decided to set out by the most direct route to Tincup. He then threatened to shoot Ben because there was no one else handy to kill. He raged, "Damn you Ben, you are a friend of Jake's. If I find out you knew that damn traitor was a double-crosser, I'll kill you so slow you will beg for the bullet in your head. Did you know he would take my gold?"

Ben immediately stammered out, "Quirt, I swear to you and everything that is holy, I am as surprised as you are about Jake. We don't know he stole your gold. He may have just wondered off in the desert or thought he could get to town for help. Shoot me if you want, but I expected to find him at the cave as you instructed."

"Alright, I'll let it rest for now." Quirt half-smiled and acted friendly again.

Quirt and Ben arrived in town and wasted no time finding out that the village had only one constable and he was more often than not drunk in the saloon. After asking a few polite questions they learned that a man with bullet wounds had come into town and was treated by the barber who was also the town undertaker.

Then Quirt went directly to Clymer Duncan's funeral parlor, which also doubled as a barbershop and examining room for all types of ailments. There were three or four men sitting in chairs against the wall of the small room killing time or gossiping. When Quirt and Ben entered the room they immediately found the need to go elsewhere. Quirt motioned for the fellow in the chair getting a haircut to leave; he jumped up, grabbed his hat, and rushed out of the building. Quirt stared at Duncan and asked, "Did you see or treat a man with two bullets holes in the last few days?"

Duncan asked, "Who wants to know?" Then he was staring down the barrel of Quirt's pistol. Quirt said nothing more.

Duncan shakily offered, "As a matter of fact I did see a fellow with gangrene who was closer to death than living just three or four days ago. He died before I could help him."

Quirt snarled, "Did he have anything with him? Where is his horse and gear?"

"He had nothing except the ragged clothes he wore that I remember."

Quirt said, "He come here carrying something that belongs to me. You have three seconds to tell me where it is, or you can bury your own body."

"I did not see anything he had except what he wore. I understand his horse is down in the livery and is for sale. No one will pay me for my service in trying to help the fellow. And that's all I know. Please don't shoot me." Duncan replied shakily.

Quirt lowered his pistol and said, "Let's go to the livery stables. And you tell me everything that bastard had to say, and don't try lying."

Duncan was now sure his time was near, "Well, he asked if someone would take his letter to the stagecoach office. He was very concerned that it go out on the next stage. Those were his last words. He died on my table. After I covered him, I took the letter to the stage. It was just leaving and the letter went into the mailbag just before the stage left."

Quirt asked, "Who was the letter going to?"

"I think it was going to his kin. I remember he mentioned his brother." He replied.

"What was the name on the letter? Did you read it?" Quirt wanted to know.

Duncan glanced at the cocked pistol; he was now beyond being scared, he was terrified. He stuttered, "Why no, that would be dishonest. I did no such thing."

Quirt waved his pistol in front of the undertaker's eyes and demanded, "I asked you the name on the letter. Also tell me quickly what town it was going to?"

"Best I remember it was Leach or something like that. I think it was going to Abilene, Yes, yes, it was Abilene. It was sent to the U.S. Marshal office." The scared man replied.

Quirt turned to Ben and said, "Let's take this dead man to the livery and look at the horse." They arrived at the livery and the stable owner a man named Jobe; an aged grizzly looking fellow roused from a half-sleep, looked at Quirt's pistol pointed at the undertaker's head and was immediately fully awake, his eyeballs almost protruding from their sockets.

The outlaw leader asked the stable owner, "Where is the horse and gear left by the fellow that had a couple of bullet holes and they say died in this hombre's parlor?"

"His horse is in that stall over there; he's mostly done for and not worth his hay."

"Where is his saddle and gear?"

"He rode bareback, no gear, just the old bridle?"

Quirt turned to Ben and said, "Tear this damn place down and look under every stack of hay. I want that gear and anything else he brought in. Get at it."

Then he looked at his two captives and snarled, "You both better hope he finds nothing that I am looking for. If you are lying, now is the time to tell me."

An hour later, Quirt was convinced that the gold was not in the stable. He suspected Jake had hid the gold before he got to town or somewhere else after he got here. He didn't believe these two in front of him, scared out of their wits, knew where the gold was hidden. They could cause him trouble if he let them go.

He said, "I'll never know if you two lie to me; I don't need either of you anymore, you're worthless, say your last words." As he raised his revolver, both scared men began to beg for their lives, protesting they did nothing against him. They dropped to their knees praying and begging for mercy. Quirt was not touched. He first shot Duncan between his eyes, and then with his other revolver shot the stable owner.

Quirt Evans felt no remorse in killing the two men. He was so intent on finding what he called his gold that human life meant nothing to him. By now he had worked himself up to an angry breaking point; he was yelling every cuss word known to man. He yelled that Jake had double-crossed him. He continued to rave about loyalty and honesty; he'd never trust another dumb gunslinger. He accused himself of being crazy to trust him or anyone else. What hurt him the most was that someone he considered dumb had outsmarted him. Jake had hid the gold. It might be in town somewhere or maybe it went on the stage with the letter, Quirt was determined to find out where the traitor stashed the gold. He knew from experience that scared people told all they knew after seeing a few of their friends shot. He decided that he would leave his mark on this vile town of Tincup even if he could find the gold.

If the gold was not in Tincup he'd go to Abilene and find that damn lawman brother and make him talk. Jake must have hid the gold and told his brother where to find it. Quirt knew that back trailing and looking for the gold would be useless. The gold could be hidden anywhere. Spending time looking for it would be useless. That would not do. He had to find someone that knew where that bastard hid the gold. He told Ben to check the barn and stables over once more. He said, "I'll look also." He had already decided that if he could not find the gold in town, he would go to Abilene and find Jake's kin. He was sure that the letter Jake sent to Abilene concerned his gold and clues where to find it. Abilene would be his next stop after he finished killing the pilgrims in Tincup.

A stable hand stood close to the thin board wall outside and heard enough to strike fear in his heart; He raced down the boardwalk whispering to everyone he could find, that Clymer Duncan and Jobe were gunned down by Quirt Evans and now he was going to kill everyone in town. That message spread like wildfire throughout the town. Hysteria gripped the spirit and hearts of the citizens. Some of them rushed back to their houses and came back on the street with their rifles and revolvers. They had heard enough to know that the killers would carry out their threats to slaughter the townsmen. There was no fast way to get out of town and away from the killers; hiding from the danger would be cowardly which was not in their nature. The courageous citizens decided to die fighting. They took some encouragement from the fact that they out numbered the killers. On the frontier threatened and scared settlers often joined together to protect their families and property. Today was no exception.

Quirt and his triggerman started at the end of the long street shooting at the buildings. Their shots were accurate, striking windows and doors, shattering glass. He was angry and thirsting for blood. Then when he saw the group of townsmen spreading out in the street in front of the saloon, he reined his horse to a slow walk and spoke to Ben, "They'll run. We'll kill every last one of them." He and Ben began firing at the citizens that were scrambling for cover behind anything they could find on each side of the street.

CHAPTER 2

THE LETTER

J ake's letter arrived in Abilene and landed on the desk of Deputy U. S. Marshal Blair Green who occupied a small office with his superior officer Marshal Tom Leach. Blair studied the soiled and wrinkled envelope and was about to put it in the box on Tom's desk, then he realized that Tom would not be back from the Indian Territory any time soon. He was aware that Tom Leach received very little personal mail. After a few moments Blair decided that the disposition of the letter should be elevated to Marshal Decker. This might be the opportunity he'd been seeking to talk with Marshal Decker about future assignments. He hoped now was the right time to make his case and return to full duty.

Marshal Andrew Decker was assigned to the Abilene area after reports reached Fort Smith that the Texians had partitioned for Statehood. President Anson Jones sent word to Washington that he needed federal law enforcement help on the frontier. At the time, President Jones said the Texas Rangers were needed for Indian wars, and word that the Rangers would soon be mustered into federal service on annexation by the United States had caused serious morale problems.

When the U.S. Marshal Service received Governor Jones request it was routinely staffed and eventually the Service was ordered to provide the requested help. The Service promoted Andrew Decker to Marshal and sent Deputy Marshal Tom Leach as his second in command to the frontier town of Abilene, which reportedly was in the center of the lawlessness in the Southwest. Marauders plagued settlers from the Mexican border to the Indian Territory on the northern boundary. They soon learned that marauders found havens in the Indian Territory and south of the Rio Grande in Mexico. Some of the western counties had not elected sheriffs and even in some towns it was hard to find brave citizens to take on the dangerous job of Town Marshal. Reports of cattle rustling, robbery bank and stagecoach hold ups and wanton killings struck stark fear in the hearts of the law-abiding settlers. Farms and ranches on the edge of the western frontier were easy targets for outlaws; many brave settlers had only a single rifle to protect their families, which was no match for the killers and rapists.

Andrew Decker's law enforcement journey started when he was twenty-three years old. He was invited to join the U.S. Marshal Service after the Governor of Missouri recognized his bravery during a shootout with marauders attempting to rob a bank. In that gun battle he was seriously wounded, but continued to fight; he killed three of the outlaws and arrested the other two. By happenstance he was in the bank when the outlaws entered, guns drawn; then shot one clerk and threatened to kill everyone in sight. He had only recently been appointed a deputy sheriff; and when the national newspapers picked up the story of his courageous actions he immediately became a national hero. The outlaw's bullet struck him in the hip, causing damage that plagued him the rest of his life. After several months of treatment he managed to walk and ride his horse, but continued to be dogged with pain and a permanent limp. The U.S. Marshal Service insisted that his limp would not impede his work requirements. During the last five years with the Service he was often asked why he had not married. He usually answered, saying the right girl had not yet asked him.

Marshal Decker and Deputy Marshal Tom Leach were sent to the Republic of Texas on a mission to quell the lawlessness in the southwest, which was steadily increasing with each passing day. When they arrived in Abilene they immediately began the difficult task of breaking up the outlaw gangs. They learned that the fearful reports of Marauders, cattle rustlers and other criminal acts, reeking havoc on the brave settlers were not exaggerated. The isolated farms and ranches were the favorite targets of the marauders. The absence of law and order in the frontier counties encouraged the criminals; the settlers had to provide their own protection. Many died defending their families and property. Anarchy reigned on the frontier.

Soon after arriving in Abilene, Deputy Marshal Tom Leach aided by Deputy Blair Green cornered two killers near Sweetwater. In that gun battle Blair was hit by a bullet before the outlaws were killed. He incurred criticism from his superiors in that battle causing him to lose favor with Marshal Decker who had to report the incident to headquarters. But Tom Leach stood by him. Blair was accused of being reckless during a gun battle; he was wounded when he thought he was protecting Tom. In the heat of the battle, bullets were whizzing overhead, he glanced at Tom and thought that he was exposed and in great danger. Blair acted instantly; he leaped to his feet and charged the outlaw. In that split-second a bullet hit him penetrating his leg above the knee. It was a flesh wound. Even before he fell he could see that Tom had only moved to a more protected position and was firing both pistols at the outlaw. When the smoke cleared, Tom was fine, the outlaw was dead and Blair was trying to stop the flow of blood from his wound.

Later, after reading the reports Marshal Decker was disappointed as he thought Blair had showed a serious lack of judgment and failed to heed his training. Blair did not contest the harsh assessment, nor did he offer the reason for his actions under fire. Tom knew exactly why his junior partner had acted in his behalf and he took much of the blame on himself and told the investigators that Blair should not be judged so harshly. Tom Leach's support helped save Blair's career with the service.

At first, before the investigation was completed, Blair felt embarrassed and depressed and was ready to quit the Service, but Tom insisted that if he had been in the same situation, honor would have compelled him to act as Blair had. He knew that Blair actually believed he had a duty to protect his partner. That was the unspoken code of the Service. Tom did not want that incident to spoil an otherwise outstanding young career. Blair never believed for a minute that Tom would have acted so carelessly, nevertheless he wanted to stay in the U.S. Marshal Service so badly that he was willing to accept any straw that was tossed his way.

A few days after the shooting, he went to the dispensary and was surprised to see Tom there getting supplies for his first-aid kit. He said, "Tom I know damn well you would never expose yourself unnecessarily as I did. It was a foolhardy act and we both know it. Marshal Decker is right in demanding an accounting. It was a momentary fleeting glimpse of what I imagined might happen to you. That was not the real situation. As soon as I was in the open charging the killer, I realized that you had reached a protected position in the ditch and was rendering withering effective fire at the outlaw. Of all the whizzing bullets coming our way only one struck my leg. My gratitude will never fade."

Tom smiled and said, "There is nothing to be gained by going over what happened that day. I'm glad to have you on my side. So let's drop it, but thanks anyway, partner."

Tom indicated that the case was closed. Blair could only imagine the heat Tom really took from his superiors. His strong defense and recommendation that the Service retain the courageous and bright young deputy marshal saved Blair's career.

Blair managed not to limp as he entered Marshal Decker's office. Decker studied him as he neared the desk and blurted out, "Sir, this letter just arrived for Tom. I thought you should be informed."

The Marshal nodded and smiled as he took the letter and turned it over and looked at the soiled condition of the envelope, then said, "It appears this letter has taken sometime to get here. I'd guess it's something that Tom is not expecting. There's no indication of who sent the letter. But just holding it in my hand gives me the feeling it is very important to Tom. How does it strike you?"

"Sir, I had the same feeling, that's why I brought it to you." Blair said.

The Marshal stood, walked around his office holding the letter in his hand. He turned and said, "Tom will not leave the Territory until he deals with that cutthroat bunch of killers causing havoc in the settlements. It's been awhile since I've had a report from him. We need to contact him to make sure he's alright. This letter might be very important."

Blair asked, "Is he acting alone up there in the territory?"

Marshal Decker replied, "No, he has the help of several deputies from the Fort Smith office. Last I heard they had made great progress and Tom was chasing one or two outlaws that had escaped during the gun battles."

Blair remained silent while the Marshal continued to pace around his desk thinking. He turned to Blair and said, "We only know the general location he is working. So we cannot just send the letter in the usual way to him. It would take weeks. How is that gunshot wound of yours coming along?"

"Sir, that's something I was going to approach you about; I feel fine and want to get back to full service. I need to prove that I am not irresponsible and that I have learned from my mistakes."

The Marshal returned to his desk and slowly settled down in his old worn armchair. He looked up and said, "Drop your trousers and show me that gunshot wound."

Young Blair was at first astonished and somewhat caught off guard. He had never been asked to drop his pants and a shooting thought went through his mind regarding the condition of his underwear. He smiled as he remembered that he had changed that morning.

He followed his instinct and dropped his trousers without comment. He watched as the Marshal studied the reddish, scabbed wound. It was not weeping anymore and well on the way to healing. Only he knew that pain and soreness still dogged him. The Marshal said, "Alright, I know you are itching to get back in action. For your information, due mostly to Tom Leach's effort's your record has been purged of the incident that caused that wound. I am glad to hear that you have learned from your mistakes. We all make mistakes, but let us try and make sure that none of them are fatal. Get a good nights' sleep and take this letter to Tom. I'll have a note for you to deliver to him as well. Take deputy Poole with you, he's our newest member and needs the experience. Try to teach him the importance of why we serve. This letter for Tom and my instructions to him will be in the mail pouch tomorrow morning. Good luck young man." Blair left the office and went to find Deputy Poole.

Sometime later when Blair entered the small rented house he found Deputy Clem Poole cleaning his pistol. Blair said, "Clem, Marshal Decker says you are to come with me to the Indian Territory. You don't look surprised."

Clem responded, "No news travels fast. I heard about the trip more than an hour ago."

Blair could hardly believe what he was hearing, "Hell it has not been that long since I left the Marshal's office. Well no matter, I am glad to have you along. It will be a hard trip, and we will be going through some tough country and Comanche land. We may need to travel some at night. It's important we reach Tom Leach as soon as possible."

Clem smiled and said, "We'll make it. The Indians don't bother me as much as the outlaws on the Owl Hoot Trails we'll be crossing."

Blair said, "We can handle them also. Be ready to ride at first light tomorrow morning."

"I'll be ready to go when you give the word." Clem said.

On leaving, Clem was still working on his pistol. Blair Green decided to ride the eleven miles out of town to the Longmire's ranch. He discounted the thought that Tom would think he was nosing into his private affairs, as he was going out there to ask Blanche if she wanted to send Tom a letter. Actually he acknowledged, although important, that was not the real reason for his trip to the ranch; Clay Longmire's other daughter Tess would soon be eighteen, and Blair hoped she might look on his attention favorably. He had been afraid to ask her or her pa if he could come courting. But now that he was leaving, not knowing when he would return, it seemed that could not wait any longer. He could visualize her sparkling green eyes, mischievous smile, long beautiful brown hair that fell in tresses and the perfect slim body that sent his heart racing. She had yet to out shine her sister but there was little doubt in Blair's mind that she would be the beauty of the family in a year or so.

His thoughts returned to the reason that he would give Clay Longmire for coming out there; he knew that Tom had been taking Blanche to church on Sunday for the last two years. There was no talk of marriage that Blair had heard, but he could not imagine that it was not on their minds. Tom talked very little about the future, but Blair felt certain that Blanche would not let him avoid the altar of marriage much longer. She and Tess could ride and rope steers as well as the best cowboy. It was not unusual to see Blanche with her pearl handle-pistol strapped to her right side. She seldom fired the pistol, but it was well known that Clay Longmire had taught both his daughters how to use pistols and rifles. But Tess avoided firearms unless there was a contest at the annual fair. Both Blanche and Tess were total western ranch women, worshipped by their pa and all the ranch hands. Clay Longmire had started the ranch before his daughters were born. He now had a modest income from his labors, except in years when cattle rustlers hit the ranch and the lack of rain inflicted losses. Everyone who knew them admired the family.

In those early years, the girls' mother died from a rattler's poison and later they found themselves in the role of housekeepers, cooks and ranch hands. Many a disappointed cowboy had cautiously tried to court them, but they discouraged potential suitors with a friendly smile and firm words. Neither of the sisters was interested in playing the courting game. Blair knew that when Blanche started going to church with Tom, her pa and sister were always in the lead buggy. They all seemed to enjoy each other's company. Often Blair tried to get up the nerve to ask Tess to allow him to accompany her to church. But it never seemed to be the right time.

As Blair neared the Longmire corral he saw the glint of a rifle barrel from the loft door. Then he saw other armed cowboys going about their chores near the barn. Out here there was no law and the ranchers had to ever be on the alert for marauders and thieves. Isolated farmers and ranchers were prime targets of opportunity for outlaws riding the owl hoot trail. Sometimes they came alone and less successful, but it was ever more dangerous for the settlers when a dozen outlaws rode in to rape, steal and pillage. Being prepared and alert was essential for those settlers on the frontier.

Clay Longmire stepped off the long porch and greeted him. He asked Blair to dismount and come in the house. Both Blanche and Tess greeted him. Blanche took the lead as the oldest daughter, and in a musical voice offered him water or coffee. He could hardly remove his eyes from the smiling face of Tess. It took a few seconds for him to regain some composure, and then he felt tongue-tied but stammered that he was in a hurry to return to town.

He blurted out, "Marshal Decker is sending me up to the Territory with a message for Tom. Since he's been gone for a long spell, I thought perhaps you might want to get a message to him. I know it is highly presumptuous of me, but I thought friends might want to stay in touch. If I'm intruding, I apologize." Clay smiled and winked at his daughters and said, "Young man, it's a thoughtful and kind gesture. You can tell Tom for me that when he gets tired of chasing killers he has a job here on the ranch. But perhaps Blanche might want to send him a note. Would you Blanche?"

She responded, "I am very thankful for the opportunity to send Tom a note. He needs to know he has friends here who wish him well. He's out there in the wilderness of the Territory and only God knows what he faces everyday. I'll only be a minute or two. Blair, please take a seat and have a glass of water."

Tess brought two tumblers of water and Clay said, "Let's sit on the porch. I like to keep a sharp eye on the horizon this time of day." Blair noticed as he went through the door that Blanche and Tess took the stair steps two at a time while giggling.

Clay Longmire spoke of the coming roundup and little or no demand for beef.

He spoke at length about the future of running cattle. Then he switched to the possibility of farming, but there was no real market out here for any of the cash crops raised back east. Cotton might prove profitable, but the large investment for gins and other equipment discouraged that idea. Blair struggled to act interested in what was being said as he knew very little about farming. He was raised on a ranch and his family managed to get by with a small herd of cattle, catching and selling wild horses. Blair knew more about riding a bucking horse than he did about operating a farm. He found working with his hands on the ranch something he'd rather not do.

He was about to announce that he had to leave, when Tess came out and handed him a sealed envelope addressed to Tom Leach. She was smiling and Blair almost dropped the letter as he was so unnerved by her sudden appearance. He glanced at her father and noticed that he was smiling and apparently enjoying the startled look on his face.

Blair tried to regain his senses and sound normal as he said, "Thank you Tess. I'll make sure Tom gets this letter. I appreciate the hospitality. Mister Longmire, I really must get on my way."

Then Clay Longmire said, "Blair we are glad you dropped by and perhaps when you return you will join our family in church services."

Without waiting for Blair's response he continued, while opening the door to go back in house, "Be careful riding through that dense grove of cottonwoods, as it is a perfect place for an ambush, I understand there are reports of outlaws drifting through here now."

"Thank you sir, I'll be very careful going through those woods."

Blair walked toward his horse and was surprised Tess caught up with him. She kept stride with him and said, "I guess you are not interested in joining us for church, since you did not say anything when pa invited you."

He looked at her with almost tearful eyes and said, "Tess, I am sorry about not answering your pa, but nothing in this world would please me as much as escorting you to church."

She laughed, and with an unexpected impulsiveness asked, "Nothing?"

That really flustered him and he could only offer, "You know what I meant, and yes going with you to church would be a good start." She was radiant and the most beautiful sight he had ever seen.

He struggled to keep his hand on the saddle horn and then swung into the saddle. She said, "Take care of yourself; I expect to see you as soon as you return from your mission to the Territory."

He rode away at a gallop, saying loudly over his shoulder, "I'll be back as soon as I can. I'll see you then. Goodbye for now." He glanced back once more and returned her wave.

It occurred to him that it would be late when he got to Abilene. He had a lot of work to do before leaving the next morning. He never felt so good in all his life. He mused, I'll *marry that lass and have a happy life.*

Blair would have felt even better if he could have heard the conversation in the Longmire parlor. As Tess came into the room her pa said, "That was a little un-lady like of you to follow him to his horse. Don't you think?"

She blushed and looked her pa in the eyes and said, "Pa, I know it was not altogether proper, but you've always told me to catch a wild bull, I had to swing a wide loop. I'm sure you will agree that he is reserved and a little too bashful. I just thought it was time to reveal a mite of my feelings. Do you understand?"

He smiled broadly and replied, "Yes, I am afraid you have me cornered. I do understand, but having both my lovely daughters courted by men engaged in dangerous work worries me. Yet I know that they both are upstanding gentlemen and I must be content with your and Blanche's choices in life. I just don't want either of you hurt. I can only hope they live to be part of the family." Clay Longmire was extremely happy with his daughters. He did not try to hide his pride. Tess looked at his face and knew that she had his full approval.

Tess thought she was soaring in the sky to see her pa so happy. She said, "I don't know about Blanche, but I will have my mustang roped, hobbled and working on the ranch before he gets old. Pa, you know I like Blair. He is fearless, except around me, and a fine young man."

Her pa smiled and said, "Yes, I believe you are right about him being brave, although I heard that he was reckless in a shootout and perhaps stopped a bullet unnecessarily. I recognize that he is a fine young man. Now let us hope he comes back from the Territory without one of those beautiful Indian maidens following him."

She said, "Oh pa quit joshing me." She took the stairs two at a time, still laughing.

*　　*　　*

After Blair's visit to the Longmire ranch he and Clem Poole rode out of town the next morning about dawn. He had returned from the visit with a vision of Tess floating in front of his eyes. That vision slowly faded as staying on the right trails and following the direction received from Marshal Decker became a challenge at almost every mile. Out in the rough countryside so many hills and valleys looked alike; he stopped to check his notes, often looking for landmarks. After a couple of days, Blair discovered that his bullet wound had almost healed. He and Clem Poole had spent long hours in the saddle and rode on some moonlight nights.

They crossed the Red River and continued on north into the Indian Territory. They found Cedar Ridge where Marshal Decker had instructed them to stop and get directions to Tom's location. As expected they learned the location where Tom stayed when not out chasing outlaws.

Then nearing the end of their journey, they urged their mounts up a sharp incline to a large plateau. They could see off to the north a small log cabin, nestled in an oak grove, with a wisp of smoke rising almost straight up as there was no wind at the moment.

Blair studied the scene and said, "That appears to be the place we're looking for. I believe it's where we'll find Tom. The cabin and surroundings fit the description given us by the Deputy Marshal back there in the Cedar Ridge land office. Let's ride in and see if we are right. You hang back and give me support in case there's trouble. We don't want to ride into a trap."

Then as Blair neared the cabin, he had not seen any activity. The door was closed and the one window was shuttered. Blair reined in at the pole-corral, tied his mount and motioned for Clem to wait. There were four horses in the corral and Blair recognized Tom's palomino.

He cautiously approached the door and called out, "Hello in the house. I'm looking for Marshal Tom Leach."

The door opened slightly and a woman's voice asked, "Who are you?"

Blair replied in a friendly voice, "We'd just like to talk. We seek information. We're with the U.S. Marshal Service."

Blair heard some talk inside, then the door opened wide and he heard Tom say, "Blair, come on in. I've been expecting someone to show up."

Blair recognized Tom's voice and replied, "Clem Poole is with me. I'll signal him to join us inside."

Then he heard, "Take care of your mounts first and then we will talk."

Blair and Clem unsaddled their horses and noticed that the water tub was full and then he and Clem went to the cabin. As they entered the small two-room cabin they saw Tom stretched out on a makeshift bed, with his shirt off and white bandages around his chest. In the far corner, chained together and anchored to the log wall were two of the wildest and meanest looking characters they had ever seen. The Indian woman looked to be about sixty, and was busy stoking the fire in the stove. She was cooking something on the stove that smelled very good.

Tom said, "Hello fellows, it's good to see you both. Blair, I'm surprised you healed up enough to be on such a long trip."

Blair smiled and said, "That scratch is almost healed. Thanks to you, Marshal Decker cleared my records of that incident."

Tom tried to laugh, but cut it short as the pain in his side increased. He looked at Clem and asked, "How did you talk Marshal Decker into sending you on the trip?"

Clem replied, "The Marshal said I needed some field experience. I think he wanted me to be along to take care of Blair." He laughed.

Blair injected. "Clem is learning fast. He's a good officer and best of all he knows how to make coffee."

Tom asked, "Did you water and feed the horses? There's still some fodder left in the shed."

Clem answered, "We didn't find the fodder, but we did water them. I'll go back out and pitch them some hay."

Tom allowed, "Later this evening you'll need to graze all the horses and again in the morning. Morning Star has been grazing the horses, but she will be glad to be relieved of that duty.

Blair reported, "I have some messages for you in my saddlebag that I'll fetch after seeing to the horses." He and Clem left the cabin without waiting for a reply.

A short time later, after feeding the horses they returned to the cabin. Blair gave Tom the messages. Tom glanced at the messages and said, "You fellows rest while I go over these reports."

After Tom had read the messages Blair briefed him on their trip and the help they received at Cedar Ridge. Then they discussed all the happenings both in the Territory and back in Abilene.

Tom looked at the prisoners and said, "Don't mind those two in the corner. They are harmless now. I'm glad you fellows finally got here. Tomorrow you will take the prisoners to Cedar Ridge and arrange for their return to Fort Smith. They have an appointment with the hangman." There was a deep guttural animal growl from the prisoners chained to the wall, but they made no other sound.

Blair asked, "What happened to you? Is it serious?"

Tom smiled and said, "Nothing serious, a fractured and sore rib. Morning Star is helping me while I heal. The Indians in this area are friendly and help us when they can. That big culprit in the corner kicked me when I arrested him, but I'll be able to ride soon. Thanks for the mail. We'll talk about some of it later." Blair knew that he was being told to not ask about the messages, as there were other ears present.

Morning Star placed tin plates and cups on a wooden table, and then prepared hardtacks to go with the stew. When the food was on the rough wooden table Morning Star said to Tom, "Me come back tomorrow early."

Tom responded, "Thanks, I appreciate your help. Tell your Chief I appreciate him allowing you to help me." She nodded and left the cabin.

Blair was surprised how good the stew tasted. Tom joined them at the table and spoke very little while eating the stew. Blair wondered what meat was in the stew, but he dared not ask what it was as he knew Indians were known for their willingness to use a variety of ingredients in their cooking pots.

He asked Tom, "What about your prisoners over there in the corner?"

Tom said, "There are plates for them near the stove, when we're finished you or Clem can give them some of the stew. You will have to spoon feed them as I don't want to take their cuffs off. Morning Star has fed them until now, but I told her one of you would take care of the problem tonight."

The next morning, Blair and Clem left the cabin to take the horses to the creek for water and to graze. The grass was knee high in places and they knew that the horses would soon have their fill of grass and water. Blair left Clem with the horses and he returned to the cabin.

Morning Star had arrived and was cooking something on the stove. He later found out that she had cooked large slabs of beef and served it with hot hardtacks and coffee. He ate and then cut up meat in bite sizes for the prisoners and assumed the job of feeding them.

He could see the hatred in their eyes, but they kept their thoughts to themselves. He then, with instructions from Tom, unchained them one at a time and took them behind the corral to relieve themselves.

During this somewhat dangerous task, neither of them ever said a word. Blair knew they were just itching for him to make a mistake, so they could attempt to escape. It occurred to him that the trip to Cedar Ridge would not be without great risk. He had just returned the second prisoner to the corner when Clem returned and said that the horses were saddled and ready for the trip to Cedar Ridge.

Tom said, "You and Clem take the prisoners out there to the corral and chain them to a tree. Have Clem stay with them and you come back, I want to talk with you."

Then when Blair returned he heard Tom say to Morning Star, "Take the bucket and bring us some fresh water from the creek." She nodded and shuffled out with the heavy wooden bucket.

Tom wasted no time. He said, "Thanks for the letter from Blanche; she thinks you will be courting Tess when you get back. I'm pleased that Tess likes you."

Blair responded, "Well she agreed to let me take her to church when I get back there. I really like her, but she is still so young and immature."

Tom continued, "Marshal Decker has ordered me to return to Abilene. It's just as well as the prisoners outside, are the last of the Mulligan gang of cutthroats. This area will be fine for several months at least. He mentioned a big problem down near the Mexican Border. I'll need you and Clem on that mission."

Blair was pleased beyond words, he stammered, "Thank you. I will not be so rash in the future. I told Marshal Decker that I had learned my lesson. I thank you for your support."

Tom smiled and said, "Hey if another bullet comes my way, you can have it. I'm not real fond of being shot." They both laughed knowing the prior incident was behind them.

Then Tom got real serious, "The other letter is from my outlaw brother. I mentioned him to you a few times. He apparently sent the letter thinking he was dying. He said he had gangrene from two bullet wounds and that he would be gone by the time I received his letter. Here read it, it is very short."

Blair took the letter and slowly read a very sad message. It was signed, *your only kin Jake. I'm in Tincup dying.* The letter thanked Tom for trying to keep their pa from making Jake leave home. He stated his regret for, *disgracing the family name; my years on the owl hoot trail, the rustling, holdups and other crimes.* Then he said *I want to make things right as my last breath leaves me. I rode with Quirt Evans. He wanted me to wait in Bat Cave. My wounds will kill me. I wanted you to know.* There was a little more about his remorse and then he asked, *Tommy you remember the guessing games we played; one of us would say we hid something worth a lot of money, and then give some clues where it's hid. Do you remember you once said it was hid near large bunch of cactus, which twisted together at the top? You said it was southwest of our place . . . I was dumb and went to find it. I never found anything I walked all way to our cave we played in and it was not there. I hope you remember. It's important to not forget such things.* There was more.

As Blair returned the letter, Tom said, "The odd part is I never played such games with Jake. He must have been out of his mind with fever or trying to tell me something. He was a good kid and I can understand his desire to atone for his crimes. From his letter, I'd say he wanted to send me clues where he hid the gold. He'd know that if I find the gold that it would be returned it to the government. Also the other thing is he'd know that we never played such games as he described."

Blair thought for a moment and said, "If you never played games like that, then he wanted to tell you something he did not want anyone else to figure out if the letter fell in the wrong hands."

Tom said, "That's really what I thought, but I wanted your take on it. We will have plenty time to think about the clues on our return trip to Abilene. You take the prisoners to Cedar Ridge and come on back. I'll be ready to ride by the time you return."

The trip to Cedar Ridge was uneventful except that the prisoners tried to slow down the pace, hoping to find an opportunity to escape or at least carryout their threats to kill Blair and Clem. Tom had warned that the prisoners were desperate and dangerous. He said they had to be restrained at all times. The walls and floor of the jail at Cedar Ridge was constructed of huge logs with no windows and only one small door. The prisoners could be observed through a small opening in the door day and night. Blair knew that Tom would have never sent the prisoners to Cedar Ridge unless he was convinced they would be safely guarded until they got to Fort Smith to face justice. They both were killers.

Blair and Clem rested overnight and set out early the next morning on the return trip to Tom's cabin. On the trip back Clem asked, "Blair do you think Tom is up to traveling? He looked pretty weak to me."

Blair answered, "Now that you mention it, he did appear to be less than normal. But I'd guess the bruised rib and trying to guard those two killers robbed him of good sound sleep. I hope he will be better when we get back. A few nights of good rest does wonders for the body."

When they arrived back at the cabin, Tom was out in the corral feeding his horse. He looked recovered and ready to travel, but he still had his ribs tightly rapped and said the pain was slowly going away. Clem flashed Blair a thumbs' up when Tom was not looking. That he also was glad to see Tom in better condition.

Tom greeted them and said, "Take care of your mounts and then come on in, we have another large pot of Morning Star's mystery stew."

They talked very little while eating the stew. Morning Star fetched a bucket of water and then left to wherever she was staying. Blair or Clem did not ask questions about the arrangements for her, as it was very apparent that Tom respected and appreciated her help.

They all got a goodnights' sleep and early the next morning, Tom was up ahead of the others and announced as they rolled out of their blankets, "We'll cook our breakfast and get on the trail; Morning Star has returned to her tribe. I still have a little soreness, but the healing process is encouraging. I feel much better." Less than an hour later they were on the trail.

The three lawmen made good time and the first part of their trip went without meeting anyone. Then less than a two days' ride from Abilene, as they rode through narrow trails and around large boulders they were ambushed. The cowardly attack came when the lawmen rode, single-file, into a canyon with rock walls rising from each side of the trail. Small trees and brush covered the sides of the trail and in the crevices between the boulders. They had chosen to take a short cut used by riders up and across the hills rather than the stagecoach route to save a few hours. Tom had warned the others before entering the narrow trail to stay alert and be prepared for action. Even though Tom and the others were on high alert, the sudden gunfire and hail of bullets surprised all of them. Apparently, the hidden gunmen were trying for headshots as their first shots missed all three targets. The Marshals reacted as they were trained to do. They rolled out of their saddles and hit the ground scrambling to find cover. By the time they reached cover the hostile gunfire was coming missing them by inches. Tom had at first thought the outlaws might just be after their horses when they missed the first shots. Now it appeared the ambushers were trying to kill them, Tom decided that not only did they want the horses, but to kill them and take whatever their victims were carrying. This had the earmarks of desperate outlaws who were poor marksmen or had some other unknown intent.

The horses spooked on hearing the gunfire and raced on down the trail. Almost as sudden as the attack, the gunfire suddenly stopped; Tom looked around and could see that both Blair and Clem had found cover behind large boulders. He looked at the wall behind him and realized why there were no gunmen on that side of the canyon; it was too steep and there were no hiding places.

He moved and immediately was greeted with a hail of bullets. He guessed that darkness would not fall for a few hours, but knew that the killers would not wait for that to happen. He had to make a move now. Clem was about twenty feet from him, and Blair was down the trail, both visible to him. They seemed to have good cover.

He said in a low voice, "Clem, work your way down to Blair. Stay behind those large rocks and tell him to count to twenty very slowly and then both of you start slinging lead at their positions. I'll try to get under that ledge over there and work around so that I have a clean shot at them. Don't talk; raise your hand a little if you understand." Clem raised his hand and started crawling toward Blair.

Tom cautiously continued to inch forward, using every protruding rock as cover, until he was under the ledge on the opposite side of the trail. He had concerns about the thirty feet of open ground between him and the ledge. He made it across the trail without drawing fire from the outlaws. Blair and Clem kept firing; the ambushers followed their instincts and hunkered down waiting for the firing to stop. Then for a few minutes the canyon was quiet. Tom knew the lull would not last, as he was sure the ambushers thought they held the best hand. They had cover and higher ground. The best hand did not always win the prize; experience urged him to push for a showdown. Luck may have helped him and his deputies so far, but it could play out at any moment.

He decided to get as close to the ambushers as possible. He moved from behind a large bounder and headed for the next cover some ten feet away; as he raced, he was aware of bullets striking the rocks and ground all around him. Then he felt something hit him in his neck. He fell to the ground and kept crawling toward cover. Blair and Clem kept firing at the gunmen's positions. Tom had a fleeting thought that if they continue to expend their ammunition; they would soon be out of bullets. This was a situation he would soon learn if his training and experience could overcome the odds facing them at the moment. The gunmen had excellent cover with the advantage and appeared willing to stay put until they killed their victims. The next few minutes would determine the final ring of the bell for one side or the other.

CHAPTER 3

VICIOUS ATTACK

The small village of Tincup, a population of about seven hundred, was nestled between two imposing mountains with large trees and a running creek meandering down from the mountains. The town's population often changed quickly; drifters stopped for a few hours, others stayed if they found a source of money. Some of those who came through and stopped were avoiding the law or fleeing from angry fathers or husbands. There was just enough commerce, stores, saloon and cafes to provide the townsmen a steady supply of food and whiskey. The creek provided year-round water; except for the shallow wells some of the more industrious townsmen dug near their houses. The first gold and silver seekers found a pristine valley with abundant game and water. There was only a sprinkling of gold ever found and no silver. Most of the prospectors moved on, and those that stayed struggled with starting a business or small ranches. The wild game remained plentiful in the mountains.

The town experienced one extreme or another; as time wore on, merchants slowly came seeking their fortunes. They established stores, bringing new and strange merchandise, which some considered extravagant items no one could afford. Money was scarce. But then it was not long before the saloon and gambling hall became the center of activity on the south end of town. Gunplay became the choice to settle or start arguments. The townsmen often said they stayed in Tincup as 'there's no other place to go.'

Tincup thrived at times from lonesome and stray cowboys looking for adventure and an occasional job on a ranch as they drifted through the valley. But the real money flowed from the Owl Hooters who arrived with their robbed and stolen money. They spent their misbegotten wealth with no thought of the future. Most of then didn't expect to see their next birthday. Tincup's boot hill was the recipient of many such reckless and carefree outlaws.

In more recent times, due to the loud complaining of the church's congregation, mostly women, the leaders appointed a constable and built a small jail. There was little or no improvement; the shootings and killings continued. For years the town had no doctor or place to buy medicines. Then it seemed a blessing when Clymer Duncan drifted into town and announced he was a barber, doctor and undertaker. He soon had plenty of customers; the killings kept him busy burying the victims of gunfights. He claimed credentials as a doctor whose license was lost in a fire. He could remove lodged bullets, splint broken bones and prescribe certain medicines, which only he could provide. He charged whatever he thought the patient could pay. Clymer Duncan was an important man in Tincup.

This then was the town that changed forever after hearing that Quirt Evans had shot and killed Clymer Duncan and the stable owner they all called Jobe. The western spirit of justice stirred the leaders to action, but fear for their lives was the real force that pushed them to act. The threat by Quirt Evans that Tincup would long remember him and that he intended to kill everyone in town propelled the townsmen to fight. The citizens knew that they were trapped; they could not leave as there was no place to go and to stay and not fight meant death at the hands of a mad dog killer.

Then hastily a couple of leaders emerged; Lathrop Moses, owner of the Sundowner Saloon and Tim McCall who was a recent newcomer to Tincup began to speak of the need to resist the killer and stop him if possible. Together, they hurriedly organized some of the scared citizens. The plan was simple; everyone in town who could find a rifle or pistol should show up on the street immediately; plainly displaying their weapons. Lathrop Moses said a show of force could save lives. Moses also reminded them that some might die, but that would be better than have their women and children abused and murdered. The men and half-grown boys soon gathered in front of the Sundowner, all armed with rifles and pistols. In the absence of anyone else speaking up, Tim McCall assumed the lead as spokesman for the group. He told them, "Just back my play; I don't intend to give the killers a chance to carryout their threat to kill us."

They didn't have long to wait. Quirt and his sidekick appeared at the end of the street on their horses. The gunmen were throwing lead at windows and doors. At the other end of the street the brave townsmen broke into small groups taking cover on each side of the street. Quirt and his sidekick didn't seem to notice and slowly came on up the street busting shells.

Then when they noticed the townsmen, Quirt reined his horse to a halt and said to Ben, "Looks like the pilgrims want to fight. Take your buffalo gun and cut down some of them, and then they will scatter like scalded cats." Ben began firing wildly at whatever he could see at the end of the street. He smiled when he thought he had hit a pilgrim.

At the same time, Quirt drew his pistols and began to send hot lead at the crowd. Ben had reined his horse to a stop, giving him a better position to fire the rifle. Then all hell broke loose, the nervous townsmen sent volleys of pistol and rifle fire toward the killers.

Quirt looked over his shoulder and saw Ben drop his rifle and slump forward; Quirt suddenly realized that the citizens were not going to run and the bullets were striking the ground all around his and he could hear the close ones whizzing by his ears. He reined his mount around, emptied his other pistol at the defenders and then raced toward the end of town. He looked back in time to see Ben fall out of the saddle. The fight for the moment was over, but Quirt's wild and desperate firing and Ben's rifle shots killed two defenders and slightly wounded three others. The citizens had paid a very high price for the one bandit lying on the ground. Some of the citizens checked themselves to see if they had stopped a bullet. Then they began to celebrate and shout, "We won, we won."

The fear, excitement and noise calmed down a little as the defenders gathered around the writhing and dying outlaw; he was bleeding from chest and stomach wounds. Blood was flowing and he was in great pain, but still conscious. Tim McCall kicked the outlaw's rifle out of reach and removed his pistols from their holsters, and then said, "You've killed your last time hombre. Death is upon you. You don't have long. Any last words?" The killer's eyeballs rolled and mumbled, "You . . . all will . . . die. Quirt . . . come back . . . with the gang." Spasms shook his body and he died with his eyes open.

That evening in the Sundowner there was loud and noisy celebrations. The drinking and gambling kicked into high gear. In the small church there was an entirely different tone by those gathered there not to celebrate, but to offer their thanks for escaping the onslaught. After the short service Lathrop Moses spoke asking the folks to consider organizing the citizens and preparing for the threat made by the dying outlaw. The consensus of the congregation seemed more concerned with the disposition of Clymer Duncan and Jobe Parker's possessions. Then someone said don't forget the outlaw's horse and saddle.

Although no one had valid claims on the property of either Clymer Duncan or Jobe Parker they insisted those present decide what to do with all the property and possessions. Tim McCall suggested that the possessions of Clymer Duncan and Jobe Parker be left for the circuit judge. They quickly agreed, but wanted to do something with the dead outlaw's horse and gear. Tim McCall said it should go toward his burial. That settled, they moved on to Jobe's horses he had in the pasture behind the stables. Someone would have to care for the horses until the judge arrived to make final disposition. There was general agreement on that proposal and a couple of the older men volunteered to keep the livery running and take care of the horses. Then the discussion turned to the safety and protection of the town.

Tim McCall and Lathrop Moses waited for the citizens to mull over their thoughts. Then the preacher stood and said, "Well we've described the problems without mentioning what is most important to the safety of our town and citizens."

There were a few nods and verbal yeas. He continued, "We need someone to enforce the law or what we all know is decent and right. Our erstwhile constable is still drunk, passed out over in the jail cell. We don't pay him anyway, so we can't expect much from him even if he was capable, which we all know he isn't. He just likes to strut around showing the badge when he is half sober. Anybody have thoughts on the subject of enforcing the law in Tincup?"

There was general silence in the room. Lathrop Moses slowly stood and said, "I've seen good times and hard times here in Tincup; we have some rowdies, but mostly honest folks here that want nothing more than to be left to their own business; whatever that might be. For myself, I make a living in my saloon and would not have the time to devote to anything else. I'll never get rich doing what I do, because I'm too damned honest." He smiled and looked around the room to general boisterous laughter.

He then said, "I understand that several years ago, this town was well run by a mayor and councilmen. There was a levied tax and all the property owners were asked to kick in to support the town marshal and the jail. Then I'm told some of them turned bad and all were either killed or run out of town. I suggest the time has come to rethink our situation. I say we elect a mayor and three councilmen immediately. We can announce tonight that tomorrow we'll hold an election. In the meantime, I am nominating Tim McCall, who showed his guts today, as our new marshal. Let's hear if anyone has a better idea?"

One aged woman stood and asked, "Who knows anything about this mister McCall. I've heard he's a drifter that drinks and gambles all day at the saloon?"

A fellow in the far corner snickered and said, "Hell, that's what we all would like to do." Again there was general laughter.

The preacher said, "Let's hear what mister McCall has to say about the job."

Tim McCall, a tall handsome, lanky fellow wearing two pistols strapped low on his thighs, stood and said, "I'm sure to hell not asking for the job. It's right, for the last year or so I've traveled most of the trails on the frontier. Exactly what I've been seeking is my business and does not concern any of you. I guess most of you drifted in here, seeking something, but you still don't know what. I sure don't know much about the written legal stuff, I'll leave that up to the circuit judge, but I do know right from wrong. I should tell you that I've seen both sides of the law and I know that without law and order no one out here on the frontier is safe. If the citizens of this town want me, I'll give the marshal's job the best I got. That is with the understanding that I'll show no favorites; if you do wrong, you go to jail and wait for the circuit judge, and that includes my good honest friend mister Moses." They laughed and clapped.

McCall paused, raised his hand for attention then continued, "Everyone has heard of Quirt Evans and his cutthroat killer gang. His dying henchman says he will be back to kill us all. They'll have to kill me first, as I intend to fight. If we join together and fight, we can defend ourselves for a little while. I believe the elders in this town will agree we need outside help. Since the Texas Rangers are not now available, I suggest we request the U.S. Marshal Service to help us. We must stop the Evan's gang before it gets to town. That's all I have to say for now."

The room almost exploded in cheers and laughter. Someone yelled, "We got us a marshal. I don't give a damn what he's seeking or what he's done before, but if he proves bad, we'll hang him to that old tree down by the jail." The room came alive in clapping, whooping and hollering. Tim McCall's future was just determined.

Lathrop Moses again took to his feet, and asked, "Any other nominations for Town Marshal?" There was silence. He continued, "Alright Tim McCall's name will be on the ballot tomorrow. Now we need nominations for Mayor and Councilmen." There was more discussion, and two hours later those present had come up with a slate for the election. Lathrop Moses was nominated for the Mayor's job. He at first declined, but when it became clear no one else would stand for the job. He reluctantly agreed to serve one three-year term.

The next day the townsmen turned out in record numbers. There was some cheerful laughing here and there, but for the most part the scared people went quietly to the church and voted. The sun had not reached its apex before the vote was in and counted. The slate of candidates was easily elected as none had opposition. Four of the leading citizens in town were elected to serve on the Council; Preacher Zilker, William Scholl, Curry Hermes and Homer Clawson. They met immediately and took their first official action; appointed Tim McCall Town Marshal and dismissed the constable who was sober enough to understand his services were no longer needed.

He laughed and said, "That suits me fine. I'll help mister McCall if he asks." The Council thanked him for his service and willingness to help keep the town safe.

Afterwards Mayor Lathrop Moses spoke for a few minutes; about the need to write a town charter and establish a few ordinances governing taxes and whatever other requirements were necessary to establish the Town. He pointed out that all those present might already be United States Citizens as word had come in that The Republic of Texas would soon be admitted to the Union of the United States. There were some welcome comments, but others were not happy with the news. Statehood meant more inference by the government.

When Quirt Evans left Tincup under fire from the citizens, he spurred his horse unmercifully urging greater speed. He headed west knowing that his horse could not make it to the border. After a few miles he reined in and let the animal rest. The horse was sweating and breathing hard. The long trip up from Mexico and the hard ride had spent all the energy left in the animal. He remembered a small farm about three miles further west. Quirt let his horse walk slowly trying to make him last as long as possible. The afternoon sun seemed to get hotter every minute. When the farmhouse came into view, he reined his horse behind a clump of bushes, tied him and began to move toward the bush corral; there were three horses in the corral. The large roan showed spirit by running around close to the fence, kicking up its heels. He'd found his horse. A few minutes later, using as much cover as he could find, Quirt, walked quietly toward the corral.

He was about to throw a loop over the roan's neck when the door opened and a man came out and yelled, "What the hell going on?" Then he ducked back in the house. Quirt did not wait; he raced to the side of the building, flattened himself against the log wall. The man came out the door with a rifle in his hands. Quirt shot him twice; the man fell to the ground dead. Then he heard a woman scream as she burst out of the door and ran to the dead man. She was sobbing and yelling at the same time. Quirt walked over, grabbed her hair and lifted her almost off the ground. She was small and when she gained her feet she tried to turn and fight him. He laughed and said, "I like high spirited women. Let's see what you have in the house." She continued to squirm and fight.

He dragged her in the house and saw a sleeping baby in a willow crib. He said, "If you are quiet the baby will not get hurt. What is your name?"

She asked, "What do you want? You killed my man."

"I want to know your name and then I want something to eat and water for my canteens."

Sobbing she said, "My husband's name is Ted Blake and I'm Florence. What about my husband out there?"

He said, "You can do what you want after I leave. Quit talking and get me something to eat. Then if you want we can have some fun." He laughed.

About an hour later Quirt mounted the roan and rode out to where he had tied his horse. It took him only a few minutes to place his saddle on the roan and turn his spent horse loose. He mounted and headed southwest toward the border. As he rode along, he smiled recalling what he had left behind. His last glimpse of Florence Blake was on the floor beside the crib. She had resisted but soon realized that she was no match for his strength. She continued to sob quietly and stopped fighting. The ordeal did not last long. Before he left he had said, "Woman, you are lucky. I'm going to leave and let you take care of your baby. If I ever hear you give anyone a description of me, I'll come back and kill you and the baby."

She had managed to say, "Just get out of here and I'll see to my man."

In Tincup at sunrise the morning after the vicious attack, Florence Blake drove her team of horses pulling the wagon toward the center of town. She had managed after many tries to get her husband in the wagon; he was very large and heavy. When she pulled the horses to a halt in front of the Sundowner saloon, a small crowd gathered around the wagon. She sat very quietly and then raised her head and addressed the crowd in a steady but angry defiant voice, "My husband is under that blanket, he was killed in cold blood by a mad dog. He raped me and took our best horse. Only God knows why he spared the baby and me. I'm here to bury my husband and then I want to know who is going to help me hunt the killer down and hang him?" She sat straight and looked around at the faces and could see their concern.

Marshal Tim McCall climbed up on the wagon and said, "Mrs. Blake, I'm the town Marshal, please allow me to drive the team to Ethel's Boardinghouse. You can get some rest and take care of the baby while I see after your husband." Florence handed him the reins and looked once more at the people gathered around and said, "Thanks Marshal, I'm obliged for your help. I have a little money but it won't last long here in town. If any of you want to buy our farm and house with all the chickens and sheep, I'd like to talk with you. I'll use that money to track the killer down." She sobbed and held the cooing baby up for everyone to see and said, "I swear to my child that I will live to see his father's killer hanged. Decent folks should not have to live in fear of being ravaged and killed by outlaws."

Tim McCall grasped the reins and turned the horses in the direction of the Boardinghouse. He said in a very low and concerned voice, "You get some rest and leave the arrangements to me. You can tell me if you want a church service or not. I'll do as you ask."

She said, "Thank you for your kindness; I didn't know what to expect when I got in town. I just wanted to give Ted a decent funeral. I could not dig a grave out there on the farm." She started sobbing again while trying to dry her eyes.

That afternoon the townsmen gathered in the church and held services for Ted Blake and those who were killed while fighting off the attack by Quirt Evans. After the funeral the preacher asked for a collection for Widow Blake. The generous citizens gave as much as they could and then Mayor Lathrop Moses pitched in a large donation saying, "All you boys can feel proud your whiskey money is going for a good cause." They all laughed.

As Tim McCall carried the money to the Boardinghouse he added a twenty dollar gold coin. His heart went out to Florence and the baby. He vowed to help them through this rough time and that he would do everything in his power to bring Quirt Evans to justice. Florence had given him a very complete description of the killer, and McCall had no doubt it was Quirt Evans who killed her husband.

The long hard ride to the Rio Grande didn't seem to tire the roan. Quirt crossed the river cussing and raging at every step his horse took. Soon after leaving the Blake place he began to berate himself for not killing the woman. Even now after the hard ride, he could find no good reason to let her live; except seeing the baby he decided to take a chance on her. That was a mistake. He'd not do that again. Leaving witnesses was not his way. But what galled him the most, was the fact that a bunch of pilgrims killed one of his best gunmen and caused him to flee under a hail of bullets. That was something new to him. His evil mind was entirely occupied with plotting his return to Tincup with a much larger and deadly gang.

He mused, "I will hit that town with the largest gang ever assembled. I'll find the gunmen I need and kill every last pilgrim in town. After that we'll go to Abilene and find that damn brother of Jake's. His letter told where he hid my gold. I'll have that gold."

Quirt Evans had always been an angry fellow; now this defeat in Tincup and seeing one of his most trusted gunman shot out of the saddle sent him in a rage beyond measure. In short his mind had crossed the line and completely enmeshed with anger and finding the gold coins. This new rage made him even more dangerous and bloodthirsty. His known ability with weapons and a ruthless killer instinct gave his depraved mind a sense of immortality. Tincup would soon hear from Quirt Evans.

CHAPTER 4

DEATH TRAIL

M arshal Tom Leach felt his neck where a bullet had grazed him; it had stopped bleeding. The ambushers were holding their fire; the silence was deafening. Tom crawled behind another large boulder and was surprised that his movement had not drawn fire from the culprits. Then there was a prolong lull in the gun battle. While staying alert and vigilant Tom's mind drifted to his family and childhood. Oftentimes, during periods of furious gun battles, it was not unusual that god fearing men reflected on their past. Tom sometimes found it an escape from making hasty and rash decisions. Today was no exception.

Tom was born to parents who lived their lives by the Good Book. There was Bible reading after chores and the evening meal as long as Tom's mother lived. In those days his parents spoke very little about their growing up in Virginia. Tom was very young when his parents set out for the untamed western frontier. At the start of the trek in a Conestoga covered wagon Tom kept thinking in his young mind that they would soon turn around and head back to the only home he had ever known. Although a few of the covered wagons used in Virginia were called Conestoga, none were close to the original Conestoga that found its way from Lancaster County Pennsylvania. The wagon Tom's family selected for the trip had a spring seat for the driver and passenger, whereas the first Conestoga wagon had something called a lazy seat on the left side of the wagon between the wheels. Yet as the wagons had evolved some of the features of the original Conestoga were retained; large wheels to facilitate fording streams and clearing stumps where trails had been hurriedly cut through the forests.

On the trip Tom's determined parents talked mostly of what lie ahead and seldom mentioned their relatives or home. After a few weeks on the narrow and twisting trails, Tom thought less of back home and his lost playmates and began to look forward to the next day for whatever adventure might come their way. He happily helped with making camp each evening, fetching water and helping his mother ready the cook fire to prepare the meals. His father hunted for small game most evening and provided plenty of fresh meat to roast boil or fry over the hot coals. Years later, thinking back he could barely remember the long arduous trip from Virginia to the Republic of Texas except for the encounter with a couple of outlaws demanding money and threatening to kill everyone.

Tom could clearly recall what happened that rainy cold evening; one of the outlaws approached his mother and tried to take her in his grasp; she reacted immediately by striking the culprit above his right ear with a small cleaver. He reeled and stumbled back against his horse, wiping blood unbelievably from his face. He was out of the fight for the moment and Tom's father suddenly realized it was now or never; he charged the other outlaw and soon had him on the ground with a pistol pointed at his head. The outlaw with the gash above his ear was still in a daze. The fight was over. After disarming the bungling robbers, his father required them to leave their weapons and ride back down the trail. Then for the next several days, Tom remembered that their nightly campsites were selected with great care and his parents took turns standing guard at night. They learned not to camp in the open where there might be hostile attacks and water should not be their first requirement. Finding a cove or closed in area that provided good cover for defense and limited the different directions for surprise was his father's highest priority. During the attack, his parents had acted out of desperation and Tom never forgot their courage in the face of great odds.

On arriving in Red River County, The Republic of Texas, Tom's family was unable to obtain land with their meager savings they had hoarded long before setting out for the new lands. There was talk among other settlers of free land on the unsettled frontier; there also were whispers about the danger awaiting anyone who ventured into the badlands to the west. The longer Tom's family stayed in Red River County, the less money they had. So after a few days, they headed west seeking their dream and to find new opportunities on the frontier. It took several days and weeks of travel to reach the little town of Roscoe. Land was cheap and they bought three hundred and sixty acres. Their first priority was to build a cabin and till a small spot for a spring garden. That kept them occupied while hunting for game and carrying water from a stream that seemed to run clear all year.

Then after a few years of near happiness, calamity hit the family; his mother died two years after giving birth to Jake. It had been a happy, but struggling family. Then the laughter in the household ceased and replaced with grim hard work. His normally jolly and easygoing father suddenly changed and somehow found a way to associate the loss of his first and only love with Jake's birth. Tom matured early in life; with a tall slender frame, muscular arms and chest, wavy brown hair, steely blue eyes, almost perfect teeth and facial features, all complimented by an ever ready warm smile. Then as he grew older he thought it was his responsibility to be protective of Jake. It was very obvious to Tom, that Jake felt his father's indifference to him and caused him to avoid participating in conversations and other activities with Tom. Jake's resentment grew, as he got older.

During those first few years following the death of their mother, their father had several 'housekeepers' none lasted very long; a year or less. The bright side of those arrangements was the improved disposition of their father, at least in the beginning of each new housekeeper. Looking back, Tom remembered that to be fair the housekeepers were also good cooks, washed their clothes and kept the house clean. Jake never knew a real mother whose love was deep and boundless; as Tom knew their mother possessed. Their father never argued with the women he brought to the house, but never gave them much notice when it was time for them to leave. He would hitch up the horses to the wagon and wait for the unlucky woman to come out of the house with her possessions. Some would cry and hug the boys; others stalked out and never looked back. Then when both brothers were in their early teens, their father brought Maria home. Maria was much younger than their father and different from all the other women who had come before her. There was never a cross word in the house after Maria arrived.

When Jake was forced to leave home by his father, Maria was saddened, ceased to speak unless to answer a question and became very reserved. Through all the heartache and hard times, their father insisted that his boys receive a good education. There was a country schoolhouse about three miles from Roscoe, which Tom, and then later Jake, rode mules to attend. The school had a small pasture where the horses and mules could graze. Later Jake was sent to school with Tom. From the first he hated school and made rather poor grades, which caused almost continuous preaching by their father about the importance of a good education. He often said that he should have stayed in school until he learned something. He only had benefit of ten years of education. He quit school to get married. Shortly after they were married left Virginia to start a new life on the southwestern frontier.

Throughout their early years, Tom tried to help Jake everyway he could, and at least interest him in school. Jake's mind always seemed to be somewhere in the sky. He struggled with mathematics, which both Tom and their father tried to help him understand but he simply did not want to learn even the basics. He also did not care for history and the world around him.

Sometimes Maria tried to teach Tom and Jake Spanish. She was fluent in both English and Spanish. Tom caught on to the language easily and was soon conversing with Maria in her native language. She tried hard to coach Jake to give more attention to his lessons and learn as much as possible. Jake did not respond any better to Maria than he had for his father and brother. He often indicated that he was unworthy and just wanted to be left to himself. His resentment never seemed to abate; he wanted nothing to do with Tom and other handsome, strong and robust boys. He felt that Tom got all the breaks. Jake had heard the older girls in school whispering that Tom was the most handsome fellow in school. Jake did not doubt the girls were right, but those overheard compliments for his brother only served to make him more self-conscious of his plain and unimposing looks. He resented his brother, but would never voice his thoughts to anyone.

Tom was not too much surprised when Jake took the family savings and spent it on women and whiskey. The few cross words that passed between Jake and his father were the normal exchanges between father and son while taking care of the farm animals and other work on the farm. Even during the most minor of such disagreements, Tom interceded as the peace maker; often volunteering to do Jake's part of the work. Tom tried hard to include Jake in all the activities around the farm; Jake rebuffed him at almost every turn. Then suddenly everything boiled to the surface; Jake let his wild side rule his senses. Taking the family savings was an unforgivable act, it was the final straw. He did not express any remorse or regret; he acted as though he expected the confrontation with his father. Tom worried about Jake for months after he left. Then he finally came to understand that he could not live Jake's life for him. When he was old enough, he had long talks with the county sheriff and finally was assisted in making application to the U.S. Marshal's Service. To his great surprise, he was accepted for training and a probation period of one year if he successfully completed all the difficult courses. He thrived on the training and excelled in most every requirement of the Service. He was in his element.

Tom indicated in his letter accompanying his application, that his brother Jake had left home and according to reports reaching the family committed crimes while riding with various outlaw gangs. During his initial interview, he was questioned at length and could recall the sharp question he had to answer: "How would you handle a confrontation with your outlaw brother? Would you pursue him as you would any other law breaker?"

Tom remembered that he had replied, "I still love my brother as he was when he left home, but now that he is an outlaw, I would treat him the same way as any other criminal."

Then the questioner asked, "You would shoot to kill your brother?"

"Yes sir, it would be my duty to treat the situation as I would in all other cases. If the situation called for it, I would shot to kill."

He was asked to wait in the adjoining room while the board discussed his application. The interviewers took only a few minutes before asking him to come back in the room and take a seat. Then with some background remarks, the board informed him that his application was approved. But he would have to undergo ten months of hard training, followed by a year of probation. The board made it clear, that then and only then would he be given the U.S. Marshal Service badge and identification. Tom was elated at the chance to prove himself.

When Blair brought Tom his brother's letter and after reading it several times, he was puzzled by the unanswered questions in the letter. From what Tom could discern from the hurriedly scribbled words, Jake was trying to make amends for his lawlessness and to say that he was dying. His allusion to their childhood games seemed to be his way of conveying clues to something of value that Jake hoped would atone for his years on the owl hoot trail. Tom was deeply touched by Jake's attempt do say he was wrong to join the lawless gangs, rob and steal. If Jake's clues to a hidden treasure prove true and he lives, he might escape the hangman's noose. Tom knew that he would try his best to save Jake from the hangman, yet he knew that Jake would have to serve time for his crimes. Tom hoped that Jake had not taken part in the murders committed by outlaw gangs. He would leave the investigation to other officials.

After reading Jake's letter Tom decided that when he got back to Abilene, he would request that he be assigned to the Rio Grande area to break up the outlaw gangs and to hopefully find the government's gold that Jake apparently hid in the desert. He already had some idea concerning the clues Jake had tried to give him. Tom thought that Jake was actually convinced that he was dying, or he would not have written the letter seeking salvation for his crimes. Tom resolved that he would not rest until he found out exactly what Jake was trying to tell him or if he was still alive.

Many thoughts related to Jake's letter and his situation stayed with Tom while on the trail back to Abilene. The first leg of the journey was uneventful, but as they entered a narrow passage with boulders on each side of the trail suddenly all hell broke loose; the three Marshals found themselves in a deadly ambush; they rolled out of their saddles and took cover as fast as they could.

The ambushers were well hidden and had the advantage. They kept up a steady barrage of deadly revolver fire. The hot lead was striking too close for comfort; the ambushers wanted blood on the trail. Tom studied the underbrush and rocks formations looking for a position that offered the best chance of getting clean shots at the shooters. He had no time to reminisce further about his family's affairs and clues to hidden gold. As he scrambled for a boulder that offered better cover, a bullet grazed his neck and cut a small furrow; he bled some but it was not a serious wound. The deadly fire was concentrated and aimed to kill, ricocheting bullets whizzed by his ears, too close for comfort. Again, Tom decided to move to a better position even though he knew that moving would bring greater risks. He took a chance and started a slow crawl, then leaped to cover behind a pile of rocks. That move caused the ambushers to send several volleys of lead in his direction.

The ambushers had spotted him and kept the steady gunfire at his new location. Tom was puzzled about the outlaws staying in the fight. Normally, ambushers would try to escape after their initial shots missed their targets. These culprits were doggedly holding the high ground, which gave them the advantage of good cover; not having to expose themselves to gunfire probably gave them additional confidence that their devious ambush might still work.

Down on the lower rocky knoll Blair and Clem were firing intermittently, following Tom's instructions to give him a chance to get closer to the outlaws. He wanted to flush them out of their hiding places and get a clear shot at the culprits. He noticed that Blair and Clem were well deployed and had fairly good cover, he motioned for Blair to hold his position; he then rolled down a slight incline, coming to rest behind another boulder. That brought a new volley of lead kicking up dust all around where he landed. He found a small depression in the ground and surveyed the landscape; he now had a better field of fire, and he could see one of the outlaw's legs as his hiding place was too small for him to hide completely. Tom took careful aim, fired two quick shots, and heard the fellow yell in agony.

The firing stopped and to Tom's surprise he then saw Clem fully exposed, scrambling up the incline firing his pistols. Both Tom and Blair yelled for him to get down, but it was too late. The outlaw did not hesitate; he could clearly see one of his targets exposed moving slowly up the hill. He knew it was easy pickings; he fired several shots at the slow moving target, Clem fell and rolled back down the hill. Tom realized that now he had to bring the battle to end. He scrambled up the hill, moving from boulder to boulder, while trying to keep as much cover as possible. Then the outlaw made the mistake of his life; he tried to retreat back down the far slope; Tom fired three quick shots; he saw the fellow crumble to the ground. The battle was over.

Tom gained the top of the hill and found both outlaws dead. Each had taken more than one gunshot wound, but the one that Tom had hit in the leg, appeared to have shot himself in the head, probably after seeing the other outlaw fall. Tom and Blair then went back down the hill to see about Clem, but Tom knew before he got close to him that he had paid the supreme price for his last act, which could be viewed as a brave act to help his comrades, or a foolish inexperienced demonstration of courage. Tom mused to himself; *I'll let the Lord do the judging, but I know the young man was trying to play his part in a dangerous game and help his fellow officers. I'll give him the benefit of the doubt when I write his parents to tell them of the sad news.*

The outlaws had left their horses down at the bottom of the hill; Tom could see one of the horses trying to break his reins while the other lay still. When he got closer, he found that the horse on the ground was dead. Both horses showed signs of abuse and going without eating. They were skin and bones. Tom said to Blair, "Pull the saddle and bridal and let that poor animal go and perhaps he will survive. We now know why the outlaws did not retreat after their ambush failed; they wanted our horses, not just what we carried."

Blair replied, "They must have been desperate to get somewhere to abuse their mounts in such a way."

"We'll never know what brought them to their end here in the rocks." Tom rejoined.

Blair studied the faces of the dead men and said, "You know, Tom, these two could be father and son. They really have similar features and the age span appears to be some twenty years."

Tom replied, "Yes, I noticed their resemblance and the older one took his own life. He would have lived with that leg wound. I guess when he saw his son, if it is his son, fall it was too much for the old outlaw and he put the pistol to his head."

Tom and Blair spent the next few hours digging graves in the rocky ground for the two outlaws. They buried them on top of the hill where they had setup their ambush. A search of their pockets and gear failed to reveal their identities. There was less than twenty dollars among the few items the outlaws carried. All they owned would be reported and turned over to the Marshal Service. Tom looked at the small pile of coins and food items and said, "In addition to wanting our horses, I suppose the other reason they tried to kill us was for what we might be carrying. Now we will never know their names or who to notify that they have met justice on the trail. Let's take Clem with us, but we may have to bury him on the trail. Perhaps we can find a farm or settlement where we can give him a decent burial. His parents will want to know where he rests. We'll make a full report to headquarters when we return home. I'll tell you this Blair; no one knows hard cruel grief is until they see the eyes of parents when learning that their son is dead. I've had to deliver such messages, and I hope Clem's is the last."

Blair said, "I'll go with you if you want."

"Thanks, this one is my responsibility, but if you stay with the Marshal Service you can expect to get your craw full soon enough." Tom replied.

Late the next afternoon, Tom espied a small swirl of smoke off to the northwest. It appeared to be about a half a mile away. Tom remarked to Blair, "It's had to make out what the fire might be about. It does not appear to be a grass fire; it could be someone burying brush they've cleared from their farm. It certainly is not a camp fire."

"There's very little wind, so the fire probably will not spread very far. What do you want to do?" Blair asked.

"We have to check it out. It will take us out of our way, but that's a small price to pay if there's trouble and we can help." Tom said.

As they approached the cause of the smoke, they found big logs used to build the cabin and shed still smoldering. The smoke was fast dissipating. On closer inspection of the two burned structures, it appeared the few belongings of the occupants had been piled in the middle of the floor of the cabin and set afire. Sprawled in the middle of the floor was the charred body of a man. The cook stove was upside down and the coals in the firebox were still hot. Tom spoke slowly with contained anger, "Blair, check around outside and see if you can find clues to what may have happened here. I'll use one of our blankets to wrap this fellow in and get him out where we can bury him. His clothing is burned so bad I doubt there will be any clue on his body that will tell us his name. Perhaps, he lived here alone. We need to know if that is the case."

In a small cleared garden spot, Blair found a wagon, two axes, three different plows and hoes, shovels and rakes. These implements seemed to suggest that the dead man had started to clear the land to cultivate for a family garden. Cutting and placing the heavy logs in the cabin walls suggested he had help, although many of the pioneers had devised ways to lift the logs by use of pulleys and the power of their mules or horses. Blair also knew that pioneers normally established themselves on the frontier by first providing meat and vegetables for the table. For meat, most of the early settlers relied on their hunting and shooting abilities. Some did bring milk cows, chickens, pigs and goats.

He had circled the cabin and found horse tracks in the creek. He could not read much from the tracks. Then he was about to go back to the cabin when he heard a noise from the small patch of willows, further up the creek. He walked slowly toward the rather dense willows with a pistol in his hand. As he neared the large cottonwood tree growing out of the creek bank, he heard what he thought was a child sobbing. He quietly approached the area and he could indeed hear the smothered crying. At that point he almost called out for Tom, but he looked over his shoulder and knew the distance was too great for Tom to hear him unless he yelled, and he did not want to reveal his presence at the moment. He inched forward on his hands and knees and saw some dead brush pulled over the opening to a hole between the large surface roots of the giant tree. He stood and let his eyes search the area around him. There was nothing suspicious so he decided the immediate area was clear and nothing threatening. From the sounds coming from near the tree, he was sure that a child was under the brush.

In a low voice he said, "There is nothing to be afraid of now. My name is Blair and I am a Deputy Marshal. My job is to protect you. Please come on out and let's talk."

There was a period when Blair was not sure if the child had heard or even understood what he had tried to say. Then he saw the brush slowly fall away from the opening and the tear stained face of a little girl appeared, eyes wide and still very frightened.

Blair stood very still and said in a low friendly voice, "Please come on out and let's talk. You must be thirsty and hungry?" She stood and wobbled a little to get her feet under her on the uneven ground, looked up at Blair and asked, "Where is Mommy and Pa?

"We'll talk about them in just a little while. We will find out about them very soon. Please do not worry about them right now. You need food and water. When you feel better we can talk. Them we'll talk about your folks. My friend is up at your cabin. He will be glad to see you." Blair tried to use a very friendly and soft voice to gain her confidence. He didn't realize that he was still holding his pistol in his hand until the girl asked, "I got water from the creek. Why do you need that gun?"

Blair quickly placed the pistol in his holster and said, "Well, we did not know that you were here. No, I don't need the pistol anymore. Can you walk back to your house?"

"Yes, I am well, thank you. Are we going to see mommy and pa?" She asked

Blair was not experienced with children; he grew up as an only child and never had time or opportunity to play much with the school kids. The closest neighbor to his house was more then ten miles, and none of them had children under working age.

Blair was in a hurry to turn this latest problem over to his boss. He ignored the child's plea for the moment and said, "Come with me to the cabin, and we will talk with our friend Marshal Leach. He will tell you what he knows about your folks." He then asked, "Will you tell me your name?"

She looked up to him and said, "Mommy and Pa call me Sissy but my real name is Mary. I like Sissy best."

"Well Sissy it will be and you can call me Blair. Let's mosey up and see Marshal Leach."

She let him take her hand and guide her through the brush toward the cabin. Her dress was dirty and wet from the damp hideaway. Although uncombed, her blond hair fell to below her shoulders in curls. He noticed that her eyes were azure blue; he had never seen a more beautiful little girl. Her features were perfect, complemented by her suntanned face and hands. He guessed she was about five or six years old.

On nearing the cabin, Blair called out to Tom, "Marshal Leach, I've found us a friend. She wants to know about her folks." Tom was under the big oak tree, busy digging the graves for both the burned man from the cabin and for Clem. He had them rolled in blankets near the shallow graves. He answered, "I'll meet you up by the cabin. I'll be there in a few minutes. We'll talk then."

By the time Tom arrived, Blair had found some hardtacks and jerky in his saddlebag for Sissy to eat. She was hungry and did not hesitate eating what was offered. When Tom came around the corner of the burned cabin, Blair and Sissy were seated on a large stump. He did not act surprised when he saw Sissy. She stopped eating and tried to get closer to Blair. She was plainly afraid and Tom sensed as much. He slowed and said as he approached them, "Well Blair I am glad to see we have a new friend. What is your name young lady?"

"It's not a young lady. I'm Sissy." Tom put on his most friendly smile and said, "I'm sorry, my mistake, glad to know you Sissy. My name is Tom Leach. We came to visit you and your folks. Do you have brothers and sisters?"

"No, they said I was all that anyone needed." She tried to smile for the first time, but it was only a glimmer and then gone.

Blair placed his arm lightly on her shoulder and said, "Sissy, we would like to know your folks names."

She cut her eyes at him and said, "Pa is called Morgan and Mommy is called Helen."

Tom waited a few seconds and said, "That's right, Helen and Morgan, but for the moment I can't think of their surname or sometimes we say family name. Can you help me to remember?"

"Our name is Parks. All our kin is dead and gone. Pa says we're the last ones." She replied in a broken voice.

Tom waited for her to eat some more of the jerky and drink a little water from the canteen offered by Blair, and then he coached, "Can you tell us why you were hiding?"

"Some awful men made trouble this morning. I think they carried Mommy away with them. I don't know where Pa is. When Pa seen them coming, he told me to go to our special place. He told me to stay in the hidey-hole until he called me. I'm scared."

Tom asked, "About how long ago did they leave?"

"I don't know they stayed only a little while. I heard many gunshots. Then I seen the smoke and that made me scared again."

Tom asked gently, "Did you see anything that might help us find your Mommy?"

"After the shots stopped, I peeked out and heard Mommy scream and then nothing more. I peeked out again they had Mommy and then they left on the horses. They had Mommy on one of them and she was trying to get down. I wanted to help her, but Pa said for me to stay in the hiding place."

Tom said, "Sissy, please wait here on the stump while Blair helps me with some work. We'll be very close. You are safe now and nothing is going to scare you again."

Blair followed Tom around to where the horses were tied, and then he asked, "You seem to know something about the family's names?"

Tom said, "You are sharp, Blair. I knew their names, but I wanted to get her talking. She has the names right. I found a tin box hidden in the hollow of that stump she is sitting on. Morgan Parks was not only a rich man, but a careful one as well. There're deeds in the box for twelve hundred and eighty acres of land, and from the description we are standing in the middle of it, and he owned several properties in Virginia. I didn't count it, but I guess there is also several thousand dollars in the box. Now we have to get her mother back with her."

Blair looked at Tom and said, "We have to find someone to take care of Sissy and soon. I'm not very good with children."

"Why? I thought you were doing just fine with Sissy. She trusts you and I believe she has no close kin from what I could learn from the papers in the box."

Blair asked, "What's next? I've never had a problem like this before."

"I'm going to follow the killers' trail and free Helen Parks, if possible. You must take Sissy on to headquarters and give Marshal Decker this tin box. He will keep it safe and will find someone to take care of her. She is a precious child and I'm almost angry with her parents for bringing her out here in this dangerous country, but then we do not know their reasons for such foolish doings, especially since they are apparently very rich."

"We must tell her something about her father. Otherwise she will pester me all the way back to headquarters. How much will you tell her?"

Tom thought for a few minutes then replied, "I guess you are right, it's up to me to tell her she won't be seeing her pa again. I'll find a way to tell her. In the meantime you shorten the stirrups on Clem's saddle, I'm sure she has been on a horse before. But you will need to lead the horse. Don't let her have control at anytime. She might do just find, but she is now our responsibility. I must get on the trail before dark. So let's get things together."

Blair said, "Tom, I don't know if I am the right person to take this child back over the dangerous trails. There could be other ambushes and trouble seems to follow us around."

"There's a stagecoach relay station about fifteen miles east of here. You can make it before morning. There will be a full moon tonight. Take her to the stage and buy tickets for both of you. I want you to remain with her until Captain Decker finds a family where she can stay temporarily. I hope to have her mother with her before too long."

Blair asked, "Do you really believe her mother is still alive?"

"I don't have an answer for that question, but it is my duty to find out where she is. It's not only a duty, but also my responsibility. Even if the Service did not expect it, I would expect it of myself. Now get ready to leave."

They shook hands and Tom returned to tell Sissy about her father, while promising to find her mother. He knew it was not going to be pleasant or easy, but it had to be done.

Tom took a seat on the large stump by Sissy; she had not moved from where she was sitting when they had left her.

Tom said, "Sissy, we will see that you are safe until we find your mother. I'd like for you to take your time and tell me everything that happened after your Pa saw the riders approaching. It's important that you don't forget anything. I know this may be hard for you to talk about, but it will help me find your mother."

Sissy looked down at the ground, clasped her hands together in her lap and hesitatingly started, "I was in the yard and Pa wanted to work in the field, and then he saw men on horses. Pa told me to go to the hiding place. He said for me to stay there until he comes for me. Then he told Mommy to hide behind the shed. Pa said run don't walk and then he said go through the bushes, stay low to the ground so they can't see you." She stopped, looked at her hands and raised her eyes, questioningly at Tom.

"You're doing fine. You are a big girl and I need all the information you can give me. Go on with what happened."

She said, "I don't know anything else. I was in the hiding place, but I heard some shots. I thought Pa was running them off."

"What happened then?" Tom urged.

""Mommy screamed, maybe two or three times. I wanted to see, but I thought Pa will scold me for leaving the hiding place. The house was burning, a lot of smoke." She stammered and started crying. Tom waited and patted her gently on her shoulder.

Tom urged her to continue, he said, "Sissy, you don't need to worry about leaving the hiding place; I would have done the same as you. You had concern for your Mommy. It's getting late. We must get on the trail soon, but finish what you want to tell me."

"They was bad to Mommy. They put her on a horse and they left. I could not see Pa, he would've stopped them."

"What happened then?"

"I waited and the fire kept burning. I was scared and feared Pa would see me out of the hiding place. I always have to mind."

Tom said, "You were a good girl. I know you mind your folks. What happened then?"

"I guess they hurt Pa bad. He would never let them take Mommy."

Tom pressed, "What did you do after seeing them leave with your Mommy?"

"I was scared. I hid again."

Tom waited until she looked up again and he almost choked up. She looked so very pitiful and scared; Tom hated what he had to say next.

"Sissy you are a big girl and you have helped me. I will find your Mommy. I promise you that. Do you believe me?"

"Yes sir, I believe you and Mister Blair."

"That's fine. You are right about your Pa; the bad men must have been scared of your Pa and they shot him. Your pa was a brave man. Do you want to see where we buried your pa?" Tears rolled down her check and she asked, "Where is he?"

"We buried him and one of our friends under the large oak tree."

She thought a while and then said, "Pa won't be alone, and he talked about heaven a lot."

"When you are ready, I'll show you where we buried your Pa. Then I am going to find your Mommy."

She whimpered a few times and said, "I guess I'm ready."

Tom did not want to tell Sissy that her pa was burned in the fire. She stood by the mound of new dirt covering he Pa's grave. Tom rested his hand on her shoulder to let her know that she was not alone. He was a little surprised at the way she was handling this sorrowful situation. He waited for her to speak. She reached up and grasped his hand he had on her shoulder and asked, "Why did those bad men kill my pa?" Tears were running down both cheeks.

"Sissy, your Pa was a brave man. That's what you should remember and all the fine times you and your family had. We have to go now. Blair will take care of you. You can trust him. I am going to find your Mommy."

Tom took Sissy's hand and led her toward Blair standing with the waiting horses. He said, "Sissy, I'll help you up. Try the stirrups and see if I need to let them out." When she had settled in the saddle, her feet slipped easily in the stirrups. She placed her weight on her feet and rose up out of the saddle, then sat back down and leaned forward to take the reins.

Blair said, "You can take the reins and wrap the ends around the saddle horn, but to start off I will lead your horse with the rope."

"I can ride. Pa let me ride his mules. Where are the mules and our cow and little calf?" She asked.

Tom waited for them to leave and he replied when he noticed that Blair hesitated, "The bad men must have run your livestock off when they left. Blair, you and Sissy should start out. You've got some ground to cover to meet the stage. There will be a full moon tonight. I suggest you rest every once in a while and keep going so that you will be there by noon tomorrow. You have plenty time so take it easy on the horses."

He tried to inject some new thoughts, as he did not want to tell her that the mules, cow and calf had all been slaughtered. He was surprised to not find any chickens or dogs, but he did not want to ask Sissy about them. The killers butchered the calf, taking both hindquarters. Killing of the other animals was a senseless and evil act. The fact they killed Sissy's Pa, burned the buildings and then took her mother with them told Tom that the outlaws were not only vicious, but evil as well.

As they left both Blair and Sissy turned in their saddles to wave a final goodbye and then urged their mounts to canter on across the undulating prairie where a tree line could be seen far off to the east. Tom was satisfied that Blair would get Sissy to safety. He was not sure of the stagecoach schedule, which called for brief stops at the relay station where the passengers could get refreshments while the horses rested. He knew Blair and Sissy would be safer at the station than on the trail; Blair would give his life if necessary to protect the child in his charge. He took one more look around the Parks' farm, but found no new clues that would help him discover the destination of the killers. He knew from past experience that killers, such as those who killed Morgan Parks and took his wife, usually kept on the move stopping at small towns where they could find whiskey and women. But since he was not acquainted with the area up ahead, he would have to follow the killer's tracks with all its perils and places where bushwhackers could easily setup their devious traps.

Tom watched Blair and Sissy drop below the knoll; he then mounted and easily picked up the trail of the outlaws. He followed the horse's tracks for hours. From reading the track impressions, he now knew that one of the mounts had thrown a shoe, and another one was unshod and had a left front hoof with a small gap. The outlaws had stopped at a small stream and rested for several minutes; they seemed to know where they were going and in a hurry to get there.

If they kept up the present pace, their horses would soon tire and require rest. Tom had no doubt that he was following vicious killers who had no regard or respect for human or animal life. He realized the chances of recovering Helen Parks alive was diminishing by the hour. He urged his horse to increase the pace, but remained alert to places where the killers could set up an ambush. If they discovered someone was on their back trail, they would try to eliminate the danger of being captured or killed. He followed the tracks until darkness forced him to stop. He reined into a small cove and dismounted. His thoughts were with the hapless woman carried away by the ruffians; experience told him that they would soon find her a liability, slowing the progress and kill or abandon her.

The next morning, Tom had been on the trail since daylight and had gone about three miles when he suddenly found some fresh horse droppings that were still warm. He knew that the outlaws were not far ahead and his self-defense sensors were on full alert. There were rising hills and heavy wooded areas on both sides of the trail. The large boulders strewn along the hillsides provided perfect cover for bushwhackers. Not having a choice, Tom rode on entering the rough lands. He was somewhat hearten by the fact they still carried Helen Parks with them as there was no evidence she had been left along the trail. Perhaps he could still save her life or from a fate worse than death.

The landscape was changing; the hills seemed to rise to the sky with large boulders covering the inclines. He could not see very far ahead as the trail was twisting and narrowing; trees and brush became much more dense. The hair on his neck bristled when his horse suddenly stopped, snorted and tried to turn back. He knew that the horse had sensed that other animals were nearby. Tom dismounted, led his horse into a heavy stand of brush and tied him firmly with the reins and a rope. He did not want to be left without a mount out here in the badlands. The horse may have smelled a cougar, which would cause him to flee. Caution demand he investigate what caused his horse to act up. He climbed half way up the hill on the left side of the trail as it gave more cover higher up. He slowly and quietly moved forward, watching every bush for signs of movement. Then he heard voices up ahead.

He now wanted to get in close without being discovered. Tom wanted surprise on his side, not theirs. He moved within sight of the outlaws; the three of them were standing in a small glade looking down at a woman; he had found Helen Parks. She was lying prone on the ground. She was not moving. He heard one of the killers say, "Slick, you like to kill women; shoot her." Tom could just barely hear the reply, "Nah, she is finished anyway and I told you both we have someone on our back trail. She'll be dead in an hour. Why tell someone where to find us?"

The apparent leader said, "Alright, no use wasting our bullets and drawing attention if we are being followed. Let's leave her here and get on to Tablerock. I want whiskey and a real woman." They all laughed, mounted, spurred their horses and rode on down the trail at a gallop.

In the moments before the outlaws mounted, Tom decided to let them go since they were leaving the woman. He had his rifle aimed at the outlaws, but experience told him that these culprits would not give up without a gunfight. He considered it more important to save her life than attempt to arrest or kill the outlaws and she might not be as bad off as the outlaws thought. He knew that once the bullets started to fly the woman could very well be the first victim. He had heard their destination, and would deal with them after he determined Helen Parks' condition. That had to be his first priority. After the killers disappeared down the trail, he walked swiftly to the unmoving woman. As he neared her prone body, she rolled to her side and rose up on her elbow; she said, "You are another one of those killers. Just shot me now and be done with it." Tom was surprised. She appeared to be just a young girl, but on closer look he realized that Sissy had many of her mother's features. Under other circumstances, this would be a beautiful woman. Her dress was up above her knees and had tears along the sides. He looked away and said, "Take it easy. I'm a U.S. Marshal. Are you Helen Parks?"

She showed no emotion and replied in a low subdued voice, "Yes, how did you know my name?"

"Thank the Lord they left you here. I've been trailing your tormentors since yesterday. Are you hurt badly? What can I do for you?"

She looked at him and said, "I've been through hell, but since last night I have feigned unconsciousness and acted as if I was dying. It may have saved my life, and I know it saved me from some of their devilment."

Tom said, "Perhaps that was the reason they decided to leave you here. We'll have to add your tactics to our training manuals. Are you able to travel?"

"I think so. I'll never be the same again. They ruined my life and killed my husband and I don't know what's come of my child."

"Sissy is well and on her way with my deputy Blair Green to a safe place. She is just fine and a real strong young lady."

She looked at him, studying his face. After more than a minute she said, "I guess you are who you say you are and I'll have to trust you. But what do you know about my baby and husband?"

"Sissy is fine. We buried your husband at your place under the large tree. He had several bullets wounds and must have died instantly without pain. Sissy asked about her pa. I told her that her pa had gone to heaven. She was sad, but seemed to understand that she would not see him again."

"Thank the Lord you found her. Was she still in the hiding place?"

"Yes, she was doing what you all had told her to do. She is an extremely brave, well-mannered and knowledgeable young lady. She handles herself much better than some adults I've known."

She hesitated for a moment and then said, "They killed Morgan and then shot the animals."

Tom said, "Madam, we have to think about the future and getting you to safety so that Sissy will know that you are alright. Are sure you can travel?"

"Yes, I'll be fine. I've been abused and mistreated. I need to clean up and get some thorns to hold this dress together. I'll never get the filth off me. But I have to go back to the house."

"Let me help you to the shade. Then I'll get my horse and you can have my slicker. Will you be alright for a few minutes until I return?"

"Yes, go ahead. I want to go back to the house. There's something I have to get, it will help Sissy and me get through this awful time."

He said, "If you are worried about the box hidden in the stump, I found it and sent it with my deputy and Sissy. It will be safeguarded for you. I looked at the contents, but it is all there as I found it. Try to rest and we will talk after I get back."

When Tom returned she was huddled against the tree trunk; she had managed to straighten her hair out some, wipe a little of the dirt from her face. He was again taken by her youthful appearance even under such extreme circumstances and maltreatment. She was composed, smiled slightly and asked, "Do you have any water in those canteens?"

"Yes, I was just going to tie my horse and bring you a drink. I don't know this country, so we have to use the water sparingly. However, there must be water around with so many cottonwoods and willows." She took the canteen and sipped the water. He thought, she is smart and has the drive to survive no matter the hardship.

She asked, "Marshal, when can we see my little girl? I know she is worried sick."

"Please call me Tom. I must be honest with you. It will take sometime for us to catch up with Blair and Sissy. Blair is a good man and a brave officer. He will make sure Sissy is safe. She knows that you were alive when they took you away. I told her that I would bring you back. Now it seems I can keep my promise. Do you feel like riding now?"

She looked at him and asked, "Where are you taking me? I want to see Sissy."

"I would guess the nearest town is Tablerock. We'll try to find it or a settler's house."

She said, "That's where the killers were going. I hope we catch up with them.

They need killing."

"Let me help you get on the horse and I will walk. We can make pretty good time, but not as fast as the killers unless they stop."

What Tom and Helen did not know was that the killers were just a little more than two miles down the trail. They had found a running stream with a pool of deep water in the bend of the stream and could not resist stopping and making a cook fire. They still carried some of the meat from the calf and cans of fruit they found in the house they burned. It was cool and peaceful under the large evergreens growing on the bank.

Back down the trail, Tom first smelled wood burning, and a little later heard their horses grazing. He eased forward, motioning for Helen to remain quiet. He located the horses; three of them grazing on tall grass and hobbled. He led his horse into a clump of bushes, assisted Helen to dismount, and asked in a hushed voice, "Do you know how to use a gun?"

"Yes, Morgan said I was a pretty good shot."

"Then take this pistol and use it if you need it to get away. You stay here and if you don't hear from me in a few minutes, get on the horse and go down the trail as fast as you can."

He took his rifle, pulled the other pistol from its holster, and went silently toward the small campfire. He expected that the killers would be close by. Two of them were sitting against a tree trunk and the other was in the water pool up to his waist, fully clothed. But before Tom could duck down, he knew that they had discovered him. The one who had seen him first, rolled to his side slinging lead, while the other outlaw was still getting his pistol clear; Tom took aim with the rifle and shot the one spouting lead at him; then the second outlaw was shooting. Tom rolled to a small rock and fired as his target scrambled for cover. He knew that the outlaw was hit; he glanced at the one in the creek, but had lost sight of him while dealing with the other two; then Tom saw the outlaw crouched and running toward the horses. He had a clear shot; he fired and the outlaw died before he hit the ground. Now to find out about the one he knew was wounded. He could not see where he fell.

Then suddenly, behind him he heard a crazed voice hissing, "You bastard, stand up and drop your guns. You killed my friends. You got me in the leg and I'm bleeding to death, but you will die a slow death. I want to hear you yell and beg for your life after I gut shoot you."

Tom had heard desperate and wounded outlaws a few times and knew this one meant to kill him. He had to buy time. Standing very still, he said in a calm voice, "Things are not as bad as you may think, I can tend your wounds and you may live a long life."

The outlaw said, "You bastard, I'm not so easy to fool, drop those guns and keep your hands in the air, turn around, I want to see your damn face before I kill you; don't make any fast moves, I might shoot you in the back."

The outlaw's voice indicated he was breathing heavily, in pain and very edgy. The situation was not in his favor. Tom was very concerned about the woman in his care. If it ended here for him, what would happen to Helen? He had to keep the outlaw talking, his chances of getting the upper hand increased with every minute of delay. This was no time for heroics. He felt almost certain his time had come and that he was a dead man, killed by a cowardly outlaw. He had to act, but how?

CHAPTER 5

BLOOD THIRST

Quirt Evans crossed the Rio Grande and spurred his horse to a gallop. He was anxious to reach Tincup and turn it to ashes. Following close behind Quirt was the most ferocious and violent gang of outlaws that he could assemble, each armed with rifles, pistols, knives and dynamite. He glanced over his shoulder and snarled to himself, *the bastards that killed Ben must die. I'll take every dollar in that rundown town.* His rage was not new as it come on him at an early age, but the recent defeats had increased his rage after leaving Tincup under a hail of bullets. He never had to take flight until he faced the guns in Tincup; the bastards killed Ben and now they would pay for his life. Ben was not that important, but having his plans ruined made Quirt's blood boil.

After the showdown with Quirt Evans and the outlaw they killed, the citizens of Tincup had not just sat idle waiting to be slaughtered. There was very little doubt that Quirt Evans would try to carryout his threats to kill everyone in town. His reputation was well known throughout the frontier. The new town Marshal Tim McCall, had demonstrated to the town that he knew something about military tactics and planning. He called a meeting of the town's elders and on a chalkboard drew the boundaries of the town; he then divided it in four parts. He marked defensive positions surrounding the town, showing field of fire from each.

Tim McCall said, "I believe that if we all hang together we will be able to hold our own, defeat and send the gang of cutthroats' running back to Mexico. It will not be like a well-organized assault by trained military men. This will not be a cakewalk in the church. When Quirt Evans returns he will mostly likely have a large gang of killers leading the charge against our town. I suspect we can deal with his large gang of cutthroats, but we must prepare our defensive gun positions and ask those who man them to give us notice of any strangers approaching town. From now on we must have at least four riflemen, one from each section on guard at the approaches to town. We'll have to depend on them to raise the alarm. Each of us must be alert to unusual incidents or strangers drifting into town. If they decide to come disguised one or two at a time, we will pick them up and put them in jail, or deal with them in the street or saloon, wherever we find them." There were many nervous questions, but no one seemed to question the need for proactive precautions offered by the town marshal.

It was late afternoon and Evans and his outlaw gang were hot, tired and anxious to argue and take exception to almost every little thing that displeased them; the rider in front kicking up too much dust, being bumped by someone riding too close, grumbling about lack of sleep and rest. There was very little loyalty to each other except for a few with relatives in the gang. They tended to hang together, no matter what the circumstance and would fight like tigers when crossed. Fights often happen in outlaw gangs; the fastest draw may not be the survivor in such temper, jealous or alcohol driven confrontations. Quirt Evans ruled with an iron hand, paying little attention to their arguments while keeping the gang members in fear of his wrath. None wanted to openly cross Quirt Evans. He had not made his mark as an outlaw leader without knowing his gang members, and kept one or two trusted gunmen watching his back at all times. He knew that it was still a hard ride to Tincup and he also knew some of the gang members were not anxious to destroy Tincup for what they considered such a small payment. Most of them had by now heard about the killing of Ben and Quirt's departure from Tincup under a hail of bullets. They grumbled and stopped their usual bantering, as they could see very little benefit to themselves with a high risk of catching a bullet scared the hell of them. Knowing all this, Evans decided that considering the present mood of the gang they needed a diversion.

He signaled a stop near a large boulder, which provided just enough shade for his horse. The gang gathered close and he said, "I've heard about enough grumbling and complaining. There will be money and women for all. Before we get to Tincup, we'll rest up at the Singletary place it is out of the way but there's food, whiskey and at least two women. Old Moss Singletary has some hired guns working as cowpunchers, but we will use all of them for target practice. I have a plan to get some of us into the house and barns before they suspect what we have in mind. It should be easy to fool them as they will not want a gun battle if they can talk their way out of it."

A little later, Quirt and his gang approached the far side of a knoll overlooking the Singletary ranch house and out buildings. Again, Quirt called a halt and motioned for the gang to gather around. He said. "Over that hill is the Singletary house. They're just waiting for our visit. Old Moss may have lookouts and they may have already seen us. Shotgun, you take two of these dogs with you and amble off down there as if you're just coming to water your horses. If they start shooting, we'll come on down. There're enough of us to kill them like rabbits. They will be well fixed for food and whiskey. Don't kill the women until we finish with them." With a wolfish grinned and a snarl, he to motioned Shotgun and said, "Go on and open the gates, we'll be waiting to see what you find out."

Some thirty minutes later, Evans and his gang had not heard from Shotgun; nor had there been any shooting. Quirt knew they were close enough to the ranch house to hear shooting if it had occurred. He knew something had gone wrong. He turned to the anxious faces of his killers and said, "Shotgun must have run into a bad streak of luck. We'll go back to that creek we crossed and wait for dark. I want all of you to be as quiet as possible; no fires but let the horses graze and water. I will slip down there and see what is going on after they bed down. Carlos you will come with me. Your knife throwing may come in handy to get rid of lookouts."

He then spoke to the gang, "If you don't hear from us, or hear shooting, come down with your guns blazing. We'll take care of ourselves."

It was dark when Quirt and Carlos approached the barn from the creek near the west side of the buildings. There were some bushes that had not been tromped down by the livestock. Both killers were experienced night prowlers and knew how to take advantage of every bush and sprig of grass. The fleeting clouds opened up suddenly and the full moon illuminated the area around the house and barn. Nothing moved. Quirt whispered to Carlos, "There may be dogs on the place, but if so they are asleep too. You stay here and watch the back door and I will try to get to that window that shows light."

When he reached the area below the window, he slowly raised up so that he could see under the blinds. A quick look told him that Shotgun and the other two were prisoners; they were lined against the far wall, tied to chairs and gagged. Before Quirt could decide his next move he heard the report of a six-gun and a bullet struck the window facing. He fell to the ground and rolled half under the house; shooting at where he thought the flash came from. Then all hell broke loose. The house was off the ground just high enough for Quirt to scramble under it and to the other side. He was fierce that he had been such an easy target. While crawling out at the other side of the house, he realized that they had been waiting to trap more of the gang. Old Moss was a hard man and a smart fighter. Quirt made it to the creek and ran up the sand bed to find his horse. There was no sign of Carlos, and then he heard from the big tree, "That was a damn trap. Did you see anything in the house?"

"Shotgun and the others are prisoners. They're tied to chairs and gagged. Moss was using them for bait. What the hell is keeping the others? I told them to come in shooting." Then he heard the guns open up. His gang had arrived. In the moonlight he saw his men come into the yard, guns blasting away. He saw several of his men fall out of their saddles; one yelling, "Get out of here. This is a trap."

Then the intense exchange of gunfire stopped suddenly. After a few minutes of silence, Quirt said, "Come on, let's get out of here, they have the advantage from their hidden gun positions. I'll get even with old Moss Singletary if it is the last thing I ever do."

Carlos asked, "What about Shotgun and the others in there?"

"What about them? They stumbled into a trap and almost got me killed trying to help them. Moss will probably kill or let them go in the morning after they horse whip them."

The gathering clouds and sandstorm hid the moon and it was pitch dark when Quirt and some of his stragglers slowly urged their mounts over the knoll. He gathered the few outlaws around him at the steam where they had stopped before attacking Singletary's ranch. He decided to wait and see if any more of the gang made it away from the intense gunfire at the ranch. A few found their way back to camp. Quirt finally decided that no more would be coming in, so he rolled up in his blanket and waited for daylight.

Long before sunrise he roused, took a swift glance at the sleeping figures around him. He fumed when he realized less than half his gang had returned. He kicked Carlos and said, "Get them on their feet, we're leaving."

Carlos asked, "Where to boss?"

Quirt was still angry and foaming at the mouth, he snarled, "Back across the river and get some more gunslingers. I'll come back and send that damn Moss Singletary and the bastards in Tincup to hell with bullet holes."

Carlos looked around at the gang members and said, "It looks like a couple of our boys have some bullet holes, and I doubt they will make it to the river. They need doctoring."

The killer boss stared at Carlos and said, "Tell them if they can't keep up. They're on their own."

Carlos replied, "Boss, we need money, whiskey and women. These gunslingers will fight when they know something is in it for them. What about Shotgun?"

Quirt said, "Moss probably killed Shotgun and the others. Let's go back to the river; I've got to find more gunslingers. After we take care of Singletary and squeeze all the money and whiskey we can get out of those wimps in Tincup, we'll go to Abilene and find where my gold is hidden. That's too much money to let go without a fight."

Later that afternoon, Moss Singletary and three of his Lazy S cowpunchers arrived in Tincup and pulled up at the Town Marshal's office; Tim McCall came out of the door and asked, "Now what Moss? Did you have trouble at your place?"

"Just a little disagreement, I'd say. A passel of killers tried to burns us out. But we got the drop on them and some are in the wagon. They need burying soon. I think you will find twelve in there that won't ever bother anyone again." Singletary replied.

"What about the other three you have trussed to their saddles? Looks like you had some trouble getting them on their horses." The Marshal responded.

Singletary smiled for the first time, "Let's just say they've learned that Moss Singletary knows a thing or two about skulking night crawlers. You can see they've been tamed some. May be the Judge will find them worthy of a good rope. They're anxious to meet their maker."

"Bring them in. The jail needs reinforcing, and I'll need extra guards, as the Circuit Judge won't be here for another three weeks. Can you spare a few of your cowpunchers?"

"I'll send in two of my punchers when I return to the ranch. But I can tell you now that I regret not hanging them. I lost three of my best men defending the ranch and have two more nursing bullet wounds. If I'd known it was going to be a bother to you and the town, these killers would have been in the wagon with the other bodies instead of my riding my good horses. They'll guilty as hell of killing people, stealing and raiding and living off the sweat and hard work of decent citizens. We ought to hang them here and now and put an end to their sorry lives."

The Marshal responded, "There'll be no hanging in this town without a court order. Since I don't have jurisdiction outside Tincup, I will ask the U.S. Marshal Service to investigate whether you acted lawfully in killing the men you have stacked on your wagon like cordwood."

"Well the hell you say, I didn't come in here to hear your lecture. These killers are now your problem." Singletary turned to his cowpunchers and continued, "Throw those damn bodies off the wagon and let's get the hell out of here before I lose my temper with this whippersnapper." He wheeled his horse and rode out of town without looking back. He was angry.

Instead of unloading the dead bodies in the street as Singletary had instructed, Marshal McCall told the driver to take them to the undertaker. Some of the townsmen gathered around the wagon with the bodies protested burying the outlaws in the town cemetery. There were suggestions to burn the bodies and save digging graves and cost of boxes. Marshal McCall called out to the group, "I'll hear no more of such talk. We are decent people and we will respect the dead, no matter of their sins." The crowd slowly withdrew and the driver urged the team of mules toward the undertaker's office. Then McCall marched the three captives to the jail. When they were locked in the small cells, Shotgun bragged, "You damn badge toters better get ready to die. Quirt will be here and wipe this town out. Better turn us loose and we'll try to keep Quirt from killing all of you."

"Just simmer down; we'll be ready for your killer boss if he shows up in town. When the Judge arrives, you three will hear your fate." Tim said as he locked and checked the door, "I don't like hangings, but I may change my mind in your case."

Shotgun tried to mask his fear and snarled, "Hell is waiting for all of us and that includes you. So be careful how you treat us. Your judge may have a mishap before he gets to town."

Later that evening, two of Moss Singletary's Lazy S riders arrived at the jail. Tim McCall looked them over and frowned, but held his thoughts to himself. These were no ordinary cowpunchers; their boots and belts were obviously expensive and their revolvers rested in well-oiled low-slung holsters strapped to their thighs. These Lazy S riders would be hard to peg; they could be just young honest cowpunchers taking on their version of hard cases or very dangerous riders of the Owl Hoot Trail. The Marshal stood and offered his hand, saying, "I'm Tim McCall, I don't believe I've seen you boys in town?"

The tall rangy fellow said, "We stay pretty close to the ranch. We save our money to buy land for a ranch. We're the Sutton brothers. I'm Steve and this ornery kid is Layton. The boss said you would tell us what you want us to do."

"We are pretty well set for tonight, but I will need you both tomorrow. We'll work out a schedule tomorrow for guarding the misfits you see in the cells back there." Tim said.

Layton laughed and said, "I believe they know us; we helped capture them. The boss said we made a mistake; we should have finished them off when we had them in our sights."

"I've told your boss that I am asking the U.S. Marshal Service to investigate whether killing those raiders was justified. From what you just said, I am given to understand that there was little effort made to avoid those killings."

Steve said, "Now just a damn minute, Layton is known for shooting off his mouth. They attacked the ranch and got themselves killed during the fight last night. It was mostly dark and we all shot at anything that moved. I guess there was no mention that several good horses were also killed. Bullets were flying like bees and I'm surprised that more of our own folks were not killed."

"Let it rest for now. You all will have a chance to tell your stories when the U.S. Marshal arrives. Where do you fellows come from?"

"Our folks had a spread up near Red Bluff on the Pecos; our parents and little sister got slaughtered by killers dressed like Indians. We later learned that most of the killers were white bastards."

The door to the cells was ajar, and Steve Sutton's words were interrupted from one of the prisoners, who laughed and said, "That was Quirt Evans, he brags a lot about riding high around Red Bluff; I believe he later learned you boys were missed and he intended to come back for you. So don't get in a hurry to meet him." The prisoners all laughed and hooted.

Steve and Layton started toward the cell with their revolvers in their hands. Tim McCall jumped in front of the door and said, "Put those revolvers away. You don't know if they are just telling you something to make you angry or telling the truth; in either case we will make sure the judge hears about their confessed involvement in the killing of your folks." They put the revolvers back in the holsters and sat down, still angry.

Tim McCall closed the door to the cell area. Poured a cup of coffee and asked in a low voice, "How did the killers miss you boys?

"Me and Layton was away selling some of our longhorns. We have a few clues about the killers of our folks, and now that we know Quirt Evans gang was involved we intend to hunt them down and kill every last one of them."

The Marshal said, "I know it is hard to live with the burden you boys carry, but at some point you both need to get on with your lives and leave the killers to justice of the law."

"You may be right. I guess we were lucky to be away at the time, but it shore don't feel like it. I guess you think we are outlaws; well we're not. We always look for honest work. That's the way Pa raised us." Steve replied in an aggressive voice.

Tim studied the floor a full minute and said, "Hate to hear about your folks; as I've said, I know it is hard on both of you. Go get something to eat and I'll see you in the morning."

Steve replied, "I'm pretty sure that I've seen you before; maybe around Pecos?"

"Well that's possible, although I don't recall meeting you. I was a deputy sheriff for a spell down there. I left that area a few years ago," the Marshal replied.

"Well I'll be damn. Now it comes to me you killed several of the bastards that murdered our folks. I remember now, you got shot up something bad they said. I've wanted to shake your hand Mister McCall." Steve walked forward with an extended hand.

Tim took his hand in a firm handshake and said, "Let's not make too much out of what I done down there. I was never able to connect Quirt Evans to the killings around Pecos, but I heard his name often enough. You boys may be looking for the same killers that I've been chasing. I'd just as soon you boys would keep all this to yourselves, at least for now. I've learned some things are better not talked about."

"Marshal, you can depend on us, we'll be around as long as you need us," Steve replied.

The next night Layton insisted on taking the midnight to six duty of guarding the jail and the three outlaws. Toward the end of his shift Shotgun yelled for help, saying they needed a doctor immediately. Layton keys in hand, still drowsy and about half asleep went to the cell door and saw one of the prisoners rolling and groaning on the floor, holding his stomach. His groans grew louder when he saw Layton. Layton was now very close to the barred door he turned to get a better view of the sick man and in a split second realized he had made a mistake; Shotgun grabbed him and jerked him up against the iron door; then it was over in less than a minute. Shotgun had easily broken Layton's neck, and then picked up the keys, which had fallen near the bottom of the door. They placed Layton's body in the cell, locked it, found their revolvers, and took several boxes of ammunition. At the Livery, they were again lucky and found it easy to kill the night watchman, saddle three of the best horses in the corral and unhurriedly ride of town.

Tim McCall blamed himself for permitting the outlaws to escape and kill Layton. He had mentioned to him about assigning another guard to help and was rebuffed. Both he and Steve had really believed that Layton was capable to handle the situation at the jail. When Tim mentioned to Steve that perhaps Layton should have some help, Steve assured him that Layton would do just fine and would resent any help. On finding his brother dead in the jail Steve vowed to bring his killers to justice. He prepared to leave and chase the outlaws immediately.

Steve said, "I'm going after the killers; they will head for Mexico and I intend to catch them before they get there. Please tell Moss Singletary that I will be back after I put those three culprits in their graves."

Tim McCall said, "Steve, they have too much of a head start and you don't know what trail they are following to Mexico. My jurisdiction ends at the town's boundary and I cannot go with you, but if you could find the place the Evans' gang crosses the Rio Grande and watch it to see when they come back this way, as you know Evans has threatened, then ride like hell to let us know that they are their way. That would be a great help to save lives here in Tincup. What do you think about that as a starter plan?"

"I feel certain I can track them. But if I don't catch the killers before they cross into Mexico, I'd hang around a while and see if they come back across. Right now I have to make arrangements to bury my brother."

Tim said, "Come along, I will help with the arrangements."

Meanwhile Shotgun and the two cutthroats wasted no time in getting back to the hideout across the Rio Grande. They arrived after dark and headed straight to the only cantina in the out of way village. On entering Shotgun was not surprised to find Quirt and several of the outlaws drunk with women on their laps. Quirt pushed the girl off his lap, snarled at Shotgun, "What kept you so long? We waited an extra day at the Singletary ranch and decided you had high tailed it."

"Like hell you did, I know you seen us roped to them damn chairs and then you all left; it was not much of a gunfight as far as I could tell. Me and the boys here are lucky, Singletary killed a dozen of our friends. What you got to say about that?" Shotgun asked.

"I may have to kill you, but right now I say cool down and grab a woman. We have money so get a bottle." Quirt put on his most friendly grin.

Shotgun was about to pull back an empty chair when Quirt's bullet struck him high in his chest; the second bullet knocked out his left eye. He was dead by the time he hit the floor.

Quirt looked at the other two who had come in with Shotgun and asked, "What will it be? You want to join that loudmouth on the floor or have a drink and ride with us when we go back to Tincup to settle the score?"

The two scared outlaws assured him that they would ride with him. Quirt stared at them and said, "That's sensible, I got to find a few more gunslingers before we leave here, so get a bottle and a woman."

After two weeks of boozing and abusing village girls, Quirt and his gang approached the Rio Grande during a thunderstorm and down pour. He had to settle for some drunks and gamblers, as he could not find enough killers, but he was satisfied that each one of them was ruthless and would fight. Quirt pulled up under some trees on the bank to wait for the rain and wind to let up before crossing the river.

Hidden several hundred yards from the Rio Grande crossing Steve Sutton watched the outlaws climb the north bank and form a single file following a well-used trail. He had the sudden impulse to start shooting and killing as many of the gang as he could. But he knew that at best he could only get a few of them before they came after him. Tim McCall had cautioned against taking action by himself; he had promised to follow the gang and when he knew where they intended to strike, he would ride ahead and give the alarm. Steve knew that McCall's plan was much better than attacking the gang here. He waited until the gang passed then followed their trail.

On the trail north Quirt's outlaws became extremely disgruntled and irritated. The gang found fault with everything; their horses, the weather, and heading into the desert where there were no whiskey or women. Most outlaws are by nature lazy and ill tempered even in good times. The anger of the gang's boss had not lessened and he knew that his unruly gang of cutthroats riding behind him was unpredictable and any one of them was capable of shooting him in the back. He had decided to tread lightly and not show his high state of anger. After crossing the Rio Grande he reined his mount to a halt and waited for the gang to come in close; the storm had paused for the moment and he wanted to test the mood of the gang. When they circled around him, and over the noise the horses were making snorting from the rain, he smiled and asked, "Should we attack those bastards in Tincup first, wipe them out and then go to Moss Singletary's ranch and burn it to the ground or deal with the Singletary ranch first? I don't give a damn, which is first. Just tell me what you all want to do."

The outlaws did not take long to respond, as they knew he was playing a game; several of them spoke up and said they would ride with him. It made no difference who died first. Then someone in the back offered, "Boss, Singletary's ranch is closer. Kill them and rest up where there's plenty food and then ride on to Tincup."

"Just remember you all picked old Moss Singletary. He may still have an army of gunslingers, but who the hell cares? Let's ride, kill all of them and leave the place in flames."

He took his suppressed wrath out on his horse; he really had intended to hit Tincup first, but decided to play along with the gang. He jabbed his spurs with the large silver rowels in the horse's flanks and kicked his sides viciously.

Quirt had no intention of sparing any living thing at the ranch or in Tincup. He would kill people, animals and everything that moved. He wanted revenge. He again, spurred his horse unmercifully as they topped the next hill, urged the stallion to run. His outlaw gang consisted of convicted killers, horse thieves, rapist, robbers and abusers of women. Quirt's confidence was now restored and riding high, as he knew that the gang enjoyed seeing their victims die. Yes, they would enjoy killing the pilgrims and burning the ranch and town. It was a bloodthirsty, ruthless bunch that rode toward what they hoped would be fun.

A few miles down the trail it started to rain again. Quirt wanted to stay on the trail and spend the night in his hideaway cave. Then he thought of his mistake in trusting that damn Jake Leach. Now the gang would stop overnight at the cave where Jake was to leave the gold. He fumed and cussed. He resolved to find the kin of that damn traitor and get his gold back. It did not just disappear; hell it might be hidden in the cave after all. He'd check every damn inch of that cave. He had to find the gold.

Death rode with Quirt Evans as he urged his horse along the desert trail toward Bat Cave.

CHAPTER 6

TREACHERY

U.S. Marshal Tom Leach's mind was racing to find a way to turn this deadly situation to his advantage. He expected a bullet any moment; no training manual ever written provided answers to instant life and death decisions. Then he heard the injured outlaw hiss, "I'm not going to tell you again; you bastard, stand up and drop your guns. Act real tame like I might let you live."

Tom's mind raced to find a way out, he recognized fear and hate in the culprit's voice; the odds were too high for any sudden move on his part as it would bring a bullet to his back. He realized lady luck would have to be riding with him now. Somehow, he had to buy time to get out of this fix. He calculated his chances of suddenly falling to the ground, roll and try to get a shot off; but he was standing on the edge of dense underbrush which limited him to falling forward, thus giving the outlaw a better chance of shooting him. He decided that was not a very good chance.

Tom decided to play along, with one hand; he cautiously unbuckled his gun belt and dropped it to the ground. Just as his gun belt struck the ground, the outlaw snarled, "You killed my friends. You got me in the leg and I'm bleeding to death, but before I die, you'll die a slow death. I want to hear you yell and beg for your life after I gut shoot you. Here's a bullet for my friends."

Tom said, "I'm unarmed, let's palaver, you can shoot me anytime you want after we talk this thing out. What do you think about that Idea?

The outlaw yelled, "No more talk, you die."

The next thing Tom heard was a loud gunshot; he flinched, but felt no pain, as he turned he saw the outlaw crumble to the ground. His revolver fell harmlessly near his outstretched hand.

Helen was standing some twenty feet away; neck high in vines and bushes. She just stood there like a statue; she held a revolver high over her head. Her face was chalky-white. Tears streamed down her face and she suddenly dropped and disappeared in the undergrowth. As she fell, Tom heard her gasp for breath, and then a long low moan.

Tom rapidly checked the outlaw to make sure he would not cause anymore trouble; the outlaw was dead, the bullet had entered behind his left ear. Blood oozed out of his mouth and nose. Tom found Helen lying on the ground, dazed and about half-conscious; she was crying and praying for God's grace and forgiveness. Tom gently helped Helen sit up and patted her shoulder saying, "He left you no choice; if you had made a sound he would have killed me and then shot you. I will always be in your debt for saving my life. I'm sure he did not know that you were nearby, and he was just taunting me, before killing me. There's no doubt about that."

She tried to dry her eyes and managed, "That was dastardly thing to do. I just knew he was going to kill you. God help me, I've never killed a human being before. What happens to me now?"

"After burying these killers, we will go and find your daughter. Now please pull yourself together. You can refresh yourself in the stream below while I am searching these culprits and burying them. I need to identify them if possible for my report and notification of their kin."

Less than two hours later, Tom had buried the outlaws and caught their horses. He picked out the best sorrel for Helen to ride, and tied the others in tandem so they could be led without much difficulty. Tom decided to cut across country, taking the most direct route, back to headquarters. Helen had revived somewhat, her natural tan color had returned to her face and she even timidly smiled when he helped her onto her horse. He estimated that it would be late the next day before they reached headquarters.

Meanwhile a conversation was heatedly taking place between Blanche and her father in the Longmire ranch house. Clay Longmire was very upset as he asked, "Blanche, what has come over you? I'd hoped you and Tom would one day run this ranch. If your Mommy had lived, she would like that."

"Papa, I can't help it. Tom is always gone for months at a time and I live in fear of hearing he is either hurt or killed. I cannot take that any more."

"These are tough times, but law and order is slowly coming to the frontier and there will be peace for everyone. Tom is doing more than his part in bringing that about. You should be supporting him instead of holding company with that young scamp Gus Leonard. Hell, I don't know that much about that fellow. He drifted in here two years ago and has made less than a fair hand. He's lazy. Perhaps, I should let him go now, something I should have done last year."

"Papa, if you let him go, I will go with him, married or not." Tears were streaming down her cheeks and she was silently sobbing.

"Blanche, it grieves me to see you carrying on this way. Let's leave things as they are until Tom returns and talks some sense in your head. Now dry up those tears and let's have breakfast." Clay slowly got out of his chair and started toward the kitchen.

But Blanche would not let it go; she said, "Another thing Papa you should quit grieving Mommy's loss, she would not want you to just waste away. There's plenty of ladies in town who would welcome it if you come calling."

"Now you listen to me young lady, I don't need no preaching by you or anyone else about my private feelings for your Mommy. She was my life and she left me you and Tess. I will always cherish her and I'll see that you both are properly married in due time as that is what she would want. In the meantime, you will not see that no good Leonard again, leastwise not until I find out more about him. Is that understood?"

"No, Papa that is not understood, but I will obey you as long as I live here. Whatever you learn about him, I just know it will all be good. Then I hope you will give us your blessing."

"Blanche, I hate to ask this, but tell me how far this courting has gone between you two. It is all so sudden; I don't know what to think."

"I'm a grown woman Papa, but I'll tell you this: he wanted to kiss me, but I refused. There, are you happy with that?"

"I'm not surprised that you have the gumption your Mommy gave you, but I needed to hear you confirm it."

Tess came into the room and acted as if she had not heard any of the heated discussion. She asked, "What's all the fuss about. I thought breakfast was ready. But I guess I'll have to cook the biscuits myself." She swiftly walked to the kitchen, not looking back.

During breakfast there was very little talk, except Tess chatted away about some strange birds she had seen yesterday in the barn. She said, "They were so beautiful, black with red markings on their wings and breasts. One minute they were there and the next they just flew away. I wanted them to stay."

Clay said, "Child, that is the way of life; not only for birds, but for the rest of us as well. I want to make sure you and Blanche have a good and decent life without having to work your selves to an early grave like so many other pioneer women out here." Blanche remained silent, with a sad face.

Tess smiled and said, "Papa, we'll marry those lawmen and they will see to our safety." She laughed and looked at Blanche with a big smile.

Blanche managed to smile and said, "Sister, speak for yourself, and quit acting like you don't know what's going on around here. Papa will decide who we marry." She hung her head in her arms crossed over the top of the table.

That really riled Clay, but he tried to control his fear and anger. He calmly said with the best smile he could muster, "You know better than that Blanche; I hope you know what you are seeking in life. I make no secret that I like Tom Leach, but whether you marry him is up to you, and you know it. If you choose otherwise when you regain your senses, I will make the best of it." He left the room without another word.

Tess looked at Blanche and asked, "Was all that necessary with Papa. You know how much he loves and wants to protect us. I may be younger than you, but I know in my heart that Gus Leonard is a no good tramp. I can just feel it the way he looks at us. He is hiding something."

Blanche said, "Now it's you and Papa. I don't see anything but good in Gus. But I must tell you, I am confused about my feelings for Tom."

"Why not wait until Tom comes back and talk with him?" Tess asked.

"I'm afraid that he will change my mind. Then I will be waiting the rest of my life for him to quit the running around shooting at outlaws. I live in mortal fear that he will be killed."

"Well anyway, Papa says you cannot see Gus anymore until he looks into his background. When that's done, I don't think you will want to see him. Come on help me with the dishes and quit fretting." Tess started to clear the table and Blanche slowly stood and helped her.

A little after sunrise the next morning, Clay saddled his horse and rode out to the range, and decided to stop at the cabin the wranglers used on some occasions while branding and rounding up cattle. He had sent four of his wranglers to the north range, including Gus Leonard, to brand the spring calves. During the ride out his mind could not let go of Blanche's sudden infatuation with Gus Leonard. This was all new to him, as Blanche had often spoken of her future with Tom Leach. Then she suddenly announced her interest in Gus Leonard; now Clay was mentally whipping himself for keeping that young fellow around. He had suspected for sometime that something seriously was not right with him. The fact year around wranglers was hard to find should not have been reason to keep him on. His choice was clear. Gus Leonard would have to go and the sooner the better. Blanche would kick up some dust for a while, but he knew she was sensible and would come to accept his decision in this matter.

As he rode up to the cabin he noticed Leonard's horse tied to the pole corral gatepost. He scanned the surrounding area looking for the other wranglers and then went to the cabin, opened the door and found Gus Leonard asleep on the floor; he was snoring. Clay saw an empty whiskey bottle close to the sleeping figure. He nudged Gus with his foot and said, "Get up; I want to talk to you."

Gus rose up on an elbow and looked at Clay with a wide grin, "Boss, I was just resting, been working real hard out here."

Temper mounting Clay asked, "Where are the other men?"

"Out a ways on the range branding calves, I'd guess." Gus was still smiling.

"Well what in hell makes you think you can get drunk and not work? I believe you have a half month's pay coming." Clay took his wallet from his pocket and then tossed Gus twenty dollars, saying, "That's more than you got coming. Now get your drunken body up and off my land."

"I'll go back to the bunkhouse and get my things. Blanche will go with me."

Clay said, "Like hell you will, I'll send one of the men to the ranch house and fetch whatever you have there. I don't want you near my daughter, ever again. You got that?"

Gus continued to smile and said, "Whatever you say boss, Blanche don't mean that much to me anyway. She knows you want her to marry that damn lawman Tom Leach. That's all I've heard for the last several months. I heard his brother is an outlaw. Maybe he is too."

"None of that is of concern to you. Both my girls talk too much. I should shoot you right now; I don't know why I let you stay on the ranch so long. You keep your butt right here until your things arrive. Then I want you off my land."

"Well, that suits me fine. I'll just go back to sleep until I get my things and then I'll mosey on. You should think of her, instead of having your way all the time." He lay back down and turned his face to the wall.

Clay was walking back to his horse in deep thought and trying to control his anger. His first inclination in there was to shoot the scamp and be done with it, but as he neared his horse he decided that he had handled the situation the best he could. At that point he sensed something wrong; the fierce blow struck him on the right side of his head. His horse spooked but did not break loose. Clay fell to the ground, killed with a stick of hardwood by the man he had just fired.

Leonard looked around and made sure that he had not been seen. He checked to see if his Boss was dead, took his money and then struggled to get the heavy body onto the saddle. He tied the body in the saddle, mounted his horse and rode toward the ranch house, leading Clay's horse. About a mile from the cabin, he stopped, pulled the body to the ground. He hurriedly, while looking all around, pushed Clay's foot through the stirrup, wrapped the reins loosely around the saddle horn and using his rope whipped the horse, causing him to break and run toward the ranch house, pulling Clay, whose dangling body spooked the horse causing him to run faster. Leonard smiled, satisfied with himself and his work on this day. Now the ranch would be his; Blanche might want to wait a few days before getting married, but she would come around. He rode out to join the other wranglers branding calves. He had not gone very far until he begin to have second thoughts about being able to keep the secret of Clay's death.

He pulled up under a tree and checked himself over. He cursed when he discovered that he had Clay's blood on his shirt. He sat thinking which way to ride. He had no feelings about killing his boss. He mused to himself, of the five he had killed, old man Longmire was the easiest. He stopped at the creek and tried to wash the blood off his shirt without success. Now he knew that he could not go out where the other men were working. They would notice the blood and start asking questions; then when Longmire's body was discover, he would be the first suspect. No, he could not go back at that point;, he counted the money again, and decided that he'd better head for the border. He had enough money to have a good time along the trail. He mused to himself, *"Now I'll have to come up with another name; never got used to Gus Leonard moniker anyway."* Lester Toler had killed the father of a young girl back in Missouri and been on the run ever since; He had used several different names and so far he had dodged the law and then took to the Owl Hoot Trail whenever it got too hot. He smiled, mounted and rode to the southwest.

As the miles passed he tried to get his mind off Blanche, but he knew that he really wanted Tess. He would come back someday and take both of them into the badlands. He fantasized taking them to the cave he had holed up in a few years back when he was just a kid while recovering from a bullet wound in his leg. He tried to remember the names of the two other outlaws who helped while he was healing from a bank teller's bullet. They had left him food and water then went on to Mexico. At the time he hated them for leaving him alone, still not able to ride. But later he realized he would have done the same thing in that situation. His mind returned to the Longmire girls; yes, they would be fun as long as he wanted them. He realized he would need help, but once he got the girls in the cave he could eliminate whoever helped him get them there. He hummed an off key tune as he happily rode on. He was once again on the Owl Hoot Trail. He felt free again.

A few days later, Leonard led his horse into the large cool cave. He was exhausted, about out of water and food, but he still had some whiskey. He spread his bedroll, sprawled on it, smiled, and wished he could have seen Blanche when she'd discovered old Longmire had been killed by his horse.

Later on that fateful day, Leonard had cowardly murdered Clay Longmire. Blanche had been in the barn gathering eggs when she'd heard a horse coming at full speed. By the time she got to the barn door, the horse had stopped in front of the corral gate, lathered almost white, and blowing like a steam engine. Then she noticed something under the horse; she looked again, and then screamed for help. Two of the ranch wranglers were left behind to work on the fences and repair the hayloft; both heard Blanche's call for help.

Clay Longmire's left foot was still in the stirrup, he was almost unrecognizable; Larsen, the oldest and most experience hand on the ranch reached the horse first. One glance at the mangled body and he turned to Blanche and said, "Blanche you and Tess go to the house." She shook her head and said, "No I want to help him."

Larsen walked over to where she stood like a statue, unmoving and eyes wide open. He took her arm and once again told her and Tess to wait in the house and that he would come and see them in a few minutes. He said, "I have work to do here. Please do as I ask."

The sisters walked slowly back to the house, each holding on to the other. Tess asked, "Who is that under Papa's horse?"

"God help me, it's Papa." Blanche sobbed.

Larsen recognized the mangled body of his boss immediately; he and his helper managed to get Clay's foot out of the stirrup, but in doing so Larsen said, "Look his foot is in the stirrup backwards. You know that the Boss would never try to mount his horse like that. This is foul play, if I've ever seen it."

The other wrangler asked, "What should we do now?"

"Let's get him in the wagon and I will take him to town. You ride out and have all the hands come in. You tell them what has happened and to wait for me to get back from town. I'm sure the Marshal will have something to say about all this. I'll see if the girls want to go with me to town. Tell the cook to keep a sharp eye out for anything unusual until the hands get back."

When Larsen entered the house with his hat in his hand, he was met by Blanche who had changed clothes and now wearing boots, one of her father's shirts, trousers and a felt hat. She had a neckerchief tied loosely around her neck. She also had strapped on her colt Clay had presented to her a few years back. She appeared completely in control of her emotions. Larsen was surprised to see the change that had taken place in such a short time. She said, "Papa always said if something happened to him that I should take control of the ranch and take care of Tess. I want you to stay close to the house and see that Tess remains here, also send for all the ranch hands to come on in. I will take Papa to town and when I return I want to talk to each of the hands. Tell Gus Leonard that he is in charge until I return."

Larsen thought a moment then said, "You can tell the Marshal that your Pa's death was no accident; his left foot was in the stirrup backwards. By the horse dragging him so far might have caused the top of his head to be caved in, but I don't think so. No, I believe he was murdered."

"My good Lord, do you know what you are saying. Who would do such a thing? Papa was respected and had friends all over the range. That's hard for me to believe. I'll see what the Marshal says." Blanche walked toward the door not looking back. But Larsen knew she was moved by what he had just told her.

Larsen replied, "I don't know who would do such a thing, but I do know whoever murdered your Pa was careless and in a big hurry. Else he would not have made the mistake of placing his foot in the stirrup backwards. I done a little law work for a spell once and I've only seen this stunt pulled once before; that fellow admitted what he had done before he was hanged."

Blanche paused in the door and said, "This really complicates what has to be done. If you are right, I will chase whoever killed my Papa to the end of the earth and kill him with my own hands. Or if there's more than one, they will be killed as well. Now you send out and tell Gus Leonard to make sure every last hand on this ranch is in the bunkhouse when I return." She whirled and swiftly walked toward the waiting wagon with her Pa.

When Blanche arrived in town, she pulled up in front of the funeral parlor, jumped down from the springboard seat and tied the horses to the hitch rail. When she turned, she was facing Tom Leach and a woman she had never seen. He stopped spoke to the woman and then came toward her. He said, "Blanche, what a pleasant surprise to find you in town this time of day. What's with the revolver and your new way of dressing to come to town? Where's Clay?"

Blanche glanced at the bedraggled woman who was leaning against the wall, and snapped, "I'd just bet you are surprised. As for Papa he is in the wagon. Dragged and killed by his horse. I've brought him in to prepare his funeral. As for the way I dress, that is no concern of yours." Tom did not reply.

He walked toward the wagon, but Blanche said, "Don't bother yourself with my troubles. I can handle this very well by myself."

He stopped and stared at her for a moment and asked, "Blanche, suddenly I don't understand you and your hostile attitude. What has come over you?"

She glanced at the woman again and said, "That should be fairly obvious even for you."

Tom continued on to the wagon, raised the blanket and studied the condition of his friend Clay Longmire. He turned and said to Blanche, "Come on and I'll bring Mrs. Parks with us. I was taking her to see Marshal Decker, but that can wait until we make the arrangements for your Papa. I'm hoping that Blair is here with her daughter. It's a long story, but it will keep. Come on."

Tom called out to Helen, "Helen, please come with us, this won't take long and then we'll see what the Marshal knows about your daughter."

Blanche did not move, she looked at Tom and snapped, "You go about your business. I can take care of Papa. It looks like we both have other interests now."

"Blanche, you and I have an understanding about our future, until I'm told different I shall do what is best for you and Tess. Now come down off that mustang and we'll make what ever arrangements you consider appropriate for you Father." He took her arm and led her toward the funeral parlor. She did not resist.

Helen followed them into the parlor and took a chair in the far corner. After Blanche and the undertaker talked for a few minutes, she turned to Tom and asked, "Will day after tomorrow be suitable for Papa's funeral?"

"That should give us time to get out the word to all his many friends, who will want to know of his tragic death. We'd be remiss if we did not spread the word about the funeral."

Blanche glanced once more at the woman in the corner chair and asked, "Where are you going from here. You mentioned going to see the Marshal?"

At that moment the door opened and Marshal Decker looked in and said, "Hello Tom, word travels fast, I was told you were in town. I also heard that Clay Longmire's horse dragged him to death."

He then turned to Blanche and said, "Miss Longmire, I'm truly sad to hear about your father, and I offer my heartfelt condolences. I need to talk with Tom for just a minute and then you can have him."

Before he could turn back to Tom she said, "Thank you Marshal, one of our wranglers who took Papa's foot out of the stirrup, believes Papa was murdered." She finally broke down, covered her face with her hands and neckerchief and sobbed.

Tom took her in his arms and said to Marshal Decker, "I just got here as Blanche drove up, and I have no details on anything about this problem. I'll do whatever is necessary to get to the bottom of this if it is foul play." Blanche continued to sob against his chest until he gently released her.

Saying, "Just give me a minute with Marshal Decker and then I'll see you back to the ranch."

Tom and the Marshal Decker stepped out on the porch and he explained about Helen Parks and that she was anxious to see her daughter, and then asked, "When did Blair get in with the girl?"

Marshal Decker dropped his voice to a whisper and said, "Bad news, some outlaw gang calling themselves the Prairie Wolves say they are holding Blair and a young girl in the badlands. They want twenty thousand dollars in gold for their safe release. When I got that demand my first thought was what happened to you and Clem Poole?"

"I'll make a full report later. But on our way back from the Territory we encountered an ambush and in the fire fight Clem Poole was killed. After killing the ambushers and burying them, we started back bringing Clem's body with us. We were not on the trail very long until we saw smoke. We investigated and found the trouble at the Parks farm. We buried Clem along with Mr. Parks. I then asked Blair to take the girl to the nearest stage line and see that she got back here safely. When Blair started back here with the young girl, I went after the outlaws who had kidnapped Helen Parks. That in summary is where we are now. How much information did you get about Blair?"

"I don't know how long they have held them as I just got the message yesterday. I was surprised that a child was also being held by them; I sent a message to the Service asking for the twenty thousands dollars."

Tom turned and spoke to Helen, "Please stay here a few minutes more until I return."

He followed Marshal Decker out the door and said, "Andrew I have a letter from my brother Jake saying that he was dying. Do have any information about him?"

"We understand he died in Tincup. There have been numerous murders down that way. Quirt Evans gang uses Mexico for a sanctuary and raids unchecked on our side. We must do something about bringing him to justice and breaking up that gang." The Marshal replied.

Tom thought a moment and said, "I also have some information about my outlaw brother that I will share with you later. Concerning the problem around Tincup, what does headquarters say about sending help to that area to quell Evans gang?"

"I'm told we should not expect any more manpower from the Service; to make things worse the Texas Rangers are not yet ready to take to the field and many of the counties down there on the border either have not elected sheriffs or the sheriffs have been killed trying to fight the gangs with very little help." Marshal Decker paused and then continued, "Our first priority right now is to find Blair and that girl."

Tom went to the door and asked Blanche to join him and the Marshal Decker. Blanche came out and Tom could see that she was fighting to control her emotions. His heart ached for her and the loss of her father. He also knew she had many questions about him arriving in town with a woman. He had not expected to learn that Blair and Sissy had not made it to town.

When Blanche came close Tom said, "Marshal Decker, I'll carry the ransom money to them. I'll do all I can to free Blair and Sissy. The woman in there is Helen Parks; the mother of Sissy who I hope is still with Blair. First, I need to find Helen a place to stay, and then break the news to her that her daughter is not here as she expected. She is going to take this real hard. She had to watch while the outlaws murdered her husband, burned their house, barns and killed all the animals on the farm. Then the outlaws took her captive and mistreated her for more than a day before I caught up with them."

Marshal Decker asked, "Why didn't the outlaws take the girl when they took her mother?"

"Helen's husband told his daughter Sissy to go hide when he saw the outlaws coming; she did and that saved her life. I might add that Mrs. Parks saved my life on the trail by killing one of the outlaws who had done the killing of her husband and then abused her. She is very distraught and may go to pieces when I tell her about yet another disappointment."

Marshal Decker said, "Well we must manage somehow to make her understand that we will do everything in our power to get her daughter back to her safely. I guess we can put her up at the hotel. She may not like all the activity from the saloon, but I don't know of anything better, do you?"

Tom was about to speak when Blanche said, "I'll take her home with me. Papa would have me do nothing less than offer a helping hand. Tom Leach sometimes I could just scratch your eyes out; you stay away for weeks on end, seldom any word from you. I never know whether you are alive are shot to pieces in some godforsaken town. But that does not lessen my upbringing, which demands that I offer that poor mother shelter until her daughter is returned to her. Now go tell her what you must then let me talk with her."

"Blanche, I appreciate your help. It is needed in this case. When you see her daughter you will know what a great and generous deed you have offered. Sissy deserves to have her mother alive and well when we bring her here." He turned to the Marshal Decker and continued, "I know most of the mountains in the badlands and I will carry the gold to them. I'll see you the first thing in the morning, right now I have two ladies to see back to the ranch." Marshal Decker excused himself and limped down the street toward his office.

Blanche grasped Tom's arm and said, "I must tell you something you may not like." She paused took a deep breath and continued, "One of the ranch hands tried to court me. I did not discourage him as I thought you might not come back. I had all kinds of silly thoughts. Papa objected and we had words before he left the house for the last time. I shall always regret my words to him. Now I can't tell him how foolish I was. I did not even allow Gus to kiss me, so there was nothing to be ashamed of other than being foolish and worrying about you."

Tom pulled her to his chest and said, "Enough of that. I know you, and that you would never disgrace yourself or family. Nothing is changed between us. Now I have to tell Helen about her daughter. Will you wait here?"

"Yes, Tom I will be here. But I don't want you going out to the ranch with us. I have a ranch to run and a sister I must care for. But I'll take Helen with me. When I get back to the ranch, I intend to tell Gus Leonard that if he wants to keep his job, he must stay away from me and work harder in the future. I know you have to go after Blair and that little girl. I'll be waiting for you no matter how long it may take. I want you to forgive for my silly thoughts." Blanche dried her eyes and tried to smile.

Tom replied, "There's nothing to forgive. I am obliged for your understanding that I must get Sissy and Blair back safely. I regret that I will not be here for Clay's services." He walked back to the funeral parlor.

Helen Parks calmly sat through hearing about Sissy being held by outlaws; then she asked Tom, "How much worse can it get? I don't want to live if something happens to Sissy."

"Helen, I will bring your daughter back to you. I want you to go with Blanche to her ranch and stay there until I get back with Sissy.

These are troubled times out here and we must bring law and order to the frontier or perish at the end of outlaw guns. I'm asking you to be patient and help Blanche as much as you can. She has just lost her father, who may have been murdered and now left to run a ranch while looking out for her younger sister. Will you go with Blanche?"

"Yes, I have no choice it seems. I want to pay my way. What happened to our money and papers?" She asked.

"Helen that is just one of many questions, I do not have the answers yet. I hope Blair managed to do something with your money before he was taken prisoner, but I have no way of knowing. I will try to let you know just as soon as I find out." Tom then took her arm and led her out to Blanche's wagon.

Blanche greeted Helen and said, "Let's go to the ranch and let Tom free your daughter. I know he will do just that." Neither of the women required assistance in getting upon the jump seat and Tom waved at them as they went down the street toward the ranch.

Tom was dead tired, but he wanted to learn as much as Marshal Decker knew about Blair and Sissy. He learned that a rock was tossed through the Marshal's window with a note that said, *your depety Blair Green and Sissy Parks will be releesed if you bring $20,000 in gold to the southwest box canyon that is called Wilbur's haunt. It easy to find. We wait one week and then keled them. We will be watching.*

Tom looked at the note and said, "Well we know what kind of culprits that are holding Blair and Sissy. I'd say they are just crazy enough to carryout their threat. Where in Wilbur's haunt? I'm not familiar with that name?"

"It is about thirty miles down the old Pecos trail. It just happens that the canyon is between here and Tincup where all hell broke out. We need more help, but when we clear up this matter with Blair, our attention must be focused the killers roaming the desert around Tincup. I'm sure you've heard of killer Quirt Evans who hangs out in Mexico and raids far into the frontier. He has already attacked the town of Tincup and the Singletary ranch. Several citizens and some raiders have been killed in those battles. I've also learned that Quirt Evans has made it clear that he plans to kill everyone on the Singletary ranch and in Tincup. The Service has asked the Governor to send a contingent of Rangers out there. But they are just now being reorganized and it will be a few weeks before they arrive. That leaves us to quell the trouble down there." Decker went on to inform Tom of all the information that the Marshal Service had sent out about the Quirt Evans' gang.

Tom thought a few minutes, digesting what he had learned. Then he said, "Blair was carrying a small tin box containing the deed to the Parks land and a large sum of money as well as other important papers. Mrs. Parks was depending on the money to see her through this mess. I'd guess if Blair had the time and opportunity he would think of something to safeguard it. I don't think he would let himself be taken hostage if he had a fighting chance to avoid it."

"Well Tom I hope you are right, but we must find someway to free Blair and the girl. I'll see if we can get some help from Austin. This is getting much too involved and dangerous for just the two of us." Then Decker explained that the Marshal's Service had been hit hard by resignations and agents killed in the line of duty. He said, "I'd like to send someone with you, or go with you myself, but as you know I would be breaking the Marshal's Service rules. What are your thoughts on all this?"

Tom had listened intently and said, "In this case, I believe working alone will have a better chance of success. I will go down there as soon as you get the gold. If I don't come back, please see to Mrs. Parks as she deserves all the help we can give her."

When Blanche and Helen Parks arrived at the ranch, Tess and Larsen met them in the yard. Blanche introduced Helen and told Tess to take her in the house and warm up some food and then show her one of the guest rooms. She turned to Larsen and asked, "Are they all in the bunkhouse?"

Larsen hesitated a moment and then said, "Yes, all but one. We don't know where Gus Leonard might be. The men said the last time they saw him he was sleeping in the line shack." She stared at him for a minute and then said, "Well let's go talk to the men."

She entered the bunkhouse and all of the wranglers stood with their hats in their hands; she wasted no time.

"You all know that Papa was dragged to death today. Larsen seems to think it was not an accident. I believe most of you know Papa carried a few hundred dollars at all times; there was no money on him when he came in. Now I want you to tell me all you know about Papa's visit to the range this morning and if you seen or heard anything that might tells us what happened to him. I am in charge of the ranch and will make all the decisions, all of you can stay on as long as you want, but what I say goes without question. Now I will start with Larsen and let him give his theory."

The next hour and half she listened to the very talkative wranglers. None had actually seen her father that day on the range, but all three of the men who were branding calves near the line shack had about the same theory; that Mr. Longmire discovered Gus Leonard in the shack drunk and asleep. They could have had words and Gus Leonard's temper led him to murder Mr. Longmire and then carried him away from the shack; placed his foot in the stirrup and spooked the horse. Then Leonard fled the area.

She was almost pale with anger and grief, but still very much in control of her emotions. Blanche turned to Larsen and said, "Larsen Moyer, you have been here with Papa from the start. I want you to be the ranch ramrod. I'm sure any one of you could easily be a good ramrod, but I'm asking all of you to give Larsen as much help as you can and remember what he says goes. Now Larsen, your first assignment is to go see Tom Leach and tell him that I want to see him out here before he leaves town tomorrow. All of you except one can come to Papa's services. Larsen will decide who stays here. Goodnight, I'll see all of you tomorrow morning." She wheeled and left the bunkhouse.

Tom was knocking on the door at sunrise the next morning. Blanche greeted him and said, "Hot coffee is waiting." She led him to the kitchen and poured him a steaming cup of coffee.

"You sent word that you wanted to see me?" Tom asked.

"Yes, the boys make a very strong case that Gus Leonard killed Papa and then took his money. I've asked Larsen to brief Marshal Decker and the local officials. I also know that you must try to free Blair and Helen's daughter. I wanted to hear what you have to say about bringing Leonard in?"

"Blanche you and Tess are very important to me. It will take me and all the help I can get another few months to quell the raiding and killing. I will find Gus Leonard and bring him to justice. In the meantime, you have a big job keeping things together on the ranch. I know Clay would want you to hold things together until at least after the roundup and you have the benefit of the money from the cattle. I'll try to get back as often as I can." Tom finished his coffee then continued, "Blanche, I've got to get on the trail."

She said, "I want you to take one or more of the wranglers with you. Some of them are very good with their revolvers and all have the guts and hardness to be of help to you. Will you listen to reason and take some help with you?"

"Blanche, I work best alone. I appreciate your offer, but you will need every hand you have for the roundup. I'll try to be back and help on the cattle drive to market."

He started out of the door and she took his arm and said, "I told you about Gus Leonard trying to court me and you don't seem to care. I was wrong to welcome his attention and I regret not being able to tell Papa that he was right, but I want to tell you here and now that I love you and will wait as long as it takes; you are a stubborn man, just like Papa." She turned and brushed the tears from her eyes and said, "Damn you, at least kiss me before you leave."

Tom took her gently in his arms and tenderly kissed her willing lips. Their embrace was interrupted by Tess who had just come in the room. She laughed and said, "What a sneaking pair of lovers you two turned out to be. I'll get Papa's shotgun and march you both to the preacher. We'll not have Papa's house disgraced." She continued to smile and laugh with her eyes sparkling.

Blanche decided to go along with Tess and chide Tom a little more. She said, "Little sister, keep that shotgun loaded and when Tom comes back I want you to keep your promise." She laughed for the first time since she found her father.

Tom joined in and said laughingly, "I promise the shotgun will not be necessary, but we will find that preacher and make an honest woman out of Blanche. I know she will be busy fending off attention of passing wranglers."

Tess dropped the smile and said, "Tom, I hope you can free Blair. He already got his foolish self shot up once; don't let him be a hero and get more lead in his hide."

Helen came in the room and said, "Marshal, I too plea with you to bring my daughter and deputy Blair back. I know how scared and lonely Sissy must be. I can only pray that she is not being mistreated. Please hurry back soon. I'm slowly dying with anxiety."

Tom said, "Helen, I will do my very best. I don't think the culprits holding Blair and Sissy will harm them; they want money and I have it in my saddle bags. I'll insist that before they get the ransom, Sissy and Blair be released. I don't want any of you to get discouraged. I will return with Sissy and Blair."

Blanche, Tess and Helen stood in the yard waving as Tom disappeared over the knoll to the southwest. Larsen watched him leave from the hayloft. He worried about his new role as ramrod; the boys all seemed to like him, but they knew his knees would not allow him to fork a horse without severe pain. He often wished that he had a family; he'd never married, but loved Blanche and Tess as if they were his daughters. The ranch could operate without a ramrod; all the wranglers knew what had to be done daily to keep the ranch profitable. He considered it his first duty to watch over the girls.

Later that week Tom arrived in sight of what he took to be the box canyon described by the kidnappers; he rode to the top of a knoll and studied the landscape, the sun was dropping fast behind the rising hills to the west. He had checked his back trail often but could not shake the feeling that he was being followed. He dismounted and looked for a sign of dust or noise on the back trail, but he saw nothing to indicate he was being followed. If he was being followed he was sure that they knew the lay of the land better than he did. He had become more alert and apprehensive the closer he came to the rising rock walls of the box canyon where Blair and Sissy were supposedly being held. The fact that the outlaws gave the location of the place where they said their captives were held, was cause real concern. Tom thought rather than have their captives in the box canyon, the outlaw's scheme was to pin him down in the canyon, kill him and get the gold. Well he had no intention of blundering into another ambush.

He also knew that outlaws always try to grab the advantage; they shoot first and ask questions later. He'd be a fool to think they would reveal where the captives are held. When he entered the box canyon, he was sure they would be watching and try to outsmart him. At the moment he guessed that he was fairly close to the canyon, but they would have lookouts to spot him long before he got there. This was for big stakes, and the outlaws would be prepared. The sun fell behind the hills and at dusk he made dry camp in a small cove. The night passed and he managed a few minutes of sleep.

Early the next morning at sunrise he was saddling his horse when a bullet whizzed by his head, he heard the report of the rifle and fell to the ground and scrambled toward a large log. The bullet had missed him by inches. His horse reared and tried to break away but the reins held and the horse calmed down, shaking his head and snorting. Tom heard two more rifle shots coming from somewhere on the high ground to the southeast. He knew that he was in serious trouble. Judging the time between the rifles shots, Tom guessed that the shooter was a lone assassin.

Tom guessed that he was a few hours ride from the box canyon where the kidnappers said they were holding Blair and Sissy. This attack was too far away from the box canyon to make sense. His next thought was someone must have followed him after he left the Longmire ranch. He had watched his back trail often for any sign of someone following him out of town. In most ransom cases, outlaws usually wanted to know if their demands were being followed. As he waited for the shooter's next move, he studied his surroundings; there was good cover about twenty feet from his present position. If he could reach that area without taking a bullet, his chances of getting out of this fix alive would be much improved. He did not believe the assassin could see him in his present position. He began the slow move to reach the more protected cover, hoping that his luck would hold. After moving a few feet he heard, "Lawman, you can walk out of here alive. Just leave the gold and get started, you have ten minutes."

Tom yelled, "Why don't you come and get me. Are you afraid? I'm waiting to send you to hell."

That brought another volley of bullets, some hitting the ground not far from Tom and kicking up dirt. Tom was now pretty sure this was a lone gunman doing the shooting. This will be a test of courage and knowledge. He waited.

CHAPTER 7

CAPTURED

Deputy Marshal Blair Green rode away from the Parks farm, leading Sissy's horse in deep thought. He had mixed emotions about Tom going after the killers alone to free Sissy's mother, but he recognized and appreciated the wisdom of Tom's decision to get Sissy to safety without delay; and not to lose more time in following the killers fleeing with Helen Parks. It would not have been right to take Sissy on such a dangerous mission. Blair knew that Tom's utmost concern at this point was for Sissy's safety. Blair's concern for the child was no less than Tom's. Blair urged his horse away from the burned house leading Sissy's horse. He glanced back and Sissy tried to smile. He thought she is a brave child.

The narrow and winding animal trail over the rock-strewn hills slowed their progress. After riding awhile, Sissy asked to stop and rest. She wanted some private time she said. Blair thought that was a very grown up and ladylike request. When she returned from behind a clump of bushes she asked, "Will I see my Mommy soon?"

Blair said, "We have to believe that Tom will free your Mommy. I know of no one else who I'd rather have than Tom, if it was my Mommy they carried away. Sissy, we must have faith in Tom. He will bring your Mommy to you. I feel certain."

Blair hoped she could not detect his reservations about Tom's situation. He was going against great odds and would have to have some luck to pull it off. He waited until Sissy was back on her horse and then asked, "You do believe me that Tom will bring your Mommy to you, don't you?"

She looked at him in the moonlight and said, "I believe you. But I want my Mommy." At the moment she seemed to accept that her mother would be freed and they would soon be together.

The trip to the stagecoach relay station was made in record time; Blair kept moving and encouraged Sissy to stay awake. At one point he stopped and asked her, "Sissy, can you stay awake another two hours? We'll be at the stagecoach station by then."

She replied, "Yes, I will stay awake and not fall off the horse. I know you are worried that I will fall off. Well, I won't." Blair appreciated her courage.

They arrived at the relay station the next morning. The station manager, a very talkative fellow came forward and introduced himself, "I'm Jack Doty, you just missed breakfast. Looks like your tike is a bit tired. Been traveling long?"

Blair said, "Glad to meet you, I'm Blair Green and this young lady is Sissy Parks. She's a real hearty pioneer. We're on our way to Abilene. Hoping to catch the stage here and let you keep our horses until I get back for them." Blair noticed the frown on Doty's face.

He turned to the stove and said, "Mabel, these folks look hungry. You still have some eggs and fatback for these folks?"

Mabel came over and took Sissy's hand said, "You're a beautiful girl. Come to the table and I'll have something for you to eat very soon. I have some biscuits left and I'll fry eggs to go with the fatback." Mabel continued to talk to Sissy. She acted as if she had found a long lost daughter. Sissy revived from her tiresome trip and appeared very pleased with the attention Mabel was giving her. Blair began to relax, thankful that they had made the first leg of the journey without incident, but he could not help showing his disappointment when Jack Doty refused Blair's request to keep the horses until he could return for them. He said he did not have enough grain to feed them.

Blair asked, "Would it make any difference to know that I am with the U.S. Marshal's Service and responsible to get this young girl to her folks? I must get her to our headquarters as soon as possible."

Jack said, "Mister, grain is grain and I don't have enough of it for your horses. I'd like to help you and I know you want the child to ride the stage rather than going by horseback. I don't even have a pasture to hold the horses."

Blair replied, "Well, that leaves only one acceptable option, and that is to ride the horses to town. I was hoping to provide Sissy with a more comfortable journey. If you don't mind, we will rest up and start out the first thing tomorrow morning."

"Suit yourself. You can most likely make better time and beat the stage there by going across country. The stage has to skirt the hills because of the large boulders, creeks and washed out ditches. By horseback you will make good time. That child seems to be right at home in the saddle." Doty replied.

Blair said, "I sure don't want to take a chance on getting lost in the hills; the Marshal's service would be very disappointed and I would always blame myself for not following the stage route."

Doty thought a minute or so and said, "Well, you might get Lafe to guide you through those hills; he has made the trip several times in the last few months. He is a relative from back east who helps us out around here with chores. If you want I will speak with him?"

"I'd feel much better about having someone who has covered the ground before to show us the way. I will pay him a reasonable sum for his troubles, if he agrees."

Blair was unaware that their conversation was overheard through the wall's thin ill-fitted siding. Lafe Wolfe a relative of the station manager's wife was leaning against the side of the building listening to what was being said inside. He made a habit of eavesdropping as he often heard useful information, which awarded him with money, even though in one recent case he had to kill the victim to get it. His relatives at the station knew very little about him, they had never seen him until he showed up some six months ago. He talked about his life back east and said that when he had made enough money he would bring his mother to the frontier.

In fact, Lafe had fled Virginia when he heard that the sheriff was coming for him. He had robbed a poker game in the local saloon and killed one of the players who objected to being robbed of his winnings. So far he had been successful in intercepting his mother's letters; each of them told of Lafe's problems with the law and warned them that he was dangerous and could not be trusted. Through his efforts Jack and Mabel Doty never suspected his lawlessness. They often bragged to the customers who came through about their hard working cousin. Even before he arrived, Lafe was planning to make his relatives disappear and then he would own the station. So far they had stalled about making out papers passing their property on to him. Now perhaps he could let them live as they might be helpful sometime in the future. That U.S. Marshal and the girl would be his ticket to prosperity. He would need someone to help him, and he knew exactly where to find him. All those murderous ideas floated through his twisted mind like a desert windstorm. He grinned, slapped his leg and said to himself, *here is money waiting to harvest. Yes the money tree I've sought has jumped up right here in front of me. That young lawman and the girl are worth thousands to the U.S. Marshal Service.*

Lafe went out to the henhouse and gathered a few eggs in his hat and carried them into the station. He wanted an excuse to get his dastardly scheme in play. On entering he did not wait for an introduction, he announced to Blair, "I'm Lafe, you just passing through?"

Blair shook his hand and said, "Yes we are going to Abilene. I'd hoped to catch the stage and leave my horses here. I've learned that there's no grain or feed for the horses. So that leaves no choice, we must to ride our horses on to town."

Doty interrupted and said, "Lafe, I mentioned that you know the trails and might guide Marshal Blair through the hills. What do you think about that?"

Lafe put on his most friendly smile and said, "Well, if Mabel can get along without me for six or seven days, I could help him out, if that is what he wants."

Blair hesitated a moment, thinking this fellow seems sincere enough, but his eyes are filled with contempt and mockery which could indicate that he might be less than trustworthy. Then Blair dismissed the thought, as he had no other evidence that the fellow was anything other than someone willing to help. Blair remembered that on a few occasions in the past he had misread first impressions, but then also had been right a few times. In any event, this fellow would bear some watching.

"Lafe, we would be obliged to have you show us the way through the hills. Have either of you heard any recent reports of lawlessness causing problems around here?" Blair watched both men very closely.

Neither hesitated and the manager said, "Lafe has not been here all that long, but I can tell you that once in awhile the stage gets held up, and ranchers in the valley complain of losing cattle to rustlers. Also there was a murder a short time ago that has not been solved. Such reports are certainly worrisome."

Lafe added, "Even if we run into trouble, I'm sure you and me can handle it. I've learned how to shoot this old revolver pretty good." He patted a well-oiled holster, laughed and winked at Jack.

Blair said, "I can't ask you to make such a trip without recompense and I don't like misunderstandings, so please tell me what you consider a fair payment for your trouble?"

Lafe smiled as he was leaving the room, looked back over his shoulder and said, "I'll accept no money as I wanted to make the trip to town anyway. I've intended to say something about going, but had not made up my mind. See you in the morning." He eased out the door pulling it shut as he left.

Two hours later, Lafe was at a small shack in the hills to the north that he visited often; today he would not be just drinking homebrew, but would firm up his scheme to get rich. Indian Joe, known for miles around for his whiskey and homebrew, did not have a drop of Indian blood; his cold black hair and dark skin served his masquerade as an Indian well. He was reared in the mountains by parents who made their living off the weakness of other people. First his mother died one cold winter and then his father got kicked in the chest by a mule, and he died leaving the sixteen-year son to forge for himself. He picked up where his parents left off; stealing, making whiskey and homebrew. Now he listened intently to Lafe's scheme. Lafe's plan to hold the U.S. Marshal and little girl for a large ransom sounded good to him. Indian Joe was no fool and he did not trust Lafe. He asked, "What's the plan after we get the money? Are you just going to turn the captives loose to help run us down?"

Lafe laughed and said, "They won't be the first to take the final trip. Don't worry yourself about that. You stay out of sight, trailing us like a good Indian until I signal for you to show yourself. We'll wait until I lead them past the town to the west. Then you can throw the rock with my demand for money through the Marshal's window. Then get the hell out of there."

Indian Joe said, "I guess we have to keep them alive until we get the money. That U.S. Marshal may demand something showing they are alive, but I say when we get the money, we head for Mexico. We can live like kings down there"

"We have to keep them alive until we have the money. We will then go to Mexico. We'll skirt the town to get close to that box canyon that you say everyone knows where it is. After we get the money we will head for Mexico. We can work out the details after I tie them up and signal you to come in. Just stay out of sight until I signal you."

"If they don't know the hills, it will be easy to get them west of the town; you just make sure that you are not planning to have the money for yourself. I'll be real hard to kill, just remember that."

Lafe nervously said, "Now why would you think that. I can't do this thing by myself. We need each other to make it work. I don't want to have a rope around my neck."

Indian Joe replied, "If we get caught, we both will meet the hangman. Just don't get any ideas. We half the money and go on to Mexico."

"I don't intend for either of us to get our necks stretched. You will get your share. Now I've got to get back to the relay station. We start out early tomorrow morning. You can already be in the hills waiting for us to come through. You stay out of sight and follow us. I'll stay on the trail that we took last month to town. I feel rich already." Lafe was still laughing when he rode away from the shack and he said to himself, *yea Indian Joe you will get what's coming to you. It won't be money.* He slapped his leg, spurred the horse and could already count his riches.

The next morning when Sissy came to the table for breakfast, Blair noticed that her face was red and that she almost fell, then grasped the back of the chair and managed to sit down. Blair asked, "Sissy, is something wrong? Are you ill?"

She whispered in a hoarse voice, "I don't feel so good. I'm not hungry."

Blair asked Mabel who was holding her hand on Sissy's forehead, "Does she have a fever?"

Mabel replied, "No, but she needs rest. I heard her tossing and turning all night. Why not stay another day? I enjoy having Sissy visit us."

Sissy spoke up and said, "I want to see my Mommy. She may already be in town waiting for us."

Blair waited a few moments and said, "Sissy, another day will not make that much difference. Anyway, I don't think Tom has had time to reach Abilene yet, but if you want to go on today, then we shall."

"Yes, let's go after breakfast." Sissy said firmly.

Lafe who was sitting quietly at the table said, "Do you want me to get your horses? Jack gave up some of his grain just for your horses. They been fed and watered."

Blair turned to Jack and said, "I appreciate the grain. The horses needed a good feed. I'll pay you for the grain."

"That's not necessary; I still have enough for our animals and the mules' pulling the stage until another load gets here. I always try to help folks in need; you must take it easy on the horses going through the hills and let them graze wherever you find good grass."

"Thanks for all your courtesies, and for seeing after Sissy. Perhaps she and her mother will pay you all visit sometime in the future." Mabel smiled and said, "Sissy that would be very nice. I always wanted a daughter just like you. Please take care and come back if you can."

Lafe was already in the saddle and his horse prancing around, rearing to get on the trail. As they left both Blair and Sissy waved to the couple standing the yard, unsmiling but waving.

Blair noticed during the first several hours that Lafe was selecting the trail through boulders and undergrowth very carefully. He often asked Sissy if she was doing alright and was the ride tiring her too much. Blair began to soften his feelings toward Lafe as he appreciated the consideration he was showing for Sissy. But he could not shake the feeling that they were being watched. Blair often stopped and studied the horizon, tree lines and looked for any sign of dust in the air. He saw nothing.

Lafe pulled up at a bend in a creek that had a large deep clear pool of water. He suggested that they make camp as the wind was increasing and there was plenty of good grass for the horses. Blair agreed. They ate the prepared food Mabel sent with them, so there was no need for a fire. Soon after eating Sissy said she would like to get in her bedroll. Blair found her a spot a few feet from where he intended to sleep. Lafe said he would scout the area ahead before dark so they would not lose and time tomorrow. Blair asked, "Is that necessary, I thought you knew the trail through these hills?"

"Well I do, but there may be a short cut and save us time. I'm not tired just thought I would look around." He replied. He led his horse through some bushes, mounted and urged the animal forward with a gentle kick in the flanks.

During the trip Blair became disturbed by Lafe's tendency to scan the tree lines every few minutes. His manner did not suggest he was fearful of anything; just that he seemed more concerned than a normal person would be out here in the hills. When Blair fell behind and told Sissy to stay close to Lafe, he looked back and slowed his horse. Blair's active mind and concern for Sissy would not let go of his apprehension. He leaned against a large tree trunk and resolved to stay alert and watch Lafe's every move. Mistrust was building fast. Then he remembered the tin box with the Parks family money and papers. This was a big responsibility safeguarding the money and Sissy. He walked down to the creek looking for a place to hide Sissy's family money. Blair admonished himself for being overly protective and concerned about something that was not likely to happen. He just could not push himself to trust Lafe. It would be far better to be safe than sorry. Tom Leach would understand his caution.

After several minutes searching he found what he consider a safe place for the money. He returned to his bedroll and removed the tin box made a circle around the campsite and was convinced that Lafe was nowhere near. Blair moved swiftly returning to the large tree with a hollow limb. The opening of the hollow was just large enough to let him slip the tin box down about a foot in the hole. He then gathered some leaves and stuffed them on top of the tin box. He felt sure that he could find this place without any difficulty after Sissy was safe in Abilene. He was relieved to have one less problem to worry about. He never considered that he would not live to return to the tree with the money; he had faith that he would get Sissy to Abilene and then return.

It was more than an hour before Lafe returned. Blair heard him coming in long before he quietly hobbled his horse. Blair decided to fake sleep as Lafe came close and looked at him and then looked at Sissy before he rolled out his bed and curled up as if he had no concern of danger. The night dragged on, Blair exercised every control he had to stay awake, but in spite of his efforts he nodded off a few times. It seemed that time stood still as it dragged on mostly without sleep, he kept telling himself, just get through this and we'll be in Abilene tomorrow night.

The next morning, after eating some canned fruit and dried beef, they prepared to break camp. Lafe seemed jolly and joked about the trails ahead; he said, "We have to be aware of rattlesnakes and cougars. From here on in, we better keep a sharp eye for danger. I've found a short cut through some real rough ground. This is bandit country from here on to Abilene, so we need to make sure we don't let Sissy ride into an ambush." He had directed these statements to Blair.

Blair said, "I've never heard that this stretch of hills had bandits. I think we're pretty close to Abilene, and if there had been such reports out here, I'm sure the Marshal would have told us. Where did you hear about these reports?"

"Well I have not been out here in this part of the world all that long, but word gets around. I hope we don't have any trouble, I am only warning you to be on guard. I will ride ahead after I show you the trail through the hills; I want to make sure we don't ride into an ambush."

Blair considered Lafe's concern and thought he should have thanked him instead of doubting his good intentions. Also he did not want to alarm Sissy and played down what he thought could be real trouble. Late that evening toward sundown, Blair had been following the tracks of Lafe's horse. He was getting concerned that Lafe had not waited for them. Suddenly, the trail narrowed with large boulders and trees and each side. He was about to rein in when he heard a deep course voice say, "Pull up and put your hands in the air, and I mean high. You too girl." Blair's first thought was to fall out of the saddle and shoot it out with the culprit, but Sissy was behind him and she might get caught in the cross fire. He slowly raised his hands. Then he heard, "Make a wrong move and we shoot both of you. Do as you're told and you both live."

Blair said in the steadiest voice he could muster, "Sissy, let's do what the fellow says. This must be a misunderstanding or something. We have no money other that a few coins. If they want our horses we can walk to Abilene."

"We don't want your horses; you should be worth something. They'll pay us to turn you loose. You and the girl ought to bring us at least twenty thousand dollars. We already threw a rock through the Marshal's office giving instructions where to bring the money. What they don't know is if you are alive or dead; it matters little to me whether they pay for your dead carcass. So don't get brave and give me a reason to shoot you both. Now get down and drop your gun belt. Then move away from your horse."

Sissy turned in her saddle and asked, "Who are you?"

"They call me the prairie bandit. My partner has a gun pointed at your friend's guts. Now you get down and both of you walk toward that big tree. Just remember, I'd just as soon shoot you as not."

Sissy asked, "Did you kill my Papa?" Her voice was firm and unafraid.

He asked, "When did your Papa get killed? I haven't killed anyone for sometime now. So I'd guess it wasn't me. Now get down and shut up." Sissy stared at him and them grasped the saddle horn and eased down to the ground. She walked slowly to the tree without comment or looking back.

Blair said, "If its money you want, perhaps I could write the Marshal a note asking him provide the money. But if you decide to kill me, please let the little girl go. She could not possibly identify you. With that mask it would also be hard for me to identify you."

Sissy turned and stared at the prairie bandit and said, "Everything was alright until someone like you killed my Papa and took my Mommy away. I'll never forgive you."

Blair wondered what had happened to Lafe. May be he would show up and help get them out of this mess. Somehow Blair did not expect Lafe to take a hand; he hoped he was wrong for Sissy's sake.

The prairie bandit said, "I told you to shut up. Not another word out of you. Do you understand?"

"You said not another word out of me than you ask if I understand. No, I don't understand."

"Well you damn sure better do as I say. I'm getting mad, that's not good for either of you. Now shut up." He kicked the ground.

Then he looked at Blair and said, "Alright mister, if you have a hideaway or knife you, best you throw it down now. If I search you and find any weapon, I'm going to pistol whip you. Is that understood?"

Blair said, "You have my gun belt and rifle; I have no other weapon."

"Alright, put everything you have in your pockets on the ground." Blair did as ordered.

Then he made Blair turn on to his stomach and carefully searched him. When he finished he said, "It's good thing you don't have anything on you; I was looking forward to beating you up a mite." He laughed one of the most evil laughs Blair had ever heard. Blair was now pretty sure that this evil bandit had no intentions of letting them live. He was sick at heart for Sissy.

The prairie bandit then ordered them to sit on the ground with their backs to the tree. While holding a cocked revolver aimed at Blair's chest, he expertly and swiftly tied Blair's hands and feet using rawhide with ready made loops which allowed him to work mostly with one hand until he had Blair's feet and hands tied firmly. Then he tied Sissy in the same manner. He used heavy strips of canvas to blindfold Blair and Sissy. He said, "That might save your life if you don't get too smart." He then went to his horse and brought back two ropes. He used those to firmly tie his captives to the tree. He was rough with Sissy. He wanted her to know he was not happy with her questions. Then Blair knew that another bandit had come close although he did not speak. The prairie bandit spoke to him, "We'll wait until dark and move them to the cabin." There was no answer from the second person.

Blair had a very good idea why the second bandit did not say anything. He did not want to be identified. That meant he could very well be Lafe. The fact they were trying to hide their identity gave Blair some hope that they did not want their captives to identify them later. That meant they had not yet decided to kill them.

Blair heard the prairie bandit say, "Let's go get your horse and decide our next move." He obviously was speaking to the newcomer. There was no response. Blair could hear them as they stalked down the trail. Blair then waited until he was sure the bandits were out of hearing distance and he whispered to Sissy, "Sissy no matter what happens, don't say anything to make them think you can identify them. Let me do all the talking."

Sissy whispered back, "Lafe is with him. I smelled him"

Blair said, "I thought so too, but they will kill us if they think we know. So don't say anything."

She said, "I'm scared, but I won't let them know."

The outlaws soon returned with the horses; first tying Blair in the saddle face down, then placing Sissy on a horse and tying her feet under the horse's belly. Neither of the outlaws spoke. They had made their plans while getting the horses.

Blair thought they had been on the trail about two hours when they stopped. One of the bandits roughly threw him to the ground. He heard Sissy crying and asking about her mother. Blair's heart melted every time he heard that child begging the outlaws to let them go. He sensed that they were dragging him through a door; he had heard them pull the door open. He was on a dirt floor up against the wall. He heard Sissy say, "You're hurting me. Please let me go to my Mommy. Please let me see, this thing is too tight around my face."

The outlaw said, "This will hold you two until we get the money. Stay quiet and nothing will happen to you. You both will be killed if you yell or cause us trouble. We'll be gone a while so be quiet and when we come back you can go."

Blair asked, "Why the blindfolds? At least let us see while you are gone."

"Just sit tight; the blindfolds will be removed when I get back. You make a wrong move and I'll kill you both. Is that understood?"

Blair said, "There's no need to have the law after you for murder. I guess you will get whatever it is that you want from us."

"I said shut up and be quiet, one more word and I'll cut your throat."

Blair remained silent and then heard them leave, closing the door behind them. He waited several minutes and did not hear anything. He whispered to Sissy, who he sensed was only a few feet from him, "Sissy, are you tied to the wall?"

She whispered back, "I don't think so; I can turn over on my stomach."

"Are your hand tied behind you?"

"Yes, but I am getting them loose. Pa played games with Mommy and me, showing us how to hold out hands when being tied. There I have my hands free. I'll get this blindfold."

Blair's first thought was what they would do to her if they came back and found them free of the ropes and the blindfold. He said, "Sissy, hurry and come over here and free my hands. We have to get out of this situation before they come back."

She said, I can see, its daylight. I'm having trouble getting the ropes off my feet."

CHAPTER 8

KILLERS RETURN

Quirt Evans' gang had ridden hard all day trying to reach Bat Cave before nightfall. Quirt called the cave his hideaway. He claims the cave for himself, but many other outlaws use it for stopovers while riding the Owl Hoot Trail. Evans knows that the cave is often used by others and that the cave is called many different names; outlaw roost, bat heaven, bat shit cave and others. He found the cave several years ago and stopped there often times on his travels from Mexico to targets further north.

When he entered the cave some of the other outlaws had dismounted and were close behind trying to adjust their eyes to the darken cave. He suddenly stopped and said, "What the hell do we have here." He walked over to a motionless figure curled up in the corner. He kicked the man in the side and yelled, "I was hoping you're Jake Leach, but I guess it's not my lucky day. You're stinking up my cave. Wake up and say your last words." Gus Leonard tried to gain his feet but was too weak and drunk to get all the way up. He fell back to the damp floor and looked up into the eyes of the most furious mean looking fellow he had ever seen, now hovering over him like a large vulture. Leonard's mind almost went blank, but he said, "Give me a minute and I will explain what I'm doing here. My head is busting open."

Quirt said, "Your head won't bother you very long." He turned to one of his henchmen standing close by and said, "Drag this bastard out and shoot him. I don't want his lousy blood on the floor of my cave. Now hurry."

They were dragging Leonard outside by his heels, when one the outlaws said, "Hey Quirt, I know this fellow. He's Lester Toler. I rode with him a few years back down Sonora way. Give me a chance to talk to him and let him say his peace."

Quirt said, "What makes you think I care if you rode with this bastard after he brings his horse in my cave?"

"He is wanted by the hangman in Missouri and Texas. He can help us."

"Alright, I'll give him two minutes to sing his last song." Quirt replied.

Lester Toler alias Gus Leonard was sobering up fast; suddenly the faces of those he had killed floated in front of his foggy vision as shapeless eerie clouds. He could feel the bullets striking his body. He starkly remembered that some of those he had killed died instantly while others jerked and writhed until life left them. All these thought brought him back to looking up at the only familiar face in the cave; Killer Harve Steadman was asking him a question and he struggled to answer. In a flash he decided to live as long as he could, he asked, "Harve, is that really you? You're Harve Steadman. I sure did not expect to see you again. That posse that chased us out of Sonora, I thought for sure caught you. I would have been with you, but you insisted that we split up. How did you get away?"

Quirt said, "Enough of that palaver; I'm not interested in what happened with a damn posse. He probably is another damn Jake Leach, who runs off with my gold. Shoot him and get over with it."

Harve nervously said, "Boss, if he must be shot, why not let me shoot him after we hear his story; I'd like to know where he has been since they run us out of Sonora, also if you let him live he can help us." Quirt just looked at him and motioned to go on with it.

Lester Toler's foggy mind tried to recall what the outlaw leader had said; it came to him slowly. He asked, "Did you say something about Jake Leach?"

Quirt almost pounced on him and asked, "What do you know about that traitor Jake Leach?

"Well, I don't know much about him. I rode with him on the owl hoot for a spell, and I know his brother is Tom Leach and a U.S. Marshal who thinks he owns my girl friend."

Quirt spoke to all those gathered around, "All of you except Harve clear out. Take care of the horses and get that horse out from the back of my cave. Harve bring this dog on in, I want to find out what he really knows about my gold. Seems to me if he knows Jake Leach and he is here in my cave, he knows about the gold. So by the time you get him back in the cave he better be ready to tell me everything he knows and no tricks."

It took more than an hour of questioning before Quirt said, "I'll let you live and join my gang, but your first way to prove yourself is to bring Jake Leach's brother to me. I want him alive so that I can find my gold. Jake sent a letter to him I'm told just before he died. I want to know what the letter said about my gold."

Both Leonard and Harve Steadman had talked fast and hard to convince Quirt that they could bait a trap for Jake's brother and force him to tell where the gold is hidden.

Lester Toler said, "I know how to get the marshal to come to you; we go to the Longmire ranch and bring back Blanche Longmire who the marshal thinks he will marry."

Quirt asked, "What makes you thing the marshal will chase after you and the girl?"

Lester Toler said, "I'm sure of it. He would follow us to the end of the world for that girl. When you see her, you'll know what I mean. We'll leave information how to follow us with her sister. He'll come."

Quirt ended the discussion by saying, "Harve, I'll hold you responsible to find my gold. After we kill all those pilgrims on the Singletary ranch, you and Toler will bring that damn marshal to me. After the raids I will return here and wait for you to get him here alive; he'll talk when I get finished with him. If he knows where my gold is hidden, he'll tell me."

Harve asked, "Don't you want us to be in on the Tincup raid?"

Quirt replied, "I've changed my mind about raiding Tincup right now; we'll rest up at the Singletary ranch. There'll be money in the safe and the bodies of his gunmen should also have money on them. You two start figuring how you are going to grab that girl and get Leach to follow you."

At first when Lester Toler heard them mention the Singletary ranch it did not registered on his mind that was the sign he saw over the gate at the ranch he had stopped at a day or so ago trying to find work or get a free meal. That old man was down right mean and suspicious. He decided he better tell them what he observed at the ranch on his very short stay there. He looked at Quirt and said, "I stopped at a ranch over the hills to the northwest and I am sure the sign said it was the Singletary ranch. I tried to hire on, but the old man would not even let me get out of the saddle. I asked for food and he said that he would feed me some hot lead if I did not get off his land."

Quirt said, "Tell us something we don't know about that bastard and his gunmen. He would never give anyone a helping hand, that why he needs killing."

"That place is a fortress. He has gun pits all around the buildings. They did not mind showing themselves; there was rifle barrels pointing at me from every direction. There were so many rifle barrels that they looked like a porcupine showing all his quills." Lester Toler shakily told them.

"Hell, we know he has an army of gunmen, but if we are smart this time they will be very busy when we attack. You are not scared to go back are you?"

"No, I have to die sometime and I sure as hell don't want to face a damn hangman unless there is a good reason to be killed at that crazy man's ranch, I rather live a little longer."

Quirt said, "I do the thinking; maybe I should have had you shot."

Toler turned white in the face and stammered, "Boss I will lead the charge against those rifles if that is what you want. I was just trying to let you know what I saw."

"Alright I'll let it pass; you and Harve light a shuck to the Longmire Ranch and bring that woman back here. I don't like failures; if you don't get her here and bait that Marshal to follow, you both better get the hell out of the country. Now get."

He turned to Cisco and said, "Since you and Lemmon had a look at the Singletary house and barns, I want you to set fire to everything in sight. You'll find two gallons of kerosene on the pack mule. Just don't let them capture you again."

Cisco replied, "It was not our fault. Shotgun led us in the trap."

"I don't give a damn, you know what happened to Shotgun, just make sure you do your job. The rest of us will be near the top of that high knoll until we see the flames. Then we'll attack in force. The fire will draw most of them to it, you and Lemmon pickoff the gunmen when they try to put out the fire." Quirt seemed to be over his angry spell. He even smiled at the thought of the pending raid.

Quirt Evans' evil mind was never very far from the gold he wanted to start a new life in Portugal with Silvia. He was convinced that Jake did not make it to Tincup with the gold. So it has to be in the cave on somewhere along the way to Tincup. Jake was too weak and feverish to stray too far from a direct path to Tincup. He decided to make one more search of the cave and the area around it. That would delay attacking the Singletary ranch a day, but if he found the gold it would be worth the time lost. He would do the searching himself. He even considered not attacking the Singletary ranch and taking his gang to Abilene and finding Jake's brother. Then he realized that Abilene had many lawmen and armed citizens and his gang could be thinned out fast. No that was too much of a risk at this time.

Steve Sutton's sharp eyes had watched the Quirt Evans' gang cross the Rio Grande. He waited until they were well out of sight before he slowly picked up their trail. His mission was to find out where they were going. The citizens of Tincup would have a better chance of defeating the Evans' gang if he could warn them that the attack was coming. If gang headed to the Singletary ranch first, then he had to carry the warning to Moss Singletary. As he followed the trail his mind shifted to why he was down here risking his life.

He remembered that after burying his brother Layton, he and Marshal McCall had a long serious talk about the escaped prisoners who killed his brother and the Quirt Evans gang; they agreed that Evans' cutthroat killers had to be stopped. Their threats to attack the Singletary ranch or Tincup could not be ignored. He had told the Marshal, "My first concern is to bring those culprits that killed Layton to justice."

McCall had replied, "I understand your grief and hurry to get after the killers. But we need to be sensible; you cannot fight that gang by yourself. We know they scurry back to Mexico after raids on this side of the border. It would help if we knew when they start back this way. Advance notice would be of great help in preparing the defenses and alerting the citizens. We also have to be concerned about the farmers and ranchers, especially the Singletary ranch which Evans has threatened to wipe out; old Moss may be a little too fast to mete out his kind of justice, but we all respect his honesty." He had then explained that he could not leave Tincup, but he had mentioned to several of the leading citizens about electing a Sheriff for the county. They seemed to agree, but did not want him to give up the Marshal's job right now. McCall asked if he would accept the Town Marshal job.

He had said, "Well, I'm obliged for your consideration, but as I've said my first job is to settle with those who killed Layton. After that I would be pleased to accept the appointment. But why do you want to be the sheriff?"

McCall had replied, "Well this county has not yet elected a sheriff which we need right now. As town marshal I am limited to the town's boundaries. As sheriff of the county I could be much more effective in protecting not only the town and its citizens, but the ranchers and farmers as well."

Tim McCall had said he served as a deputy sheriff for a spell and learned the background on the establishment of county sheriffs in the Republic of Texas; beginning in 1836 the Texas Constitution guaranteed that county sheriffs have no bosses other than the voters who elected them. The independence of the sheriffs' office appealed to him.

Steve Sutton tried to clear his mind of the conversation with Tim McCall and give all his attention to following the Evans' gang heading into the desert like terrain, but he could not shake the discussion he had with Tim McCall; it now seemed a lifetime ago. When his brother Layton was savagely murdered he resolved to find the killers and bring them to justice. He still believed in the power of the law and did not want to become a killer or work outside the law, but regardless of the consequences to him, the murderers of his brother had to pay for their crimes. He was not sure that any of the culprits who murdered his brother were in the gang ahead, but it continued to occupy his mind. He was sure that if he saw any of the killers he would recognize them. He cursed his luck in not having binoculars. He never seemed to have the money to spare, but today he wished he had found money for the binoculars.

As the gang advanced north, following the tracks of the horses was becoming increasingly more difficult over the hard rocky areas. At times he had to ride in large circles to cut the trail of the gang. Sometimes the gang cut across country leaving the trails, but he knew they were still heading in the direction of either the Singletary ranch or Tincup. Tim McCall had asked him to follow the outlaw gang and try to find out where they intended to attack next. He had said, "Evans and his gang have threatened the citizens of the Singletary ranch and Tincup, but outlaws are unpredictable and may decide to attack elsewhere. We need to know as much as possible about their plans."

When he had watched the gang cross the river; he was not close enough to determine if the killers of his brother were among them. He watched as the gang crossed the river; just seeing the gang caused his anger to reach a boiling point. It was difficult to restrain himself from attacking the gang with both revolvers spitting lead, but he knew that would be foolish and he would never know whether or not he evened the score for his brother. He trailed them and it appeared they were going toward Bat Cave. He took advantage of the small hills and large boulders for cover and that slowed his progress. But he was successful in staying fairly close to the gang. It became obvious after several miles that the gang was not concerned with their back trail and were heading toward Bat Cave.

Steve Sutton followed the gang to Bat Cave and then found a vantage point behind a large boulder near the top of the hill; he spent most of the hours of the night crawling on his belly to a position so that he could watch the cave entrance. He got close enough that he had heard bits and pieces of what they said while saddling their horses the next morning. He heard them mention the Singletary ranch and could even make out that one of them said he could hardly wait to string up old Moss Singletary. Now that he was sure the gang would attack the Singletary ranch, he had to remain in his position until the gang was out of sight. His legs and arms were stiff from cold night air, but he made good time running to his horse that he had tied at the bottom of the hill. He next caught sight of the gang, they were on the trail heading toward the Singletary ranch. That forced him to cut across the hills through rough country. He was determined to beat the gang to the ranch, so he pushed his horse to punishing speed.

It was nearing sundown when Steve arrived to the knoll overlooking the Lazy S; he reined his horse to a stop and stood up in the stirrups, took of his hat and waved. He knew Moss had sentries out around the clock everyday. He saw no signal in return, but sure that he had been spotted. He rode on at a gallop and pulled up at the corral gate. Moss Singletary stepped out from the barn and asked, "Why are you trying to kill that horse? He looks like you rode the life right out of him."

Steve replied, "I hate myself for punishing the best horse I ever forked. No time to waste. Evans is leading his gang this way; they intend to strike the ranch. He threatens to kill every living thing on the ranch and burn it down to ashes. I need to water my horse and take on a barrel of it myself."

Moss said, "Never mind about the horse, he'll be cared for. Go in the house and get whatever you need. I'll be along shortly."

Then Moss turned and called out, "Listen up. Pass the word; I want every hand at the corral in fifteen minutes. Evans and his gang of cutthroats want blood, so they will get blood, not ours but theirs."

Moss Singletary walked swiftly back to the house and found Steve still drinking water. He asked, "You feel any better? Tell me how you know the Evans gang will attack us."

Steve took a deep breath and spoke slowly as he was exhausted, "I watched the gang cross river from Mexico and then followed them to Bat Cave, where they stayed overnight. I slipped in close to the cave entrance during the night and heard some of what they said while saddling their mounts. They are coming here first then going to Tincup and burn it to the ground." He stopped and Moss asked, "When do you think they well get here?"

"I'd think they will attack tonight or early tomorrow morning. But they are crazy and could do anything. I asked Marshal McCall to let you know that I was going after the killers of my brother. Did he tell you?"

"Yes, he came to see me and we had a very pleasant talk. I would have done the same thing if someone killed my brother. You are still riding for Lazy S and your pay has not stopped. I'm sorry about Layton; he was a good cowman and hard worker. Come we have work to do."

He walked out to the corral where the wranglers were gathered near the corral gate. He looked around the group and said, "I guess we are all here. Thanks to Steve, we have notice that Quirt Evans and his gang are on their way to finish us off. Unless the gang decides to come in over the southwest mountain range, which is hard riding, they must come by the trail through the gap. My guess is they will approach through the old riverbed. That's how they got here before. Now instead of them surprising us, we'll have a little lead reception for them. One of you fork the fastest horse in the corral, go to the north range and tell the men I want them to ride like hell and join us in the positions in the gully. There's good cover down there and if we can get several of them they might stampede back over the mountain."

He paused and looked around at Steve and said, "Steve I want you and three of the men to stay here and guard the house and barns, I know that deceitful bunch and they might try sneaking past our positions and burn us out."

Steve said, "Boss, please let me come with you. The killers of my brother may be riding with that gang, and I will know them on sight. I want a chance to even the score."

Moss thought a moment and said, "We are obliged you alerted us that those disciples of the devil will try to kill us. And I can't blame you for wanting to find the killers of Layton. I noticed when you rode in that you had about reached your limits. But if you can still fork a horse, let's go. We need to prevent the attack from reaching the house and barns. They won't be expecting a reception more than a mile from the ranch. I hope we can send those mad dogs running back to their hiding places. We cannot let them get close to the ranch before we start the dance."

When Moss was satisfied that his wranglers had all selected good cover and wide field of fire, he spoke to one of the men, "Trent, lead all the horses back to the corral; loosen the cinches and help defend the house if it comes to that."

Trent said, "Boss, seems like the shooting will be out here, I'd like to stay."

"Boy, I don't remember asking what you want to do. Now get to it." Moss grinned at the young wrangler and motioned for him to gather the horses and go. He then said loud enough to be heard by the closest wranglers, "Pass the word, we all are afoot and I know we will give the killers a good fight. Pay is doubled for all of you this month, whether or not you survive this little set-to. Remain quiet and good hunting."

Moss heard muffled laughter and one wrangler said, "If I cash in my chips out here make sure Lady Fluffy in the Sundowner gets my pay." There was more snickering which got a friendly admonition from Moss, "That's enough talk. But I'll help Fluffy spend your money if that comes to pass." There was more suppressed laughter.

The reception for Quirt Evans' cutthroat gang is set.

CHAPTER 9

THE RANSOM

Lafe Wolfe and Indian Joe remained silent until they were sure Blair and the girl could not hear them; Lafe said, "Let's get the horses and go to the cutoff; we can catch whoever is bringing the money before he gets in the canyon. I spotted a good place to set an ambush and get the money. I hope it's not another U.S. Marshal."

"What do we care if it's a U.S. Marshal? He'll die just as easy as anyone else. We'd be stupid to let who brings the money to ride out and put a posse on out tails. Why I think you're going soft on me?"

"Like hell I am. But I'll leave the killing to you since you like it so much. I kill when I have to, but I'm not concerned with anyone's life, including yours."

Indian Joe laughed and said, "If you had any sense you would let me kill those two back there. They're nothing but trouble. Just so you know I'm not concerned with my life; just lookout for yours. It could end very sudden like, if you cross me."

Lafe replied, "If we kill the prisoners, what would we bargain with if the money isn't sent? I'd say that is short thinking."

Indian Joe scowled and said, "We should've turned their horses loose. They won't need them anymore. You best not say anything more about short thinking on my part. It could get you killed."

"Here we are about to get rich and we're talking about killing each other. We'll split the money fifty-fifty and live it up in Laredo or any place we decide."

The sun had peeped over the mountain top in the east; Lafe reined his horse to a stop and asked, "Was that rifle shots?"

Indian Joe said, "Yes, sounds like it's coming from close to the cutoff where we want to set the ambush. No one shoots that much killing a rabbit for breakfast. Let's ride."

The gunfire Lafe and Indian Joe heard sent U.S. Marshal Tom Leach scrambling to gain the protection of a large boulder. When he reached the boulder and paused to get his breath, the gunfire ceased. He lay still while waiting for the shooter to reveal his location. He sensed that the shooter was trying to get in close using the overhanging rocks protruding from the steep walls. Then he heard what he recognized as a cougar's scream followed immediately by a loud piercing scream. Tom did not have to see what was happening to the shooter; he could hear the continued child like whimpers and painful yells from the victim and deep throaty growling by the cougar. Tom jumped to his feet while trusting his instinct and raced toward the life and death struggle. As he neared the noise he saw the cougar on top of the man who had not ceased his struggle and yelling.

Tom used his revolver and shot the cougar. The man on the ground was covered in blood and gasping for air. Tom noticed that he had sustained among other wounds a large gash on his neck and blood was flowing freely. Tom came near and heard the man gasp out, "I'm dying."

Tom said, "You're from the bank, you were there when I picked up the money. Why did you try to kill me?"

"It is getting dark. I wanted the money to go back to civilization. Feel no pain." His eyes widened and he died.

Tom found the assassin's horse tied to a bush several hundred yards back down the trail in a dense mesquite and chaparral grove. He didn't remember the culprit's name, but realized that he had no time to bury him. He tied him on his horse, removed the bridle, tying it to the saddle horn, slapped the horse on his rear and sent him back down the trail toward town. He regretted sending him home like that, but he did not have time for the dead, when he might be able to save the lives of

Blair and the child. He would make a full report of the incident when he got back to headquarters. At the moment he was due in the box canyon. Tom returned to his horse, mounted and rode slowly toward the canyon where he was instructed to bring the ransom money.

Indian Joe cautioned Lafe to slow down since they were getting close to where he thought the shots came from. When he heard Tom's shot that killed the cougar he reined his horse in and said to Lafe, "Something tells me that shot ended the fight. I heard rifle and a pistol shots spaced and that indicates someone was trading bullets at each other; course there may be a passel of them but I don't think so. We need to make sure what's ahead."

Lafe replied, "I want that money and if we have to kill more than one of them to get it, then let's get at it. Come on, I'm going down that hill and find out what's going on down there." He jerked the reins and jammed his spurs in the flanks of his horse, causing him to jump; the slope fell off into a deep ravine, Lafe and his horse tumbled down the rocky hill. Indian Joe took his time getting to the bottom of the hill and was surprised to see both Lafe and his horse on their feet. Lafe was skinned and bleeding slightly from scratches on his face and arms, but otherwise seemed not be hurt. He was walking his horse in a circle trying to learn if the was hurt. The horse was still shying and scared.

Indian Joe said, "Your stupid anger is going to get you killed. If there is anyone within a half mile of here they heard the noise and may be eyeing us now." He pulled his revolver from its holster and pointed it at Lafe saying, "Either you swear you will do as I say until we get the money or you die here and now. You tell me if you want to die?"

Lafe was still shook from the tumble down the hill and he knew Indian Joe would kill him in a wink of the eye. He said, "Damn it to hell, I thought you're my friend. If it makes you feel better, I'll do what you say. Just lead me to the money."

"That's more like it." Indian Joe started to say something else but his attention had shifted to the tree line across the ravine. He said, "Mount up; see that horse that has some one tied in the saddle. Let's catch him. It might be our money on that horse."

They caught the horse after a chase over rough ground. Their horses were winded and blowing when Indian Joe roped the running stallion, bringing him to a halt. Lafe was the first to raise the dead man's head and looked at his face, seeing the gash still oozing blood. He said, "Let's get him down and search his pockets and the bedroll; he may have the money."

Indian Joe said, "Search him if you want, but someone killed him and has the money. See if he is a lawman." After several minutes of desperate searching Lafe said, "There's no badge or name on. You say you are in charge, so what's next?"

"We leave him and take the saddle off the horse and turn him loose. Then go after the money."

Tom had heard the commotion when the horse and Lafe tumbled down the hill. He led his horse in a deep cut bank and tied him to a limb, then began advancing in the direction of the commotion. He was about a hundred yards away when he saw the dead man being searched. He worked his way closer and found a fair sized boulder offering good cover and called out, "You on the horse dismount on this side of your horse, real slow like and keep your hands in the air. I'm a U. S. Marshal and a wrong move invites a bullet."

Instead of dismounting, Indian Joe spurred his horse and guided him into some high bushes. He was gone in a twinkle of the eye. Tom held his fire and said to the other one, "Step away from the horse and drop your gun belt." Lafe did as he was told. Tom approached him and asked, "Do you mind telling me what you're doing out here?"

Lafe studied Tom for a few minutes, deciding to bluff it out he asked, "Did you bring the money?"

Tom knew then that he was looking at one of the kidnapers. He said, "You don't think we are crazy do you? I brought the money and hid it. I'll need to see your captives before I tell you where to find the money, that is if you can describe the captives and if you can't we don't have anything to talk about."

"The man's name is Blair and the girl is called Sissy. Does that sound like who you want?"

"Yes, that sounds about right. Where are they?"

Lafe tried to laugh and said, "You must think I'm crazy. First I get the money then I tell you where to find them. How does that sound?"

"Well, that just about what I expected from someone with your intelligence level. I'm going to put my rope around your neck and drag you back to town. I bet before we get there you will tell me where to find my friends and the name of your partner in crime. Start walking down that slope. My horse is not far off and then we head for town."

During the time Tom was talking with Lafe he was scanning the surrounding area looking for the culprit that fled. He used the dead man's horse as a shield from getting a bullet in his back.

Lafe's mind kept searching for a way out of his present situation; he knew that he was in serious trouble. He asked, "If I take you where they are, would you let me go? I don't want the money. I just want to go home."

"It might make a difference to the judge if I told him that you cooperated after I captured you, but you will face a judge regardless of what you do now. Make up your mind fast."

"They're in a cabin a mile or so to the west. I'll show you the way." Lafe was playing for time hoping that Indian Joe would come to his rescue, but Indian Joe was no fool; he was smart enough to know when the game was over. He had debated the thought of sneaking back and trying to get a lucky shot at the lawman, but he decided to head north. He stopped in a gully and counted what money he had on him; just a little under a hundred dollars.

He muttered to himself, "To hell with that crazy stupid Lafe; let him swing, I'll wait for a better day." He forced his horse up a steep bank and urged him toward the rising hills to the north.

Meanwhile Blair and Sissy's situation was improving. She had managed to untie her feet and crawled over to Blair. He tried to roll on his side so that Sissy could untie the ropes holding him to the wall. She said, "The ropes seem tight. I'm looking for the knot." He could feel the ropes loosening around his risk; she worked fast and soon his hands were free. It only took a couple of minutes to free himself. He stood and said, "Thanks Sissy, you are a real fine partner. Now you stay here until I get a look around outside; I don't see anywhere in here that they could put our gear and my revolvers. I'll just be a minute or two."

Sissy said, "Please hurry I need some private time." She looked at him with trusting eyes and continued, "Well hurry up." Then she half smiled and walked to the other end of the cabin.

Blair found his and Sissy's horses in a rope corral tied to the trees. Saddles were still on the horses. He almost ran to his horse hoping to find his revolvers; the revolvers were gone. They took everything of value with them. He returned to the cabin and said, "Sissy, come on out and take what time you need behind the cabin. I'll get our horses ready to ride." She glanced at him, waved her hand and ran behind the cabin. He checked the sun for direction; normally he would follow whatever trail he could find, but with Sissy to think about he decided to cut across country toward town avoiding further encounter with Lafe and Indian Joe. He would deal with them later. After riding through some rough country, he recognized for the first time where he was. He said, "Sissy, you'll be safe soon. I know the way to town from here, but we are closer to the Longmire Ranch. We can get food and water there."

Sissy asked, "When will I see my mommy?"

He replied, "We probably will have to wait until we get to town to find out about her. Let's go."

At that very moment, Tom Leach wanted to make sure Lafe could not escape or cause him trouble so he tied his hands to the saddle horn. As an added precaution he dropped a loop over the horse's neck, giving the horse just enough rope to stay a few feet behind as he headed out in the direction Lafe had indicated. It did not take very long to find the cabin. When they arrived Lafe exclaimed, "The horses are gone. I bet that bastard got loose."

Tom replied, "Get down and lead the way through the door." Tom had his revolver in his hand and let Lafe enter ahead of him, his hands remained firmly tied together. The cabin was empty. Ropes used to secure the prisoners lay on the dirt floor. Tom looked around the cabin and asked, "What did you give them to eat? There's no stove and it looks like this place has not been used for years."

"We didn't have any food and very little water."

Tom took his arm and led him outside to the horses and assisted him to mount. Tom made a circle around the cabin studying the tracks he found where two horses had crossed some soft ground and left very visible tracks leading up the hill. He said to Lafe, "Let's go, we'll follow their trail. Looks like Blair is cutting a course across some pretty rocky hills. We may catch up with them. What do you think happened to your helper in crime? I believe you said his name is Indian Joe? Is that all the name he has?"

"I told you already I don't know anything about him. Met up with him on the trail and I'd guess he is long gone. He was no good anyway." Lafe lied with a surly snarl.

They rode on for a couple hours without speaking when Lafe suddenly asked, "Where's the money? You said it was hidden some place."

Tom turned in the saddle looking at Lafe and said, "That I did. It's hidden in my saddlebags. But don't fret too much as I never had any intention of giving you or anyone else the ransom money. That would violate our code and encourage criminals like you to try it again on some other innocent person. No, we don't pay ransom, but just use it for bait to bring vile cowards to justice."

"I'm not a coward. I've had me some real scrapes and come out the better man every time."

Tom laughed and called out over his shoulder, "I'd guess you used a sneaky trick or shot the victim in the back. You say you're the better man, not a chance. No use talking about such things as the judge will deliver the verdict, not me."

"Are you going to tell the judge that I helped you find them?"

"I'll tell the judge the truth, but I don't expect what little you helped to carry much weight with the judge. He's a no nonsense enforcer of justice." They rode on with Tom leading Lafe's horse. He did not have a chance to break loose and escape.

Following the trail left by Blair, Tom soon realized that Blair was heading toward the Longmire ranch. Tom urged his horse to increase the pace and didn't bother looking for tracks. He wanted to reach the ranch before dark.

When Tom rode into the Longmire yard leading Lafe's horse he sensed that something was amiss; then the front door swung open and Tess yelled, "Tom, Tom they got Blanche." Her face was ashen and her normally well-groomed hair was flying wildly in the wind.

Tom dismounted and took hold of her arms and said, "Slow down, tell me what happened to Blanche." Then he saw Helen Parks and Sissy come slowly toward him. He looked back at Tess and said, "I'm waiting; tell me what happened to Blanche."

"That vile Gus Leonard and another gunman came here this morning and took Blanche with them. She put up a fight; then the outlaws said they would kill us all if she kept it up. All the while the other man was holding a gun on us saying he would kill us if we come out the door. You can see the bullet holes in the door. They shot back at us as they rode off with Blanche." Tess was out of breath.

Tom turned to Helen and Sissy and said, "Sissy, I'm glad to see you with your mommy again. I'd like to talk with Blair. Where is he?"

Helen Parks said, "He left soon after he got here with Sissy; he's following the outlaws to rescue Blanche. The outlaws left a note. Blair read it and took off after them."

Tom walked over and put his hand on Sissy's shoulder and said, "It's hard to express how glad I am to see you again, young lady. Are you alright?"

"Yes, Blair got me home. I like him and you too." Tears appeared on both cheeks. She bravely wiped them off; her mother hugged her and smiled. It was the first time that Tom had seen Helen really look happy.

He turned to Tess and asked, "Where's the note? I'd like to see it."

Tess fished the note out of her pocket and passed it to Tom, it read, *Marshal Leach better come to Bat Cave alone or Blanche won't come back. Quirt won't wait long.*

Three of the wranglers stood respectful by the corral gate, not wanting to intrude on the conversations. Tom turned and recognized the ramrod, he said, "Larsen I need to have a couple of your wranglers take my prisoner to town and carry a report to Marshal Decker? I'll have the report ready in a few minutes." Larsen stepped forward and said, "Yes, I'll see to the prisoner and your message. But I should have gone with the other Marshal to bring Miss Longmire back, but he would not accept my offer. He said he works best alone. He's riding into a pit of snakes out there in the badlands."

Tom said, "Blair probably thought you should stay and protect the ranch and the rest of the family. I must get on their trail without delay. I guess most of us know Bat Cave is the largest cave ever discovered in this part of the southwest. I guess it will take sometime to get there?"

Larsen replied, "The Owl Hooters use it as their roost and hideaway. Everybody knows to stay away from that part of the country."

Tom thought a minute and said, "I'll go across the mountain and try to cut them off before they get to the cave. Blanche will slow them down all she can. My best chance to rescue Blanche is to intercept them in the open. If they reach the cave it will be very difficult to get her out without harm."

Larsen wasted no time in appointing two of his older wranglers to escort Lafe to town and carry the note to Marshal Decker. Tom Leach gathered some supplies from the house and set out to rescue Blanche. He refused to let his mind consider the vile treatment she might undergo at the hands of Gus Leonard and his cohort. Tom knew all about that killer Quirt Evans and that Jake was part of the Evans gang.

As he passed the corral gate he looked back and waved. The little sad group returned his wave until he rode out of sight. Tom's attention returned to the trail leading to the badlands. His concern was for Blanche and Blair; if Blair caught up with the kidnappers he would give his life if necessary to rescue Blanche. His courageous efforts might put Blanche in greater danger. He hoped that Blair would follow their trail and wait for an opportunity to act when he had some advantage and a good chance of success in rescuing Blanche.

Tom was tired when he left the Longmire ranch and now with evening closing in he began to look for a place his horse could graze while he dozed off for an hour or so. He glanced at the sky and was thankful that tonight he would be able to travel by moonlight. He did not think the kidnappers would try to cut across the mountain but would stay on the trails in the lowlands. Blair was on their trail and he would do everything he could to free Blanche. Tom had long since learned that his life after joining the U.S. Marshal Service had been one of luck and chance. Now he and Blair needed both to rescue the girl he intended to marry.

The girl that Marshal Leach hoped to marry had suffered a long day on the trail through dense mesquite bushes and thorny vines. Her legs were scratched and bleeding when Gus Leonard called a halt to make camp. He spoke to Harve, "You go find us a rabbit while there's still light and I'll make a small fire. I don't think we have anyone trailing us yet."

Harve asked, "Why don't you go get a rabbit and I will stay with the girl and build a fire?"

Leonard whipped out his revolver and said, "This says you go get the rabbit."

"Hell, I was just joshing you; I'll try to find us some meat." He laughed, tied his horse and slipped off down the hill and said over his shoulder, "Keep your hands off that girl or I will tell Quirt and you know how he deals with everyone he dislikes."

Gus Leonard did not look at Blanche during the exchange between him and Harve. She had managed to dismount even though her hands were tied together with rawhide strips. She found a rock and sits down. Leonard gathered some dead limbs and grass and started a small fire. He said to Blanche, "I guess we won't have much to eat for the next couple of days unless he finds a rabbit. I'm really sorry about all this; if we get out of this mess will you still marry me?"

"You bastard you killed my papa and then ask such a question. You are crazy. I'd like to see you in hell."

"I don't know where you got such an idea; I didn't kill anyone. Clay came out to the range and ordered me to leave; he wouldn't even let me come back to the bunkhouse to get my gear. I left because I didn't want to hurt you."

As she sought an opportunity to get away, Blanche's mind was racing; she knew that it would be dark in a few minutes. She calmed herself and decided that she would play along and grab the first chance he gave her. She said, "Well that not what the evidence shows, if you say you did not kill papa then I guess I believe you."

He smiled and said, "I'm glad you understand. We have to get away before Quirt Evans gets his hands on you. Tell me where the gold is and we leave now."

"What gold? I don't know anything about gold. What are you talking about?"

"Your old sweetheart Tom Leach knows where the gold is hidden somewhere near Tincup. That's the reason Quirt Evans wants you. He is a mean killer. So tell me now and I'll get you out of this if I have to kill Harve."

"I've already told you that I've not heard about gold. I thought you still liked me?" She attempted to smile.

"I do like you. I like you very much. Maybe you don't know about the gold, but I bet you could get Leach to tell you?"

"I might be able to do that, but not with my hands tied and out in the wilds with you."

"If I untie you, do you promise to like me just a little?"

"Yes, but I need to go behind that large rock for just a minute before we do anything."

He said, "I will untie your hands, but if you try to get away there will be hell to pay. Hurry up and do what you must, Harve will be back soon." He was smiling to himself.

She knew that her ploy to go behind the rock would not be the time to escape; she relieved herself and straightened her blouse. She had to play for time.

Leonard had been very close to the side of the rock and when she stepped out he tried to take her hand. She made a little gesture and whispered "later." He quickly rolled out his bedroll, dropped down in a prone position and motioned for her to join him. As she approached him, her mind was racing, and quickly resolved that this was live or die situation. She very timidly came near him, still sitting up; he pulled her down and kissed her on the lips. She put just enough in the kiss to make him think she was a willing kitten. A desperate plan formulated in her mind.

She pulled away and said, "I've never done anything like this before, but I'll not have anything more to do with you wearing those guns."

Dusk was falling fast. He said, "If that is bothering you, I'll take them off." He hurriedly unbuckled his gun belt and tossed it to the side of the bedroll.

He came at her again, and she said, "Help me out of these trousers." He laughed and said, "This is going to be fun."

She pulled both her feet together, her knees touching her chin, as if to give him room to get in position to pull her trousers off. When he was off balance in front of her feet, she kicked him in the groin with all her might. He fell backwards in pain; she grabbed his gun belt and stood up. Harve appeared in front of her and apparently did not see that she held one of Leonard's pistols in her hand. He came toward her and she raised the pistol and fired. Leonard scrambled to his feet and she saw Harve running for cover. She had a fleeting thought about bluffing it out and getting a horse, but instantly decided she was no match for both of them. She turned and raced into the heavy brush not looking back. Her one goal was to get away from that pair of killers. She heard them searching for her and cussing each other, she raced on unaware of the thorny bushes. She was free.

The outlaws searched until dark looking for Blanche. Then they returned to the camp and placed more wood on the fire, and Leonard said, "That bitch got my guns and belt. She could be anywhere out there and she would like nothing better than to put a bullet in my gut. Do you think it is safe to stay here tonight? You know we can't go back and face Quirt without her."

Harve replied, "I have no intention of letting him shoot me like he did Shotgun. We can't catch her in the woods and she won't come back if that is what you think. She has guts and will power; she'd rather die of thirst than come back to us. I say we wait for the moon to come up then take her horse and head for the Territory."

"I hate like hell to go without my guns, but I guess we have no choice. What you say sounds good to me; Quirt will have a fit and shoot us. To hell with that girl and my guns; and besides we don't know if that marshal is following us, if he does not show up Quirt will blame us. Another reason to not wait around here that shot from that bitch could draw company." Leonard said.

"We can go slowly through the woods. Let's get out of here before we get a bullet from that damn she-cat or someone else. We can camp three or four miles from here tonight and rest our horses." Harve replied.

The cowardly bandits saddled and rode away, not bothering to put out the small fire.

CHAPTER 10

LAZY S DEFENDERS

Quirt Evans and his band of cutthroats reined to a halt when they got near the Singletary ranch. He instructed Cisco and Lemmon to go start the fire. The gang would wait until they could see the flames. He said in the meantime the rest of them would cross ease in and be close to the top of the knoll overlooking the ranch. As the gang eased forward making as little noise as possible, they had the benefit of moonlight and it was late enough that every one at the ranch ought to be sleeping. Quirt wanted complete surprise if possible. Before they reached the crest of the hill, Quirt whispered to the gang that the house could be seen from the knoll.

They halted and Quirt asked, "What the hell is keeping Cisco? I'm not waiting much longer." Then they waited another fifteen minutes and Quirt could not contain his anger. He knew Cisco had had time to get to the barns. He said in an angry voice, "To hell with the fire, let's go kill some pilgrims." He spurred his horse led the gang to the creek and started up the far bank when all hell broke loose.

Moss Singletary and his wranglers had just about given up on the gang attacking as the night was wearing on and the bright moon might discourage their attack. But they had remained fully alert when the first two outlaws passed through going to the ranch. Moss whispered to pass the word that they should hold their fire and let those two through. He had anticipated something like that and three of his best fighters were positioned to catch anyone trying to get close to the ranch house. Then when he did not hear gunfire he was satisfied that those two bandits had been silently captured or killed. He was not too concerned how they were captured.

The Lazy S defenders could the horses and riders as they crossed the stream. The targets were close enough that the first volley from Singletary's men caused havoc with the gang; some screamed in pain and tried to get back across the creek. Several died. Within minutes the fight was over. Moss heard some of the horses racing back up the trail away from the deadly gunfire, he called out, "hold your fire." There was dead silence, except for horses with empty saddles milling around in the creek. Moss turned to one of his wranglers and said, "Go to the barn and bring the wagon. We'll need to escort those dead bandits to town in the morning. I don't expect any of them that fled back up the trail to come back anytime soon. You men check each of those bandits on the ground and see if they need medical attention. The rest of us will walk back to the ranch."

Steve Sutton said, "I'd like a chance to check the bodies in the creek to see if the killers of my brother are among them. If I don't find them here, I'm going after those that got away."

"Steve, that would be a foolish thing to do, if the killers of your brother escaped you are not going to catch them. Those bodies down there will be brought to the ranch and we'll look them over. Now let's all go back and get some rest. I don't think those cowards will be back anytime soon."

Two of the three outlaws Steve sought never made it to the barn; they dismounted behind a clump of mesquite, each carrying a gallon of kerosene and stealthily approached the barn from the rear. When they neared the barn door, they heard, "You boys have guns pointed at your guts; just drop whatever you are carrying and stand dead still or we shoot. Your choice." Cisco and Lemmon had ridden the Owl Hoot Trail long enough to know that taking bullets in the gut was no way to die. Without a word they dropped the kerosene cans and raised their hands. Ten minutes later they found themselves in the barn gagged and tied to centers poles. They never spoke a word while being tied to the poles. But the lantern light reflected the stark fear in their eyes.

Luck never promised repeat opportunities of escaping situations such as they were in on the last visit to the Singletary ranch, and now unless they could talk their way out of this mess the hangman would be pleased to place the noose around their necks.

Moss Singletary and his wranglers returned to the house and were told about the two prisoners in the barn. Steve said, "I'll go take a look at them."

Moss said, "Yes and I want to ask them a few questions, so I'm coming along."

Moss and Steve entered the barn and met the two wranglers watching over the prisoners. Moss said, "Light a lantern and let us have a look at what you boys caught."

Steve was the first to exclaim, "I be damned here's two of the bastards that killed my brother. Let's hang them here and now."

"Steve on this ranch we can be damn tough and hard as horseshoe nails, but we observe the western code of justice to the letter. We only hang killers when there is no court or jury available. In this case these bandits will go to town and face justice." Moss sternly replied.

"It was my brother they murdered and waiting for a jury really galls me." Steve bristled.

"I understand your feelings. But what I said goes. Let's pull the gags and see what they have to say for themselves." One of the wranglers swiftly removed the gags and the prisoners turned their eyes away from the dim lantern light.

Moss took one of them by the chin and said, "Look at me. You know where you are and how you got here. No trick on a young inexperience boy will let you loose again. Which one of you killed that young boy in the jail?"

The short dark one replied, "It was Shotgun. He choked him to death." The other one spoke up and said, "He's telling you the truth, it was Shotgun."

Steve stepped forward and demanded, "I want to know where that murderer Shotgun is?'

"Quirt shot him in the head when we got back across the river. Shotgun got smart with Quirt and he killed him. He almost killed us at the same time, but changed his mind."

Steve said, "Too bad he didn't shoot you both, now I guess we'll have to wait for the hangman to do his work." Neither of the outlaws responded but hung their heads with eyes cast to the ground.

Moss asked then, "How many did you have in your gang tonight?"

Cisco answered, "I don't know, maybe twelve or fifteen. I heard the shooting. Did any of them get away?"

"We don't rightly know yet how many got away. We'll have to count the bodies. You boys hunker down and wait for daylight. No use straining at those ropes, you'll be well guarded. You both have made the trip to town before, so you know how we treat our prisoners."

Moss turned and left the barn. Steve Sutton followed him outside and said, "I respect your code Mister Singletary, but my brother paid the price to give those murderers several days, perhaps weeks to live. Justice should be swift and final. Least ways that was the way I was raised."

Moss turned and said, "Son, I've lived a long time, and always found doing the right thing made me feel good about myself. I hope you will come to that understanding sometime soon. You are still young and have many years ahead of you. You might even become famous before you cash in your chips. You'll have a job on this ranch as long as I live. Now go some rest, I'm placing you in charge of getting the bodies and the prisoners to town. Take three wranglers with you to help the marshal guard his jail until those two killers in the barn face the judge. You stay with them and make sure one of our guards is outside the jail around the clock. The marshal can handle the goings on in the jail, but we will make sure no one leaves the jail that isn't free to travel."

"I'm obliged for your help and consideration. I do understand your code, but it is hard to swallow in this case." Steve offered.

"I know how anxious you are to see that justice is carried out. I also know that you'll do just fine. Rest assured the killers of your brother will be dealt with severely and western justice will once again prevail. Nothing will bring back your brother, but our code of justice saves other innocent lives. Your pay will not be interrupted while you stay in town and witness the final act in this tragic murder." Moss replied.

Steve offered his hand to his boss and said, "Layton was a wild kid and still learning the ropes. I appreciate your help and understanding; every hand on this ranch respects and admires you, I will never be able to repay you for tolerating Layton's and my lack of ranch experience. I do thank you."

"You're learning fast and that is what counts out here in this lawless territory. There will come a time when all these killings will cease and we all can live in peace. I'll see you in the morning."

Moss went into the house and closed the door. He mused to himself, on this night *a large dose of western justice was served and some of the killers will no longer terrorize innocent citizens. Those that fled will also receive a dose of the same medicine if they attack the ranch again.*

At the time Moss Singletary's wranglers were loading onto a wagon the outlaws killed in the attack on the ranch, several miles away two other members of the Quirt Evans gang were leading Blanche Longmire's horse, taking her to almost certain abuse and death. Moss Singletary and his wranglers were unaware that Quirt Evans had sent two of his killers to the Longmire ranch up near Abilene to kidnap and take back to Bat Cave the girl Marshal Tom Leach intended to marry. U.S. Marshal Tom Leach's name was known throughout the frontier. His reputation for honest and fair enforcement of the laws was legendary.

Quirt Evans was convinced that Tom Leach knew where his brother hid his gold as he had sent his Tom Leach a letter from Tincup before he died. Quirt Evans listened very intently to the range telegraph—word of mouth rumors—and what Gus Leonard had said about the Marshal being sweet on the Longmire girl. Leonard had told him that Tom Leach would follow instructions to come to the Bat Cave when he learned that his sweetheart was carried away. Evans believed the information he had extracted from the two Tincup idiots before he shot them. They told of a letter Jake Leach wrote to his brother just before he died, no doubt telling him about the hidden gold. Quirt intended to make Tom Leach reveal the location of the gold. Then kill him.

In pursuit of the kidnappers and Blanche Longmire, Deputy Marshal Blair Green had mixed emotions as he left the Longmire ranch to rescue Blanche. He was tired from the ordeal he and Sissy had experienced during the last several days. He had not consulted his superiors about undertaking the rescue; he was assuming the authority he hoped would be granted if there had been time to seek it.

Now on the trail, he was becoming knowledgeable in reading signs left by the fleeing outlaws. He expected to overtake the kidnappers sometime the following day as they had several hours lead on him. But plans don't always go the way expected. Later that day his horse was bitten by a rattlesnake causing him to unexpectedly start bucking and squealing; Blair was almost thrown from the saddle, but managed to hang on. Within minutes after Blair gained control his horse he noticed the horse was lame in the right front leg. He dismounted and examined the swollen leg. Blair's training had not prepared him for dealing with a horse's rattlesnake bite; it was obvious that the horse could not carry him fast enough to overtake the kidnappers.

He had nothing to treat the wound, but had heard that bleeding helped. It took all his courage to cut a small slit in the skin where the rattlesnake had left his fang marks, and then it only bled slightly. The horse never flinched. Blair now found himself in a quandary: a lame horse would not carry him fast enough to catch the kidnappers, nor did he know if the horse could survive the rattlesnake poison. If he turned the horse loose and continued the pursuit on foot the likelihood of overtaking the kidnappers was slim or none. So with a heavy heart he reluctantly started the slow return journey to the ranch, walking and leading the horse. The distance between him and Blanche's kidnappers steadily increased as he walked toward the ranch and the kidnappers continued in the other direction.

Blair did not hear Blanche's gunshot fired when escaping from Leonard, but another very interested person did hear it. Tom was looking for a place to make dry camp when he heard a single gunshot. He halted and listened for a few minutes, not hearing another shot he petted his horse's neck and said, "Boy that sounds like someone just killed a rabbit to roast, although it seems too dark for that. Let's mosey that way and find out if they will share it."

Tom Leach had ridden hard that afternoon to get ahead of the kidnappers and find a place to rescue Blanche. He wanted to intercept them before Blair caught up from the rear. He was concerned that

Blair would not use his training and caution if he caught up with the outlaws. The gunshot he just heard had to be investigated. It could be someone who made camp and intended to eat roasted rabbit tonight, but it could be the kidnappers with Blanche. He would exercise extreme caution to prevent harm to Blanche.

He rode for several minutes, stopping often and listened, there was no more shooting but he soon smelled smoke; someone had started a fire. He tied his horse to a mesquite bush, removed his boots and spurs, pulled on a pair of calf skin moccasins, wrapped a dark colored neckerchief over his head and hid his bedroll, rifle, boots and hat. He then slowly moved toward what he believed was a small fire, such as used to roast meat and make coffee. As he crawled near the edge of the brush and weeds he could see the fire. He waited. After about an hour, the fire was dying out and he was about ready to check out the area around the fire to see if the campers left anything that might indicate it was the kidnappers of Blanche. Then he saw a person approach the fire, staying away from the weak glow of the one small flame. After several minutes he watched as more wood was added to the fire; it flamed up and he recognized Blanche. He almost called out to her, but cautiously waited a few more minutes to make sure she was alone.

Tom hunkered down and watched Blanche as she continued to add sticks to the flames. He quietly moved around to the opposite side of the camp. His hundred and ninety pound body slithered through the brush noiselessly. He kept his eyes on Blanche as he proceeded to survey the ring around the campfire. When he was sure she was alone, he called out in a low voice, "Blanche, this is Tom, stay where you are, I'm coming in." She froze in place staring in the direction of his voice. She raised the pistol she held in her right hand and said, "God it sounds like you Tom, but if it is not you, I swear I'll shoot." Tom still had not moved as he did not want to frighten her. He said, "Blanche, you can keep the revolver pointed at me, but I'm coming in."

As he came in she dropped her hand holding the revolver and almost shouted, "I thought it was the end for me. God, I'm glad to see you." As her neared her, he removed the bandana from his head and asked, "Where are the bad guys?"

She ran to him, grabbed him and locked her arms around his body and sobbed. Her relief was just as unbearable as the emotion of being held captive by the two brutes that dragged her away from home. Tom said, "Let's move over to the fire and you tell how you got loose and where the kidnappers are now?"

Blanche finally gained control of her emotions and told Tom about being taken prisoner and the trip from the ranch. She cautiously left out the ruse she used to gain her freedom. She merely said that she was able to grab Gus Leonard's gun belt with his revolvers, took a shot at him and his partner and then fled in the brush. Tom noticed the deep scratches on her face, arms and hands, some still oozing blood. He asked, "Where are they now?"

She said, "It seems like I've been hiding for hours; they looked for me until it was really dark and then they returned to the fire. I had not gotten that far away from the fire, as I found a clump of dense bushes and high weeds to hide in. They returned to the fire and I heard them arguing about what to do."

Tom urged, "Go on, I need to know what to do next."

"Well, I heard them say that if they returned to the cave without me, Quirt Evans would kill them. They argued some more about trying to find hidden gold, then they left. They kept talking about where they would be safe; after several minutes they decided they'd be safe in the Indian Territory. They took all three horses and left. I followed and tried to stay in hearing distance to learn what they would do next. I heard enough to know that they seemed scared and wanted to get away. I think they thought I might slip back and shoot that murderer Gus Leonard. He killed my papa; I'm almost certain even if he denied it. Then when I was sure they were not coming back, I came back to see what they might have. I found only the one blanket. Now thank the Lord you are here."

"You took a dangerous chance in following them, but I understand why you did. I'm putting out this fire, and then we will get my horse and follow Leonard and his cohort. Do you think you can ride?"

"Tom, I'm scratched up a bit and scared to death, but now that you are here, I can do whatever is necessary to get home." Blanche almost joyfully replied.

"We'll talk some more after we find a new campsite." Tom said while putting out the fire.

Tom hurriedly distinguished the fire, smothered the coals with dirt and took Blanche's hand and led her toward where he had tied his horse. After a few step he said, "Blanche stay real close to me through this brush, I'll go slowly so that you don't get anymore scratches."

He found his horse and said to Blanche, "We'll have a full moon and I believe we ought to be able to travel by moonlight. If you can we'll make pretty good time; from what you said about the direction Leonard took it seems they intend to go between your ranch and Abilene. So we won't be going much out of our way following them. I'd like to deal with them before they reach the Territory."

"I'd like to have the first shot at that Leonard. He killed my papa. I had a chance back at the campfire, but was too frightened and anxious to getaway. I guess my shot went wild and didn't hit either one of the bastards."

Tom thought her tone belied her desire to kill someone, even the murderer of her father.

The moon seemed peeked over the mountain to the east; Tom had helped Blanche to mount and he led the horse very slow through the dense brush. It wasn't long before they came to an open prairie and was able to increase the pace. Blanche had not uttered a word after getting in the saddle. He looked back often and seen that she was grasping the saddle horn with both hands. He wanted to continue hoping that the bandits had stopped and made camp; if so they would probably start a fire. He thought it helped that the wind was from the north. On a night like this, the scent of burning wood would carry a long way. After crossing two small open areas, they were once again in tall weeds and bushes. Then his horse snorted, shook his head and stopped. Tom waited a few minutes then smelled burning wood. His next thought was what he could do with Blanche now that danger lurked ahead. A big boulder was emerged in brush and weeds; Tom decided to leave the horse and convince Blanche to stay with the horse. What he had to do, was dangerous and could very easily take a bad turn.

He whispered to Blanche, who was about half-asleep, to dismount and he would prepare the bedroll so she could get some sleep.

She asked, "Why do you have to be so secretive? I smell the smoke and know that you want me to stay here. I still have that killer's revolvers and I can help."

"I'm sure you could, but it is more important for you use the revolver to guard our horse; we don't want to be left afoot out here in the wilds. Now just take it easy, but stay alert and I'll be back in a few minutes. If you hear three shots spaced a few seconds apart bring the horse and come toward where you think the shots were fired. But if you don't hear the signal or I'm not back in an hour, take the horse and work your way back to the ranch; just keep the moon to your right until you come to something you recognize." She came close grasped his hand and said, "Alright, I guess you know what you are doing. So I'll stay here."

Tom squeezed her hand and said, "Don't worry I'll be back or you will hear the shots. I can't leave a beautiful bride to be out here in the badlands. Stay as quiet as possible and don't let the horse make noise if you can help it."

Blanche said, "That's one hell of a proposal of marriage that is if you plan on being the groom."

"Indeed I do, now stay quiet." He silently slipped into the underbrush.

It took Tom almost thirty minutes to work his way close to the small fire built between two large rocks. He continued to silently inch forward until he could hear what they were saying, "I think we should have stayed back there and killed that bitch before going to the Territory. Now we have all the lawmen in the country after our necks and nothing to show for it."

"Harve, what the hell are you worried about? She got my guns and belt. I can find other guns easier than digging a bullet out of my gut. She missed me by inches; I could hear the bullet pass my head. I've still got the rifle, but you should let me use one of your revolvers. The first rider we meet with guns, I'll replace mine."

Tom realized the hour he promised Blanche was about up; he sat up and pulled his revolvers from the holsters. The moonlight cast long shadows of the outlaws as they prepared to bed down for the night. Tom could hear their horses apparently tied nearby. The time had arrived to act. He took advantage of a boulder, yet having full vision of the targets; he called out, "Stand real still, don't move or you both are dead." One of the killers dropped to the ground, but Tom's bullet caught him in the chest as he fell. The other outlaw continued to stand still. Tom approached the fire and learned the reason only one of them tried to shoot it out; the one standing did not have revolvers and the rifle was out of reach. Tom said, "I take it you are Gus Leonard?"

"I'm called that sometimes. Who are you?"

"Leonard, you are under arrest for the murder of Clay Longmire and kidnapping of Blanche Longmire. If you don't get reckless and do something stupid, you will get a chance to defend yourself in court."

"I didn't kill anybody. You've got no proof."

"As I just said you will have a chance to give your story to the judge. But you better know that I'm personally disgusted with you and angry enough to mete out western justice and not take you to jail. So don't force me to shoot you." Then Tom ordered Leonard to get on his hands and knees, holding one of his revolvers to Leonard's head while searching him for weapons with the other. Tom removed a dagger from it's sheathe at the back of Leonard's neck. Then he stood and fired three times, counting to four between shots. He hoped Blanche understood the signal.

After a few minutes Leonard asked, "How long do I stay on my knees like a dog?"

"Just stay put, I'll tell you when to move."

Blanche had no trouble in finding the small fire. When she got near, she stopped and heard Tom say, "Come on in Blanche. You can get a look at the murderer of your father."

On seeing Leonard she raised one of the revolvers, but Tom reached out and took it from her tight grasp. He said, "Blanche, I know how you feel. But unless this jasper does something real foolish he'll face a judge. That is my obligation and yours as well." Blanche looked at the dead man and asked, "Is that one dead?"

Tom said, "Yes, I had to shoot him."

He then took rawhide strips from his saddlebag and tied Leonard's hands. Grabbed him by his arm and half-dragged him to the horses. He said to Blanche, "Bring my horse; we need to ride a few miles yet tonight. Someone may have heard those signal shoots. Are you alright?"

"Yes, I'll make it if I don't go to sleep in the saddle."

"You'll make it just fine. We can be at your ranch by mid-morning tomorrow if all goes well."

Tom hurriedly placed the dead outlaw in the saddle face down and tied his hands and feet with a rope under the horse's belly. He then spoke to Blanche, "You lead this horse and I'll lead Leonard's. That ought to keep you awake."

It was near noon the next day when Blanche almost shouted, "Tom, the ranch is just over that rise ahead. God, I'm happy to be home." Tom glanced at her and could she the tears streaming down her cheeks; she was indeed relieved to be home.

Gus Leonard also saw the happy face and said, "I guess you will be just as happy when you see them put the noose around my neck?"

Blanche stared him in the eyes and said, "You murdered my papa. What the law orders for you will suit me just fine. But for your information, not that it will do you any good, some human beings love life and will never celebrate the taking of a life regardless if it is worthless or not. My papa's blood is on your hands, you will answer for your sins."

Leonard did not respond.

CHAPTER 11

THE RIDE HOME

Tom Leach wanted to get Blanche back to the ranch without delay. She was scratched, exhausted and needed sleep and rest. He recognized that she kept going on will power alone. His heart hurt for her. Her life on the ranch had served to insulate her from showing girlish feelings. He took the most direct route back to the ranch and tried to select terrain that made it easier for her to hold on to the saddle. He avoided going down steep inclines and kept the pace. Every once and awhile he would look back and she would flash a brave smile. Her ordeal without the scratches and cuts from the brush were more than enough to cause most people to just give up. Getting Blanche home was just part of the problems ahead; there was anarchy in the Southwest near Tincup that had to be dealt with at the earliest opportunity. He would have already been down there except for the kidnapping of Blanche. Quirt Evans did not need to send him a message to confront him by taking an innocent girl away from her family. Quirt Evans and his gang were the source of the reported lawlessness on the border and Southwest. It would now be a priority.

On the ride home, Tom Leach slow walked his horse while leading the prisoner's horse; Blanche led the other horse with a dead outlaw tied in its saddle. At about the time they sighted the ranch house, they received a signal from one of the Longmire wranglers to come to the house. Then as they rode past the corral gate, the front door burst open and the family began to come out to the yard; they were jumping up and down and yelling with joy. Tom stopped and motioned for Blanche to come abreast. As she neared, he reached out and took the reins of her horse and said gently, "Jump down and go meet them. I'll take care of business and see you after awhile."

The last person out of the house was Marshal Decker. He met Tom as he dismounted in front of the barn door. He said, "I see you rescued Blanche and took a prisoner. Was he involved in kidnapping her?"

"Yes, the outlaw tied face down on the horse helped him. Where's Blair?"

"Blair is in the house recovering from walking miles without water and food. A rattlesnake bit his horse and lamed him. Blair tried to lead him back to the ranch, but the horse's leg continued to swell and walking seemed too painful for the horse. Blair turned him loose and carried his saddle and bedroll across that strip of desert to the southwest. He's one tough lawman. Tess sent a wrangler in to tell me about Blair's condition. I just left him; he's sleeping and regaining his strength. He'll be just fine in a day or so. What're going to do with the prisoner?" He eyed Leonard who stared back defiantly. Before Tom could respond to the Marshal's question Leonard spit and said, "I'm not guilty of anything except taking a job on this damn ranch. I've been dragged in here like an animal. There's going to be hell to pay if I'm jailed."

Marshal Decker disregarded Leonard's outburst as if he didn't hear him, he asked Tom, "What do you want to do with this loudmouth"

"That's up to you. What do you suggest, hang him here or send him to jail?"

Marshal Decker smiled and said, "The U. S. Marshal codes must be followed, never take a life without justification even when the evidence shows he's guilty; I'll take him off your hands. But right now a couple of the ranch hands can guard him while we talk, then I'll take him and the dead outlaw to town."

Two of the ranch hands standing nearby came over and volunteered to guard the prisoner. Then Tom and Marshal Decker walked to the house. As they walked Marshal Decker held his hand on his hip to soften the pain from limping. Finally as they approached the door he said, "I keep thinking some morning I'll wake up and not have this bothersome limp and pain, but I know that is just a dream. That's more than enough self-indulgence for one day. I have much to discuss with you. The recurring raids and killings in the Tincup area have the folks in Austin up in arms. The Governor and our superiors are demanding action. The situation around Tincup and all the way to the Rio Grande is out of control and the lawlessness is wide spread. I've put them off until now, but we must get down there and help the Town Marshal, there's no sheriff elected in that county yet. Their young Marshal named Tim McCall has organized the citizens and is doing what he can to protect the town, but that leaves the farmers and ranchers to fend for themselves. As luck will sometime have it, one rancher, Moss Singletary of the Lazy S has armed his wranglers and puts up a good fight. The Quirt Evans gang has attacked the ranch twice in the last three months and suffered great losses. Tincup is holding some members of that gang on murder charges awaiting the district judge. What do you know about Quirt Evans and his gang of cutthroats?"

"I'd say about the same as you've explained. You know Evans was behind the kidnapping of Blanche in an attempt to learn where the government gold is hidden. I understand he is waiting at Bat Cave for Blanche and me. When I've rested a few hours, I'll not disappoint him as I intend to visit the Bat Cave. If you agree, I'll first stop in Tincup as I understand one of Moss Singletary's wranglers has recently slipped in near the cave while Quirt and his gang were there. That information will be very valuable."

Marshal Decker said, "We have a message from Tincup about that brave young man. His name is Steve Sutton; Evans gang members killed his brother. In an effort to be prepared, Tim McCall sent him to the Rio Grande to watch for Evans return to our side. That young man may have saved many lives at the Singletary ranch as he almost killed a horse to alert the ranch that Quirt's gang was on the way to attack the ranch. Moss Singletary sent a message to the Governor urging him to send Rangers to quell the lawlessness in that part of the frontier. The Governor says it will be another few months before the Rangers will be trained and ready to take the field. We cannot wait for that."

Tom replied, "When we stop Quirt Evans, I believe much of the lawlessness down near the border will slowly go away as it has in other parts of the frontier. In training we learned that when the leader of a gang is brought to justice his followers generally fade away. If our information is correct Evans has lost a large number of his gang and may be getting real desperate. I'll need to rest a few hours and then I'll go down to Tincup and see what I can learn before going to Bat Cave."

Marshal Decker replied, "Tom you're going to need help to breakup that gang; you know they will fight to the end. I'd guess all of them have murder charges pending against them. They will not give up as long as they think they have a chance of escaping the noose. You are authorized to deputize qualified citizens to assist you in bringing Quirt Evans and his gang to justice. The deputies you appoint should be potential U.S. Marshal Service material and willing to undergo our training programs after you establish law and order on the border. I've already notified headquarters of my decision and I expect their unqualified support. Let's go in the house, I want to talk with Helen Parks before I return to Abilene with your prisoner and dead outlaw."

Tom said, "I dislike leaving so soon, but Quirt Evans may not wait long at the cave."

"That may be so, but now let's see if Blair is awake. He set out to rescue Blanche without my approval. I'll rein him in ways, but I admire his dedication and courage. He is an outstanding lawman."

Tom replied, "I guess that would be my task to speak to him about dashing off without orders, but I believe that he'll respond much better to your talk."

As they entered the house, Tess met them and said, "Blanche has bathed and is sleeping. She is scratched from head to toe. When I asked how she was treated, she only wanted to talk about what a brave and wonderful gentleman Tom Leach is. I would have tried to convince her otherwise but she was too tired to argue the point." Tess laughed and got a grin from Tom.

Tom asked, "Is Blair still sleeping?"

"No, he's in the kitchen eating."

Blair came into the room and said, "Well I made a mess of trying to help rescue Blanche. I see you done just fine without my fumbling everything that I touch."

Tom glanced at Marshal Decker and said, "They said you might be laid up. You look fit to me."

"Well with all the attention I got here, I'd have to recover, but I don't remember very much about getting here. I still say that I failed Blanche and the Service."

"You had no way of knowing that a rattlesnake would lame your horse. So don't be too harsh on yourself for that part of the event. I am somewhat disturbed that you undertook the rescue alone without notifying Marshal Decker. We all need to work together and minimize out exposure to dangerous situations."

Blair said, "I know the rules and I regret my haste, but I just reacted when I heard that killer had Blanche. Once more, I'll promise to not make the same mistake again."

Captain Decker spoke up and said, "Let's put all that behind us, we have work yet to do. Have you recovered sufficiently to back with Tom when he goes to Tincup and the Bat Cave?"

"I'm fine and ready to go, except, that I am the only one who knows where I hid Helen Parks' money box. Sissy knows, but I don't think she could find it."

Tom asked, "How far away is it? Or better how long do you think it would take you to fetch it?"

"I'd say it is less than a days ride or a little less on a good horse."

"If you are well enough for the trip tomorrow morning, you should go and retrieve the box. I'll set out for Tincup about the time you leave. You can come on and join me later."

Helen Parks came in the room and said, "Blair, that box can wait. You should go with Tom. Blanche and Tess say that I can stay here until other arrangements are made. Matter of fact, they want me as an employee to do the cooking and cleaning for the family. I've told them no pay is expected nor will it be accepted. My greatest concern is to get Sissy in school as soon as possible."

Marshal Decker said, "Helen, I own a small cottage on the outskirts of town that you and Sissy are welcome to use as long as you like. It is located not far from the school; it's within walking distance. The couple that rented it has gone back east, so at the moment it is empty."

"Marshal, I'm obliged and thankful for your offer, but I would not think of staying there without paying rent. Let me talk with Blanche and Sissy and then I will decide. Thank you." Helen withdrew and tried to conceal her joy at the generous offer by Marshal Decker.

Blair asked, "Well where does all this leave me? Am I coming with you Tom or do I go and return Helen Parks' valuables?"

"She seems content to delay recovery of the box, and I need you, but it's Marshal Decker's decision."

Marshal Decker replied, "Quirt Evans will not wait at Bat Cave forever he'll mount another killing spree; so Blair if you are able to go with Tom, that appears to be the best option at this time."

A little while later Marshal Decker and a Longmire wrangler rode toward town, each leading a horse; one with a prisoner and the other with a dead outlaw. Gus Leonard was still yelling invectives as they disappeared over the hill. Marshal Decker seemed not to hear his vile accusations, knowing that Leonard was facing the noose. He rode on unconcerned.

Tom and Blair slept in the bunkhouse and were summoned by Blanche before sunrise for breakfast at the house. She had prepared a big man-sized breakfast; steaming hot coffee, fried eggs, biscuits and gravy. In the center of the table she had arranged butter, jams and honey. Blanche, Tess and Helen joined them at the table, each with a cup of coffee and ate biscuits and jams. The conversation centered on Sissy who was still sleeping. After Helen had talked for awhile giving thanks to Blanche and Tess, she said, "There's no way that I can ever repay my debt to these girls, nor to you two good men. I'm sure that I would have died out there in the wilds if Tom had not rescued me. I don't want to even think about the treatment I received at the hands of those killers. God knows that I owe each of you my life as well a Sissy's." She was sobbing and tears were streaming down her face. She attempted to rise and leave the table, but Tom placed a firm hand on her shoulder and said, "No, stay with us please. Helen any one of us would feel the same as you do; you and Sissy went through real bad times; the bad times will fade as all our woes fade. Blanche also experienced near death and mistreatment. We cannot dwell on the bad times, but look forward to the future. I can tell all of you, there will come a time when the frontier will be safe and families can live in peace without fear. If Blair and I are successful in the next few weeks, that time will come sooner than you now think. In the meantime you ladies should enjoy being together and keep the faith."

Blanche said, "Tom we will be here when you and Blair come back. I know that you will come back. Tess and I will enjoy having Helen and Sissy here to keep us company. There's much we all have to talk about when you both return. But I don't think now is the time. So you two just go and do your job, but don't think you will escape what we have in mind for you when you get back. I'll take the liberty of notifying the preacher, so you don't need to bother with that little detail." She was smiling and crying. There was silence for a few minutes.

Then Tess turned to her sister and said, "That little speech of yours was the most brazen attempt I've ever heard to rope a suitor. I'd hope they can speak for themselves without such shameless hinting by my only sister." While talking Tess had turned her head away from Blanche, then Blanche was about to say something harsh until she saw the smile on Tess' face. She then said with a smile, "Little sister you can sit there prim and proper, but just remember papa said if you want to tame a wild horse, you first rope him. But I don't think that will be necessary in our efforts to tame a couple of lawmen." They all laughed. Tom and Blair were left speechless. Now was no time to make promises to beautiful girls. That could wait. There was important and dangerous work ahead. Quirt Evans and his outlaw gang holed up in Bat Cave would not just fade away; they had to be captured or killed. They would fight to their last breath rather than face justice.

Tom and Blair left the table and slowly walked to the door. They turned and faced the women, all standing expectantly. Tom spoke, "We'll be back and talk about that preacher." He and Blair waved to the emotional women and headed to the corral. Blair managed to get out the door without saying anything, as he was afraid that it would come out wrong. He and Tess had not had a chance to really talk about the future, but what he had to say should be said in private. He did not want a public refusal that would embarrass both Tess and him. Blanche and Tom's situation was different; apparently they had some kind of understanding about their future together. He was encouraged that Tess seemed to enjoy the banter and did not deny her interest in him. He resolved to wait and see what she said when he returned from Tincup. He was still weak from his ordeal in the desert, but he tried not to show it.

Within minutes following breakfast Tom and Blair rode out toward Tincup and Bat Cave; they were acutely aware that odds that either of them would see the Longmire ranch again were not in their favor. The job ahead was dangerous. Quirt Evans and his gang had to be stopped before the anarchy spread to other parts of the southwest. Both lawmen silently wondered if the women on the ranch would be safe while they were away. The fact that several wranglers maintained vigil day and night protecting the ranch gave them some comfort that they would be safe. Although unspoken, they were also aware that outlaws were crafty and skilled at slipping by sentinels.

To shake the worry about Blanche and the ranch, Tom let his mind drift to the clues Jake sent about the stolen gold. Many times during the last weeks he had studied the clues and was just about convinced that the gold had to be hidden somewhere in the desert. He guessed that since Jake rode with a bullet wound knowing that he was dying he would take the most direct route from Bat Cave to Tincup. So that narrowed the search area down somewhat. But first he had to establish law and order in the area and breakup the Quirt Evans gang. Then he would search for the government's gold.

CHAPTER 12

BAT CAVE

Some of the more wily and elusive outlaws riding the Owl Hoot Trail often used bat cave as a refuge. Its location was known to rustlers and marauders for several years before a few pioneers learned of its existence. In recent years only Quirt Evans continued to think of the cave as a hideaway. Either Evans did not care or was too stubborn to recognize that lawmen knew that desperate rustlers and killers, often fleeing a posse, stopped and rested at the cave before making the dash to Mexico. Quirt Evans usually had a large gang with enough members to guard the cave. He required one or two guards to hide in the desert approaches to the cave and sound the alarm of approaching riders.

Now after the defeat for the second time at the Lazy S ranch, he rode into the cave steaming mad; the loss of his most trusted gunslingers at the creek riled him as it was unexpected; the Lazy S gunslingers had made a stand more than a mile from the ranch and killed his best gunslingers. Then to make things worse three of those escaping the battle decided to quit the gang and ride for their lives out of his reach. When he was told that the three had fled, he threatened to shoot the messenger. But suddenly he realized that he was no longer safe and his life depended on the willingness of the last few outlaws to back him. After the defeat by Singletary, he was concerned others would flee.

Quirt paused in the entrance to the Cave and said, "Topper you and Scorpion take the first turn at guard; you know the lookout points. Make sure you stay awake and alert."

They all dismounted and removed their saddles. Quirt then signaled for Topper to take the horses down the hill to the rope corral, which was between rock walls where the ground had washed away leaving a wide ditch. The horses could not be seen from the approaches to the Cave.

Then before Topper could gather up the reins of the horses to lead them away, Scorpion asked, "How long will we stay here?"

Quirt stared at him and his anger boiled, but he checked himself from reacting with his pistols blazing; unwanted questions were never welcome to him. He said, "Until I say we leave. Do you object?"

"Hell no, but you know that we lost most of the gang and the rest of us have powder burns. A posse could be on our tails right now. I've always thought this Cave is a death trap for anyone pinned inside by a posse."

Quirt tried to sound normal, "They all are too busy licking their wounds to send a posse after us. I intend to wait for Leonard and Harve to bring that Longmire girl back and they better hope Jake's lawman brother trails them here. When we get the gold, we go to Mexico. You can ride out anytime you want, that is if you can out run a bullet in the back." He snarled.

Scorpion said, "I stay and guess the rest will also." He turned and left the Cave.

Two days later Quirt Evans' gang of bandits was becoming increasingly restive and complaining that the Cave was worse than a jail. They wanted to breakout and get some money. What little whiskey and tequila they had in their saddlebags was gone the first night in the Cave. Now their thoughts turned to senoritas and food. Quirt was no dummy. He recognized that he was about to lose control of the few outlaws still with him. He had held them together by force and fear, but now he saw unmistakable signs of revolt. They had reached a point of either shooting him in the back or slinking off during the night. He called his small gang together including those on lookout; he had his fill of complaining and arguing among themselves. His anger and impatience caused him to lash out at the missing Leonard and Harve. He said, "I don't know why I trusted Leonard, or whatever he calls himself, but I thought Harve was still loyal. They have deserted me or more likely fell into a trap. They could be either in jail or shot. I'm getting tired of waiting. That damn Marshal would be here by now if Leonard and Harve had done their job."

Scorpion asked, "When do we leave?"

"You're going to leave this morning. You go to Tincup, you said you've never been there so no one will know you, and find out if that damn town has guards posted. I want to know everything that is going on in that flea trap. I heard they organized the pilgrims." Quirt sounded nice and friendly.

Scorpion grinned and asked, "Why get killed in Tincup when there are other towns with banks between here and the river?"

Quirt looked around and saw other faces nodding approval with Scorpion, he said, "I want to find the gold that Jake took. It could be in the bank in Tincup. We don't have enough guns to attack the town in force, but when we know what we're up against we can drift in one at a time, I'll be last as the Marshal might recognize me, then we hit the bank and the general store at the same time. We'll first hit the general store and start a fire to burn it down and while they are trying to put out the fire, we'll hit the bank. But first we need to know everything you can find out. Is that understood?"

"Yeah, eighty thousand in gold is a good reason to get shot. Count me in." Scorpion had changed his mind when he saw the murderous eyes staring holes through him. Almost anything could trigger Quirt's instant rage.

"That's better; we'll wait two more days. Get going." He smiled and motioned for Scorpion to get on his way. The gunslingers standing around relaxed as they expected the exchange between Quirt and Scorpion to end with a shootout. Some of them began to believe Quirt knew something more than he was telling about the location of the gold. They felt that each of them should share in the eighty thousand. They busied themselves with the small fire cooking rattlesnake and armadillo stew.

Later that day while the outlaws enjoyed their devils stew, Marshal Tom Leach and his sidekick Deputy Blair Green climbed a steep hill and looked off to the west. Tom said, "I'd guess by this time tomorrow we can be in Tincup. If there's a full moon and no clouds, we could be there much earlier."

Blair stood up in the stirrups, stretched and asked, "Do you smell smoke?"

Tom took a few moments and said, "It can't be far off. I've noticed that we are riding in some real fertile ground, and I'm surprised we haven't come on to a farm or small ranch out here. Let's amble off to the west a little and see what we can find. We might get a good meal." They both laughed and urged their mounts to pick up the pace a little. The thoughts of a good bowl of stew or some fatback and eggs with biscuits stirred their hunger.

As they neared a grove of trees growing up the side of a hill, they caught the first sighting of smoke. It was coming from a dugout in the side of the hill. Suddenly they heard, "Hold right there. Turn around and get out of here."

They reined to a halt and Tom responded, "We mean you no harm. We are U.S. Marshals on our way to Tincup. Please be reasonable and look at out badges."

"Just sit real still, and raise your hands where I can see them." A boy of about seventeen stepped from behind a tree, holding a rifle. He had on clean clothes and appeared to be very strong. He stopped several feet from them and said, "I'll see your badge, but it'll take more than that to make me take this rifle off your guts."

Tom said, "You don't appear to be the nervous kind. We mean you no harm and if you won't fire that rifle, I'll show you our papers and badges."

Without further hesitation, Tom pulled back his vest to show him the badge, and then said, "Son, we can prove we're U.S. Marshals. Our job concerns mostly outlaws, so we understand your caution." The boy lowered his rifle and said, "I guess you are not killers. Pa is in the field over that rise there. Ma was making coffee when I espied you gents. Come on to the house." Tom and Blair dismounted and followed the boy to the house.

As they approached the wind swept small yard, Tom said in a conversational tone, "This fellow with me is Blair Green and I'm Tom Leach. We got a whiff of smoke from here and thought we should come over and see if someone was in trouble; all too often when we find smoke on the frontier there's trouble. What's your name?"

"I'm Zane, sorry about being rude, but we get all kinds through here. Are you really lawmen?"

"Yes, we are U. S. Marshals. Have you heard of the U.S. Marshal Service?"

"No, can't say that I know anything about that. There's not much talk out here except family talk." He responded.

"Zane, what's your family name?"

"I guess you mean our last name? We're Selman's from Missouri," he replied.

About then the door opened and a woman came on in the yard and asked, "Zane, I see you captured some more outlaws. But on closer look I guess they're not outlaws or you would have your rifle in their middles." She smiled and came forward to stand by Zane.

Zane said, "Ma, these fellows say they be lawmen. They have badges also."

"Well, I'll be swaney. We need some law out here in these parts, don't we Zane? My man is in the field with Van and will be coming in soon. I have coffee boiling, come in the house, you too Zane." She said.

They tied their horses to the top rail of the corral fence and followed her and Zane in the house. They both were surprised to see very large rooms dug in the hill with unfinished split timbers; the doors to the other rooms had canvas attached to the top with weights on the bottom to hold them in place. Two of the doors were open (canvas rolled up and tied to a nail over the door) and Tom could see the spacious bedrooms. He remarked, "I'm surprised to find so much room in the house. How did you all dig out so much dirt?"

Zane answered, "Shucks, it wasn't that much; pa found this large cave that cougars and other animals used for years, he built us a house here, with our help of course. He said if the wild animals liked this side of the hill it was good enough for us. Pa's a right smart man."

"I'll just bet he is. I'd be obliged to make his acquaintance." Tom said.

Zane's mother brought a pot of coffee to the table and said, "Zane, go strike that iron signal three times, now mind you." Zane immediately went out the door.

She said, "I'm Etta. Walker and Van will be here soon. Zane went to fetch them; we call the field and woods with the signal by striking it; two strikes means trouble, three strikes means dinner is ready and four strikes means come on to the house but there's no trouble. I don't know why I'm prattling on like this, but we don't see many honest folks coming through here." She wiped her hands on the apron several times while she was talking. Tom recognized that she was nervous.

He said, "Mrs. Selman, We just stopped by to make sure you folks were alright. We're headed to Tincup; do you all go there often?"

"Walker and one of the boys go ever so often for what we don't have out here and sell eggs and hog meat." She seemed more relaxed. Then she added, "Walker always leaves one of the boys here to help me. We all can shoot pretty fair."

Tom was about to ask directions to Tincup when Walker and Zane came in the door. Tom glanced at Zane and wondered why he had changed clothes; he was dirty and sweaty. Etta introduced her husband and son by saying, "Here's my man Walker and Van. These here men say they are U.S. Marshals." Tom couldn't shake the feeling that the boy she said was Van was the same boy that left the house, but then Zane came in the door.

Walker said, "I see you think you see double, these boys are spitting image twins. Both of them need cuffing now and again," He smiled and seeing the smile on the brothers' face knew that he was joshing.

Tom said, "Well, you could fool me. How do you tell them apart?"

Etta answered, "Van in the dirty clothes likes to work with his hands, while Van likes to hunt and eat." They all laughed as if it was a standard family joke.

Tom took a sip of the hot coffee and asked, "You say outlaws come through here? What happens when they get here?"

Walker responded, "I guess since you are the law, you need to know what happened to the last bandit; it was several days back when Zane and me was hunting. This fellow came in pretty as please telling Etta he would pay for food; Van was down in the bottom there tending our hogs. Etta told him to wait in the yard and she would fetch him a sack of food. When she went in the house, he followed her and tried to catch her in the corner." He turned to Van and said, "This is the law, you best tell him what happened that day."

Van said, "There's not much more to tell. I heard ma yell and I rushed in the house. This big heavy long haired fellow had ma in the corner and she was fighting for her life. I grabbed a stick of firewood and cracked him real hard on the head. It was a mite too much, it kilt him. Ma was not hurt. I guess you'll take me to jail?"

Blair spoke for the first time, "Where's his horse and gear?"

Walker replied, "I turned his horse loose as we don't want other folk's property even if they be dead. His saddle and bedroll is in the barn, I was going to take it to Tincup to the Marshal there when next I go. We don't go that often."

Blair asked Etta, "Did he give a name?"

She said, "Yes, he called himself Indian Joe; he was a big man with long black hair. You lawmen know anything about him? I hate he was killed."

Blair said to Tom "That's the other kidnaper of Sissy and me."

Tom turned and faced Walker and Etta, he said, "Folks you don't need to concern yourselves about killing him. He was an outlaw. Western justice was done in this case. Van you protected your mother. Any man would do the same thing. It's never what we want when someone gets killed. I'll make a report when I reach headquarters."

Walker said, "Van was going with me to Tincup and make a report. We're honest folks out here. If we break the law, we expect punishment."

Tom asked, "Do you think you can catch the horse?"

Zane answered, "Saw him today in the bottom down by the creek. I can fetch him for you."

"That's not necessary. I was thinking if you need another horse you could pay the government a reasonable price and keep him." Tom said.

Walker shook his head and said, "Marshal we have very little money, not enough to buy that horse, but we sure could used him."

Tom said, "I was thinking since you all had to bury the outlaw and had the trouble you didn't ask for, a fair price would be about two dollars for the horse and saddle."

Walker looked at Etta and asked, "You got that much money ma?"

Etta got up from the table and said, "I get it. All you men go wash your hands, supper will be on the table shortly."

The supper consisted of turnips and turnip greens, corn bread, fried eggs, fatback and a stew that no one asked what was in it. Tom and Blair found the stew very good and asked for a second helping. After supper Tom said to Etta, "Mrs. Selman that was a fine meal. The Service gives us an allowance for meals; I'm sure you don't charge for food at your table, if you would not think hard of me and accept it, Blair and I would be obliged to leave a small thank you." Tom took the two dollars she had given him for the horse and placed it on the table. Saying, "We'll see that the government gets paid for the horse. When I explain that it would have cost more to bring the horse to town and feed him at the livery, I'm sure they will say everyone's even."

When Tom and Blair got ready to leave, they all walked out in the yard and Tom asked, "What's the best way to Tincup?"

Walker said, "Lessen we need the wagon, we go over that hill there." He pointed and said, "Keep your eyes on that saddleback you see at the top. Go to it and you'll see Tincup from there."

Tom said, "That looks pretty rough that way, how long does it take to get to Tincup?"

"Well it is a bit rough, but passable. Going that way it's about a half day ride to town."

They exchanged goodbyes and Tom followed Blair toward the saddleback. He hoped they could reach town that day. It was nearing nightfall when they arrived between two peaks, that Walker Selman called saddleback. The climb up the incline tired the horses and riders alike; the last several hundred yards was gained by dismounting and leading their horses. When they got to the top and rested a few minutes, Blair asked, "Tom, how high is a hill before it's called a mountain?" They both laughed and Tom said, "I don't have the answer for that, but if you ask the horses, I'll lay a penny they say it's a mountain."

They laughed again and made camp. Surprisingly there was good grass for the horses; after staking the horses to graze, bedrolls were prepared. They both were tired and anxious to rest.

During the ride to Tincup the next morning they again had to dismount and lead their horses from the steep hill. Just as Walker had said Tincup could be seen from the top of the hill, they made good time following a trail that was not used very often.

Then hours later, Tom and Blair reined in at the jail, they were greeted by Marshal McCall; he obviously was cautious as he held his hand near the butt of his revolver resting in an oiled holster. He asked as they came onto the boardwalk, "Welcome to Tincup; haven't seen you gents in town before, passing through?"

Tom smiled and offered his hand, saying, "I take it you are the Marshal; we're with the U.S. Marshal Service. I'm Tom Leach and this fellow here is Blair Green. We've come to offer our help in dealing with the lawlessness in these parts."

"That is right good information. I've been expecting you. Come on in and I'll tell you what we're up against." As they entered the small office in front of the cells, which were blocked off by a wall and door; Steve Sutton stood, eyes searching the newcomers. Tim McCall turned to Tom and said, "Marshal I'd like for you to meet one of our most dedicated citizens. This is Steve Sutton, whose brother was murdered in this very jail; I'll always blame myself for not taking more precaution in handling killers."

Tom introduced himself and Blair and Tom said, "Glad to meet you. I'm sure you know that every citizen we lose to outlaw actions reflects on the government's inability to protect them. We're here to help end that situation. Please accept our condolences on the loss of your brother."

Steve Sutton had heard that the Marshals were coming to help quell the lawlessness in the desert area down to the border. He said, "Thanks Marshal, Mister McCall has done all he can do. It was not his fault my brother was killed. He has two of the three outlaws that killed my brother in cells back there. The circuit judge arrives tomorrow and I'm waiting for justice."

The next hour was spent with the lawmen exchanging information on the Quirt Evans gang. Finally, Tom said, "Last I heard Quirt Evans is waiting in Bat Cave for me. He wants to find the location of eighty thousand in gold coins, my outlaw brother hid before he died. Since I don't know where the coins are hidden, I suspect Evans and I will have a very interesting conversation."

Steve Sutton spoke up, "You'd be riding to your death by going near Bat Cave; Quirt still has several killers with him, who would take great joy in torturing you to death."

Tom said, "I'm obliged for the information. I'd like to interview each of the prisoners you say rode with the Evans gang. What are their names?"

McCall said, "One is called Cisco and the other Lemmon; they won't give any more information. They seem resigned to their fate."

"Which one appears to be the leader of the two?" Tom asked.

McCall said, "I'd give the nudge to Cisco, he is the most aggressive."

Tom said, "Bring out Cisco and I will talk with him. The information Steve gave us about the Cave and that he actually knows the trail to the overlooking plateau is highly useful, but there may be a chance we can take advantage of the prisoner's knowledge of Evans and the other outlaws. Marshal I'd like for you and the others to take a stroll while I question the prisoner, and then come back in about an hour."

McCall and Steve went into the area of the Jail cells and returned shortly with Cisco in handcuffs. McCall pushed him roughly in a chair in front of the desk and said, "This is U.S. Marshal Tom Leach, who wants to speak with you." He and the others left the room took chairs on the boardwalk.

Tom waited, watching Cisco shift positions in the chair and wiping his face with his cuffed hands. Then when Cisco couldn't stand the anxiety he blurted, "What's the hell wrong with you? Talk if that's what you have me here for."

"Tell me your full name? You know I can find out." Tom asked more to evaluate his reaction and than his answers.

He asked, "What difference does it make? No one cares what a dead outlaw's name is."

Tom stared him in the eyes and said, "It might make some difference. You know that the circuit judge will be here tomorrow and that you are charged with murder and attacking the Singletary ranch with intent to murder and burn their buildings. Those are serious charges with penalty of death by hanging."

"So they hang me. What do you care?" Cisco wanted to know.

"I asked you a simple question. What is your name?" Tom persisted.

Cisco squirmed in the chair and proudly proclaimed, "I'm Cisco Nunez, the son of a peon goat farmer. My family died before I was ten and the goats raised me. Will that keep me from the noose?"

Tom was pleased Cisco was responding, he waited a couple of minutes and said, "It's not my job to care about the disposition of prisoners charged with murder; just to bring them in for justice. I guess we don't have anything to talk about after all. I guess you care more about Quirt Evans than you do about your own neck." Tom stood as if to return him to the cell.

Cisco was wily, intelligent and sensed that there was more to this interview than he had learned. He asked in a subdued voice, "What do you want me to do?"

Tom said, "Well under certain circumstances judges give great weight to an accused that cooperates with the law and assists in preventing more killings. Mind you I'm not promising anything, but I could speak to the judge and he could cut your sentence from hanging to something far less. The decision is yours."

Cisco said nervously, "I don't want to die with a rope around my neck. For your information, I don't give a damn what happens to Quirt Evans; he got me in this jail twice. I'd shoot him on sight if I get the chance."

Tom thought a moment and asked, "Are you an American citizen? Did you kill Steve Sutton's brother?"

He replied, "I was born in Mexico and I sure as hell did not kill that boy. Shotgun killed him and we left when he did."

Tom said, "Well being born in Mexico makes no difference and I am pleased to hear that you did not help kill Layton Sutton."

Cisco thought a moment and asked, "What is it you want of me?"

I'm asking you to help end the lawlessness in the Southwest, and at the same time demonstrate to the court that you have some redeeming values; if you come with me to Bat Cave you need to know that I will shoot to kill if I determine that you take the wrong side. So make sure you understand this is not going to be easy for you or me. Does your word mean anything?"

"If I tell you I'll back your play, you can bet I'll do just that. But if I think at anytime you double-cross me, I kill you." He stared back at Tom for the first time.

Tom made a decision. He said, "That's fair enough, I keep my word and you keep yours. Just so you know what I have in mind, Quirt Evans and what's left of his gang must be dealt with harshly. My mission here is to quell the anarchy and establish law and order. I'll do that with or without your help."

Cisco said simply, "I'll do what you tell me to do."

Tom was convinced that Cisco meant what he said, but resolved to watch him very close. He went to the door and asked McCall and the others to come in the office. When they had closed the door behind them, Tom said, "Cisco Nunez has decided to help breakup Quirt Evans' gang of cutthroats. Remove his handcuffs and give him his gun belt and revolvers. I will be responsible for him. Marshal McCall please write out a release to me of Cisco Nunez and I will sign it. Show it to the judge when he arrives tomorrow. And hold it for Cisco's trial. Cisco is going to Bat Cave with me."

It took only minutes for McCall to find a release form and complete it in a very neat hand. He passed it to Tom who read it very carefully and then signed it. He spoke to Blair, "Go to the livery and get Cisco's horse and gear. Then meet me in the saloon, I want to get on the trail to Bat Cave without more delay. I don't want Quirt Evans to leave before we get there." Blair left the office without comment.

Tom turned to Steve Sutton, he said, "Marshal McCall has high praise for your help. The fact that you know the layout at Bat Cave could help. Do you want to take part in this dangerous undertaking?"

Steve did not hesitate, "Yes sir, I want to go with you. But I am not too pleased that one of the murderers of my brother is turned loose."

"No one said anything about turning Cisco loose. He tells me that he did not choke your brother, but was glad to get out of jail. He's my responsibility and if it makes you feel better I believe he will help us."

Steve said, "I trust your judgment. I want to dedicate the rest of my life to law and order, I'm sick of all these senseless killings of innocent people."

Tom said, "Glad to hear your mature intentions. I am inviting you to join the U.S. Marshal Service as a temporary Deputy Marshal. If you serve as I believe you will, when the battles out here in the desert are won, you can undergo the training and become a career U.S. Marshal. Will you accept the appointment?"

Steve said, "Sir I am honored to accept the privilege of serving with you."

The short oath of office was administered and Tom said, "Take my horse down to livery and water him while you get your gear together we will leave as soon as you all are ready. Cisco wants a drink before we leave town. I'll see you and Blair in the saloon."

Steve left the office as if he was walking on air. Cisco had heard everything that transpired. He smiled and asked Tom, "Any chance you want another deputy?"

Tom returned his smile with a friendly comment, "Cisco this life of ours has many twists and turns; you never know what's around the next turn in the trail."

Marshal McCall said, "I'd sure like to come with you, but I've promised this town I'd do my best to help protect its citizens. When things settle down, I'm going to stand for Sheriff of the County. I feel I can be more effective with the additional authority."

Tom and Cisco left the jail and walked the short distance to the saloon. Tom ordered a beer and looked at Cisco for his order, He said, "Hell a beer is fine. I can wait for hard whiskey." He laughed.

The bartender served them beers; Cisco looked round the room and then nudged Tom. He whispered, "That warty gunman close to the door with his back to the wall is Scorpion he's the trusted pal of Quirt." Cisco paused then said, "Well what do you know he just noticed me. I'll mosey over there and pull Scorpion's teeth for you."

Tom said, "Just a minute. I'd like to know why he's in town. See if you can find out and then we'll arrest him."

Cisco grinned and said, "He's tough and will draw if cornered, but I'll try to get the information."

He pushed away from the bar carrying his beer in his left hand and approached the outlaw's table. Tom could not hear what was said in the short exchange between the two outlaws, and was surprised at the reaction of Scorpion. He jumped up turning the table upside down and clawed for his pistols. He got off one shot, which missed Cisco and imbedded in the wall. Cisco was much faster and very calmly drew his revolver and fired, knocking the pistol out of Scorpion's right hand, then stepped in close and slammed his revolver to the side of Scorpion's head who crumbled to the floor. The gunplay was over.

Tom walked swiftly to the table and checked the outlaw to see if he was still among the living. He stood and said, "He's alive. Get a couple of volunteers to help carry him to jail and then we'll get him patched up. I want to talk with him when he comes around."

Cisco had no trouble getting volunteers to carry the limp body to the jail. On the boardwalk, Tom asked, "What was said that caused him to react so fast?"

"He noticed your badge when we came in. He was suspicious and accused me of being a traitor. I told him that explained my situation pretty good. I told him that I was working with U.S. Marshals, and asked him if he wanted to help bring Quirt Evans in or go to jail himself. I guess he thought that was a bad idea. You know that he pulled on me first."

Tom said. "Yes, I know that you had no choice. Before I talk with him, I want to hear all you know about him and Evans. We need to know why he was in town. Let's go."

Tom delayed leaving for Bat Cave waiting for Scorpion to recover sufficiently to question. While waiting Tom remarked to Cisco, "You say your parents died when you were ten, what happened then?"

"I lived in a convent. The Nuns were good to me. They helped me learn your language." Cisco said with his eyes downcast.

Tom said, "I suspected you had a good education from your command of the language." He smiled and went on, "Except of course when you want to assume the character of a bad guy. What happened after you left the nunnery?"

"Marshal I don't know why you seem so interested in my life."

Tom replied, "If you would rather not talk about your life, that's fine. But I do like to know a little about those I take in to dangerous situations."

"I was about sixteen when the government soldiers burned us out. I hated them the way they treated the Nuns. I've been on the Owl Hoot Trail ever since."

Tom said, "Our lives are influenced by many difference factors. The way you handled the situation with Scorpion gives me confidence that I can trust you. I hope you feel that you can trust me."

He replied, "I believe you keep your word or I'd still be in the cell waiting for the noose."

Tom said, "Let's go in and see how Scorpion is doing. He should be coming around about now."

Scorpion was awake, rubbing his head and spat at Cisco. Tom asked him, "You want to tell us why you come to town?"

He hissed and spit again, "Go to hell. I don't talk to badge toters, I kill them."

Tom said, "That's your privilege you can tell your story to the judge tomorrow."

Tom had seen enough defiant killers to know that Scorpion would go to the gallows blaming everyone for his sins except himself. It took Tom and the others only a few minutes to get on the trail to Bat Cave. The future of all four might be determined out there in the desert. Cisco rode out front; leading the way to the Cave. Tom's doubts about Cisco's new found loyalty to the law lingered, but Cisco was giving every indication that his switch from bandit to law abiding was sincere. Regardless he would continue to watch his every move. If Cisco proved that he was no longer a threat to society then he would keep his promise of asking the judge for leniency, but to what extent would be up to the judge. His duty was to see that Cisco returned and faced judgment of the court.

After a long ride Steve Sutton reined in and spoke to Tom, "Bat Cave is just over that hill in front; Cisco just told me that Quirt's guards will spot us once we're on top of it."

Tom asked, "Steve, how long will it take you and Blair to reach the advantage point on the ledge from which you say you observed the Cave entrance?"

"We'll have to do most of it on foot. I'd say about two hours." Steve replied.

"You mentioned you could also see the rope corral, where they keep their horses; If any of them try to mount up and leave, discourage them with a few warning shots."

"Yes, I'm sure we can pin them down, with rifles that will be child play until dark, then that's a different matter." Steve allowed.

Tom looked at Blair and said, "You go with Steve, we'll give you time to get in position. Then Cisco and I will ride over the hill about thirty minutes before sunset. Cisco will have a gun on me as if I am his prisoner. That's if Cisco agrees to place himself in danger."

Cisco smile and said, "I'll have the gun, it's your plan and I'll do my part."

Tom replied, "Cisco, I trust you, you will have fully loaded revolvers. I don't expect to get a bullet in my back. Can you pull this off and get me in close to Quirt Evans? I want to take him alive if that's possible."

Cisco looked Tom in the eyes and said, "You're going to both of us killed, but when I give my word, I keep it. If I decide to kill you it won't be a bullet in the back." He smiled.

Tom smiled back and stated, "Alright, we all understand each other and the plan. It's simple and I hope it works. Cisco and I will hole up behind those large cactuses and rocks over to the right. Good luck."

Just before sunset Tom and Cisco mounted and urged their horses up the sharp rise. Cisco was leading Tom's horse and it appeared that Tom's hands were tied to the saddle horn. Cisco had Tom's gun belt and revolvers hanging from his saddle horn. Tom had taken a revolver out of his saddlebag and tucked in his belt under his jacket. Cisco watched Tom hide the revolver under his jacket, smiled and said, "We may need more than a few bullets for that gang; there could be several gunslingers with Quirt."

Tom said, "If we get the drop on them maybe there'll be no need for shooting."

Cisco said, "They will fight. We'll need all our bullets. I hate to tell you this, but it might be my last chance; I've never killed anyone. But today, I'll make my bullets count."

Tom said, "Let's try and make sure that when this dance is over, you can say the same thing. Killing another human should never happen if there is a way to prevent it. You've seen enough to know that in some cases killing can be prevented. That's what we'll try to do this day."

As they started down the hill, Cisco said in a low voice, "I'm surprised that the guards have not fired warning shots. They never let anyone down this hill until they are either killed or searched and disarmed."

Tom asked, "Should we ride on in or give the warning shots?"

"Nah, let's go on to the Cave; they know my horse."

When Blair and Steve made it to the plateau overlooking the entrance to the Cave, Steve remarked, "There's only one horse in the corral. It looks like the nest is mostly empty. Should we try and signal the Marshal?"

Blair said, "No, let's wait it out, our signal might be misunderstood and put Tom in more danger. He'll let us know when to enter the fray, if there is one."

Tom reined his horse to a halt and Cisco came along side, Tom said, "I'll take my gun belt now. It would appear our charade isn't necessary."

They dismounted and Cisco led the way into the Cave; it was empty except for a lone outlaw apparently asleep in the far corner. Cisco said, "We're too late, Quirt got tired of waiting and left." He walked over to the sleeping figure and roughly nudged him with his boot-toe.

The outlaw rose and drowsily said, "What took you so long? Quirt took the others and went back to Mexico." Then he saw Tom and started to draw his pistol. Cisco kicked the pistol out of his hand and said, "Get up on your feet and keep your hands in the air." He smiled and turned to Tom and asked, "Is that the law's way of handling desperadoes?"

Tom said, "It'll do. Search him."

Cisco expertly searched the outlaw and said to Tom, "He calls himself Hawk, but he must have a moniker." Cisco found a folded wanted poster in his pocket, he handed it to Tom. Tom looked at it showing a clear image of the outlaw's face; it read Jesse Batson, Wanted for Murder $5,000 Reward Dead or Alive.

Tom looked at the now scared outlaw and asked, "Carrying this poster tells me you are proud of your crimes."

He shakily replied, "I didn't kill anyone."

Tom asked, "Jesse, where is Quirt Evans?"

"He and the others left mid-day yesterday. He made me wait and see if Harve and Leonard showed up."

Tom asked, "Where did they go?"

"They went back to Mexico he said to bring back more gunslingers. But I know they wanted women and tequila."

Tom turned to Cisco and said, "Bring him outside."

Tom went out a few paces from the entrance and waved his hand for Blair and Steve to come down from their perch. The he instructed Cisco, "Get the rawhide strings from my saddlebag and tie Jesse's hands behind him; tight, but don't cut the blood off as he will face a judge for his crimes."

Jesse began to protest and beg for mercy. Tom and Cisco ignored him.

It was more than thirty minutes before Blair and Steve came to the Cave; in the meantime Tom had formulated a plan. He would send Blair and Steve back to Tincup with Jesse Batson. He knew they would protest, but that seemed the best solution. When they arrive, Tom said, "Blair I want you and Steve to take the prisoner to Tincup. If Cisco wants he can come with me. I'll try to catch Evans and his gang before they reach the river."

Steve spoke up and said, "Tom, I'd like to come with you. I'm sure that Blair can take this culprit back to town."

Tom replied, "Yes, I'm sure either one of you could do the job alone. Blair needs to get back and take care of some other unfinished business, and you need to help Tim McCall with guarding the jail. I was concerned about cutting him short when I brought you along."

Blair said, "We'll do as you say. I wish though I could go with you. You'll be facing overwhelming odds."

Tom smiled and laughed, "I'm sure Cisco hopes they won't be overwhelming. We'll do our best. Now let's get on our separate trails." Tom walked to his horse mounted and urged him south. He looked back and saw that Cisco was very close behind him and down the far slope Blair was leading the outlaw with a rope around his waist toward the corral to get his horse.

Quirt and his gang had left clear tracks in the soft dry sand. Cisco studied the tracks and said, "Jesse said Quirt left with four others; I take that to be about right from what the tracks say. Most of the gang must have deserted him."

Tom said, "I agree, they seem to be on a straight course to the river. Do you know of a stopping place between here and the border?"

"Yeah, there's a small village with a bar and eats about forty miles from here. Women come in when the gang stops there. I'd guess they will stop there to get feed for their horses, and drink tequila."

Tom said, "Let's hope we catch them there."

Cisco laughed and asked, "Marshal did you ever catch a cougar by its tail?"

Tom smiled and said, "Can't say that I have, but I'm still young and maybe I'll do that yet."

"If you get Quirt in a corner you'll damn sure wish you had the cougar instead."

Tom said, "That could be so, but we'll see."

Cisco said, "He'll fight to his last breath and then some.

They rode on with a meager supply of water in their canteens.

CHAPTER 13

THE CHASE

Quirt Evans and his gang of four outlaws rode down the narrow dirt street, reined in at the only café and saloon in the village. The small town consisted of about fifty houses, mostly shacks, some built with mud, straw and rock, the oldest dating back a century. From the beginning of the town, no one wanted to spend time painting or carving signs proclaiming names for businesses or even the town. The locals just called it town or village.

There was no law in town nor had anyone ever voiced a need to appoint even a night watchman. A general store next door to the café provides what merchandise the local folks might need. Seldom did any of the inhabitants find a need to travel to a larger town some eighty miles north. The trips to the distant town were few, but occasionally some of the more hearty folks made the journey.

Bandits on the run often stopped in the village, as there were several unattached women who willingly entertained them for drinks and favors. What little order that existed was maintained by Cletus, the owner of the café and saloon, and his guards with sawed off shotguns. Few people in town could remember when Cletus arrived, but he said it was during a rainstorm, which lasted less than an hour. When the sun came out, Cletus was the new owner of the unnamed café and saloon.

The previous owner was tossed out in the wet street along with his wife and bartender. Since that day, no one questioned Cletus' authority. The café served food that was edible and the drinks were cheap and plentiful, but the meals and drinks were never free, the prices ranged from what a customer had in his pocket or whatever price Cletus set. Customers without money were tossed unceremoniously onto the street with broken bones. Quirt Evans and his gang always brought more money to spend than other outlaws coming through town. Cletus personally welcomed Quirt and his outlaws every time they came through the front door. Some of the citizens whispered to each other that Cletus was a member of the Evans gang.

On this stop, Quirt Evans had fewer outlaws than ever before; Cletus eyed them as they strolled to the bar; he asked Quirt, "Where's the rest of your gang?"

Quirt said, "Some got killed and others run off afraid I'd killed them. Don't worry in two weeks I'll stop here with at least twenty fighters; we'll have money to spend."

"Does that mean you are short of money now?"

"I'll stay only until tomorrow morning; we have enough to see us through the night." Quirt replied.

Cletus said, "The food is half-price, but all of you pay for your drinks and the women."

Quirt bristled, "I never pay for a woman, don't intend to start here either."

Cletus softened, "Alright, I'm making an exception this time; just come back with the customers you promised a minute ago."

Quirt could not hold his anger, "Cletus, I allow you to run this damn town and cheat everyone out of their money. So don't start telling me the rules. If I see one of your henchmen raise a shotgun, I'll kill you first. Is that understood?"

Cletus knew that he had pushed too hard, but could not back down, "That works both ways. Since we're friends you don't have to pay for anything on this trip, but the others pay as usual." He smiled and passed a bottle of tequila to Quirt.

Quirt attempted a weak smile, eyes flashing anger he took the bottle of tequila to an empty table. He was promptly joined by a pretty young girl after getting a nod from Cletus. The storm of hostility had passed for the moment. Cletus and Quirt both relied on nerves and gunpowder to survive.

Back on the trail following Quirt and his gang, Marshal Tom Leach and Cisco had ceased to waste time looking for tracks as Cisco was sure where the gang was going. They had used their last drop of water earlier that morning, and now near noon, Cisco pointed to smoke curling up from houses and said, "There's Quirt's stopping place. They may still be at Cletus' café and saloon. Cletus has guards with sawed off shotguns. Taking them in the saloon will be very risky."

Tom said, "I don't understand how they got here so fast; they had to punish their horses beyond endurance, but I guess their pleasure and comfort is more important than caring for their horses."

"Well we pushed hard and our horses are tired also but not hurt. How are we going to get that cougar and his kittens by their tails?" Cisco wanted to know.

Tom thought a moment and said, "No need to risk innocent folks getting hurt by going in the saloon for them." He smiled and added, "Also I have a responsibility to see that you get an opportunity to tell the judge your story. I'd have to leave you out of the gunfight."

Cisco laughed and tried to clear his dry throat, then said, "I'll face that judge when the time comes even with bullet holes. I'm in this fight like I told you earlier."

Tom replied, "I believe you. I take it folks know you in town. Do you want to ride in and find out the situation? Or would Quirt shoot you on sight?"

"I don't see how he could know that I'm working with you. Yes, I can pull that off, but getting away from them without a fight will be very hard." Cisco said.

Tom said, "You know the trail they usually take going out of town; tell me and I'll slip around town and take up a position on the trail. If they are still there, you come with them and I'll throw down a challenge at the right time. Then you can decide what side you will take."

Cisco showed anger for the first time, "Damn it Marshal! Either you trust me or you don't. If you don't trust me, shoot me now. Here's my pistol."

Tom smiled again and said, "Keep your hardware. Just relax, actually I do trust you, but I had to be sure before I expose myself on the trail facing a passel of guns."

Cisco seemed to get his good humor back and pointed to some landmarks off to the southeast where he said Tom would find a well used trail. He said about a mile from town the trail narrows and goes through large trees on both sides. He said, "That's a good place to wait."

Tom continued to study the landscape and said, "Alright I'll wait down the trail. Where can I get water for my horse and a drop for myself?"

"To get there, you'll be crossing a creek with water. I'll see you on the trail. If they are gone, I'll grab some food and join you out there in a little while." Cisco smiled and started to ride toward town.

Tom said, "I'll be coming in if I don't hear from you. So don't let Quirt get the drop on you."

Cisco waved and continued on his way.

After studying surrounding terrain, Tom decided to go around town to the south. He let his tired horse walk as it had been a long day. He found a creek with clear water; filled his canteens and sipped some of the cool water while his horse drank. Then found the trail Cisco described. He followed it to a sudden turn in the trail with large trees. A perfect place for an ambush; Tom had no intention of an ambush, he would step out in front of the riders and try to arrest them. If they showed fight, then a fight they'd get. He loosened the cinch, left the saddle in place and then staked his horse to graze. He waited.

Tom aroused from a light sleep to the sound of approaching rider. He swiftly moved to the side of the trail and waited until he knew the horse was close; he stepped out in the trail to see Cisco's smiling face. He pulled his mount to a halt, dismounted and offered Tom a can with a tightly closed lid and said, "Better eat it while it's still warm."

Tom asked, "Does this mean we got here too late?"

Cisco replied, "I'll tell you the story while you eat, we need to get on the trail if we want a chance to cut them off before the Rio Grande."

Tom asked, "How long ago did they leave?"

Cisco handed Tom a spoon and said, "Start eating and I'll get your horse ready to ride. They have a three-hour head start. But I think Quirt will make one more stop before reaching the border."

Tom opened the can and asked, "What's this? It smells good."

"Goat stew. It's good for you." Cisco walked toward Tom's horse.

A few minutes later they were on the trail; Cisco pulled along side Tom and said, "There's no need to spend time with tracks as Quirt will go straight to the border."

Tom asked, "What happened back there in town?"

Cisco said, "It is not a pretty sight; bodies and blood all over the saloon. No one has tried to clean up yet. Quirt had words with Cletus, the self-appointed boss of the town who has controlled everything for several years. Quirt filled him full of bullets, while his gang took on Cletus' shotgun guards. The guards got off a few shots, killing several people, including one of Quirt's gang. I counted eight bodies, two of them girls, still collecting flies."

Tom asked, "What else did you learn?"

"Quirt took all of the money and gold Cletus had. One of the bartenders, shot in the leg, said it was several thousand dollars; he was forced to tell Quirt where the money was hidden. Quirt then threatened to burn the saloon, but changed his mind at the last moment. At least one of the gang rode away bleeding from buckshot."

Tom said, "That explains the drops of blood I found on the trail. The wounded fellow got this far, but from the amount of blood it seems unlikely he'll make the border."

Cisco said, "There's nothing, but rough country between here and the border☒ many places for an ambush. If Quirt gets the sniff of us on his trail, you can bet he'll not give us a chance."

Tom said, "Just point out the most likely places before we ride into them; it's going to slow us down, but so would a bullet from behind a rock."

Very late that evening Cisco pointed to a small grove of trees and said, "There's a creek close to those trees and hidden back against the hill is a small shack; Tubby lives there; he's a mix breed, some white, Indian and Mexican he says. He lives off hunting and his goats; he always has food and tequila for Quirt's outfit when we come through.

Quirt leaves him money on his trips; Quirt never stays overnight when I was along. So I'd guess he's not there."

Tom asked, "Where would their horses be if they are there now?"

"We'll circle around that knoll to the west and come in from the outside; the brush corral is near the stream."

It was almost dark when Tom and Cisco found the corral; it held six goats and a jenny. On hearing and smelling the approaching horses; the donkey snorted, kicked up her heels and brayed loud enough to be heard for miles away.

Tom said, "I guess that announces us. You're the guide, what happens now?"

"I think Quirt has already left if he stopped. Follow me to the cabin. Tubby knows me."

As Cisco neared the door he heard a voice from behind a tree, "You there turn around and let me get a look at your sorry face."

Tom had stopped just around the corner of the shack, but he could see Cisco slowly turn and heard him say, "Tubby put that damn scattergun down and give me something to eat."

"Is that you Cisco?"

"You know damn well who it is! Where's Quirt and the boys?"

"They stayed less than ten minutes; Lefty is inside with a bullet in his chest. I tried to dig it out, but it's no use."

Cisco asked, "How long have they been gone?"

"You just missed them. Why weren't you with them?" Tubby wanted to know.

Cisco said, "Come on Tubby, do you have anything ready to eat? My friend and me could eat a whole goat."

The big fat man walked slowly toward Cisco, still apparently worried, he asked, "Where's this friend of yours?"

Tom stepped out in the dim light and said, "Right here, you can put the shotgun down, we mean you no harm."

Tubby continued to the door and went in followed by Cisco and Tom. In the corner was a small bed; an unmoving man was sprawled, uncovered on the soiled mattress. Tom went to the bed, and even in the dim light thrown out by a lantern the pallid face with eyes open indicated Lefty had died. Tubby stuck his hand on the man's throat and after a few seconds said, "He's dead. Hope you'll help bury him; I'm feeling a little poorly."

Cisco asked, "What did Quirt have to say?"

"He said that someone was on his tail and he had to cross the river before daylight. He wanted me to help his friend Lefty. I tried to help him, but knew from the start that he was dying. Quirt knew that also."

Tom said, "Cisco you can stay and help bury this culprit; I'm going on after him." He turned to Tubby and asked, "Tell me, was he alone or had others with him?"

"It was just him, Lott and one more; I don't think he said his name. Who're are you?"

"The name is Tom Leach, U. S. Marshal."

Tubby started to raised the shotgun he was still holding, and he heard Cisco say, "Don't think about using that scattergun. I'm working with Tom and you can't get us both."

Tubby smiled for the first time. He said, "Shucks, the law don't mind me and my goats. I just help anyone that comes by, including criminals like you."

Cisco said, "Put the shotgun in the corner; first take out the shells. And let's see what you have cooked up. We'll leave you money."

Tubby said, "Money's not much use out here. Got any whiskey?"

There was very little to eat; boiled goat meat and something he called pan fried bread. There was no seasoning in any of it. But it was filler and would do until they found a place to eat or kill a deer.

They soon were back on the dark trail after explaining to Tubby that time did not permit helping him with burial of the dead outlaw. As they mounted preparing to leave, Tubby said to Cisco, "If you'll bring me onions, pepper, salt and soda, I'll make sure you have the pleasure of a senorita for you two lawmen."

Cisco replied, "Tubby my friend is a promised man. But you have the girls here and you get your wish list." Tom did not comment.

On the trail, Cisco seemed to have cat eyes and had no trouble following it. After a mile or so, he stopped and Tom came along side, he said, "Unless they stop to bushwhack us, there's no way in hell we'll catch them short of the river. They're riding their horses hard, they're killing their horses."

Tom said, "We may find a dead horse on the trail if they keep pushing them. But if they cross the river, my badge and letter of resignation stays on this side and I am going after them. That bastard had my future wife dragged from her home and mistreated. That is the lesser of his crimes, but that will force me to quit the Service to bring him back for justice or leave him his dead body in Mexico. I'm not asking you to side me"

Cisco said, "You're one crazy and mad gringo. I'll be at your side. Both of us could end up in front of a government firing squad."

Tom said, "That would be a bother; I intend to take you back to face a judge and stand trial for your crimes." They both laughed.

Cisco shook his head and said, "It seems that you want to see me hang more than you want Quirt Evans and his gang busted up."

Tom said, "Both seem necessary, but first things first, I'll take care of Quirt Evans and trust that you help get yourself back for trial."

Cisco was still laughing, he said, "Like I say, you're one crazy gringo."

When Tom and Cisco reached the Rio Grande crossing to Mexico, Tom dismounted removed his saddlebag and asked, "Where's the nearest place I can send a letter?"

"There a small village where the stage comes through about every two weeks; it's less than a half mile down river; last words to your sweetheart?" Cisco wanted to know.

Tom removed the saddle and said, "We'll let the horses rest while I make out a report to the Service. I'll of course mention your help and conversion to the law."

After removing his saddle and sitting down on it, Cisco said, "I'm obliged that you concern yourself about my neck; if you go after Quirt in his den, you know I'm going with you and all those nice words about me won't make any difference to either one of us."

Tom replied, "That may be so. But if you live to cross back over here, it'll make a heap of difference. I believe that you're really not a bad person; just fell in with the wrong people, but only the court has the authority to decide justice in your case. I'll keep my word."

After a few hours of rest, Tom and Cisco mounted and rode toward the stage office. It was a short ride and Tom sent his report and badge to Marshal Decker. In his report, he asked Marshal Decker to tell Blanche why he crossed the Rio Grande to Mexico; and in case he failed to return, tell her to get on with her life. That was the hardest part of writing the report. He felt somewhat free to cross the river even though violating laws bothered him. He knew that Mexico required visitors to cross at designated places and identify themselves. There was no time for that today, but he still felt guilty and empty; yet he was determined to bring the gang of cutthroats to justice.

Quirt Evans and his killers had inflicted pain and harm on the citizens north of the border; contributing to the state of anarchy in the southwest. Knowing that Evans and his gang would never just go away without a fight, he intended to eliminate or bring them to justice. Knowing there was no alternative he must work outside the law. He shook his head to clear the last twinge of guilty feeling and urged his horse to follow Cisco down the trail. The only consolation he could muster was that the U.S. Marshal Service would retain its honor.

It took them less than an hour to reach the river. Tom looked out across the Rio Grande River toward Mexico with unsettled and mixed feelings. Even now at the last moment of decision he experienced deep regret; he was about to violate the laws he had sworn to enforce. However, he knew that Quirt Evans and his cutthroats were in a village a few kilometers south and no doubt celebrating their latest raids of ranches and towns in Southwest Texas. The gang had used the Mexican haven to escape justice from U.S. laws far too long and it was time to bring them to justice. Cisco, the reformed outlaw had volunteered to help Tom wipe out the old gang of killers he had ridden with on the Owl Hoot Trails. Tom thought he would soon learn if Cisco could be trusted in a hot gun battle. So far, on this trip, he was thankful for Cisco's help as he knew the countryside and would lead the way to the village.

They crossed the Rio Grande River and never looked back; they were in Mexico without authority. If Mexican officers stopped them, Tom resolved to try explaining why it was important to bring Quirt Evans and his killers to justice. He hoped they would listen. However, they did not meet anyone on the trail to Cisco's hideout. Cisco followed a small animal trail to a hilltop overlooking the Village. He said, "Friend, down there is big trouble. We could go back to the river." He laughed and slapped his leg. He was having fun.

"Again, Cisco you may be right, let's make sure Quirt Evans and his cutthroats feel our wrath. The fight down there in the Village is for all those good citizens that gang killed and mistreated. It all ends today." Tom quietly replied.

Cisco said, "I expected your strong head would get us killed. Let's go." Again, he was laughing and apparently enjoying himself.

On entering the village, there were only a few people in the dusty street; none of them appeared threatening. When they saw Tom and Cisco, they disappeared as if by magic. The job now was to flush the killers out in the open and cut the odds down somewhat. Tom turned to Cisco and offered his hand; Cisco grinned and shook it vigorously.

Cisco told Tom that the locals would not interfere with a gun battle as they had few firearms in the town. The Mexico Army very seldom made visits and then just passing through. If Evans was in town, he made sure the officers had drinks and women. As they came near the cantina, Cisco said in a low voice, "Maybe we should go to the stables first and see how many horses are down there. The locals have no horses, just donkeys."

Tom said, "Good idea, lead the way. We can leave our horses in the stable then find Quirt and the other cutthroats."

When they arrived at the stables, they found five horses, all showing signs of mistreatment; they were trying to recover from the long hard trip up north. The horses looked under fed and they appeared tired and hungry. When Cisco dismounted, he opened the corral gate, and Tom rode in and drove the tired horses out toward an open pasture to the south. The horses regained some of their strength and loped willingly to freedom.

Tom asked, "Cisco, where do you think the rest of the killers are if there are only five in town?"

"I heard Evans got mad and killed some of his gang, and other took off. But, who cares, we kill these five and I'm sure one of them will be Evans. I saw his horse."

"When we capture and kill Evans, the others will most likely disappear and not bother us up north." Tom replied.

Then they heard someone yell, "What the hell's going on? Them's our horses."

Cisco did not say anything until the sleepy looking outlaw, still rubbing his eyes, got nearer. Then Cisco yelled, "Meet U. S. Marshal Tom Leach, he's down here to take you all back for trial."

The bowlegged man stopped and looked at Tom still on his horse, and said, "The hell you say looks like you both want to die."

Tom replied, "Drop your guns and you will live."

In response the outlaw clawed for his holstered pistol; Cisco was smiling, Tom waited until the pistol was clear of the holster and then shot the fellow twice in the chest; he fell backwards, dead by the time, he hit the ground.

Tom said, "I think that leaves about four of them? Let's put our horses in the corral, we may need them later."

Cisco said, "No time for the horses, do you see them coming out of the Cantina? This will be a street shootout."

Tom said, "Well, that saves us the job of flushing them out. You just make sure that Evans is left for me to deal with."

Cisco agreed, "He's all yours. I'll try to help even the odds a bit. Let's go."

Tom took his rifle just in case of an expected attack from the rooftops. He had learned long ago that the unexpected happens in shootouts. He walked out into the street and yelled, "Evans, tell your gunslingers to go back to the Cantina and they live another day. This is between you and me."

Quirt yelled back, "Who are you? Tell me what makes you think you will live."

"My name is Tom Leach. Jake Leach's brother."

Evans kept walking toward Tom and talking, "Hey there, Jake was a friend of mine. He was a good compadre. I'm not going to kill you Tom Leach; I want to know where my gold is hidden."

Tom noticed that Evans appeared wobbly on his feet, but that could be an act. He waited. The other three kept coming although they had spread out across the street.

Tom said, "Tell your gunslingers to get out of the street, then we can settle our differences."

The answer came in a twinkle of an eye; Quirt's fast draw was signal for his gunslingers to start shooting. Out of the corner of his eye, Tom saw Cisco fall to the ground, still firing at the targets in front of him. Then Tom dropped his rifle, drew both revolvers and very slowly, but deliberately fired; he saw Evans hit the ground and roll toward an over turned cart that was leaning against a building. Then Tom switched his attention to the two outlaws crouched and firing in his direction; they missed and Tom's next shot killed the outlaw trying to get in a door. He saw that the other one still in the street fall as he heard Cisco's revolver speak again. The street was clear, except for the bodies of dead outlaws, but Quirt Evans had gained cover behind the over turned cart.

Tom yelled, "Evans, you don't stand a chance. Come on out and I'll take you north to stand trial."

He heard, "Go to hell gringo. It's killing time."

Tom knew that a bullet had grazed his left side; he could feel the warm blood oozing down, collecting above his belt. This had to end fast.

In the next instant he saw Quirt jump to his feet in front of the cart and start walking toward him; he waited. Evans stopped about twenty paces away and asked, "Is this close enough for you to kill me; your bullets are useless."

Suddenly, he raised his pistols and almost got them in firing position before Tom's bullets struck him; he fell and lay still. Tom watched him while he approached Cisco who was trying to sit up; Cisco smiled and said, "Marshal take me back for trial. See if the judge can send these bullets in me to jail." He coughed and died with a smile on his face.

Tom had seen many outlaws die, but this was the saddest ending to the life of an outlaw he had ever experienced. He had looked forward to getting Cisco a very light sentence, as he was indeed a reformed criminal. Redemption was his.

Tom had kept an eye on Quirt Evans; he did not seem to be moving. Tom walked to him, rolled him over to face the sky. Blood was running down the side of his mouth, his breathing labored; He managed, "Where's my gold?"

Tom said, "The government's gold is somewhere in the desert, they'll get it back soon."

Quirt Evans grimaced and died. He'd have no use for stolen gold where he was going.

Tom noticed that the street was deserted; only one woman coming toward where Quirt Evans lay.

She stopped, checked his pockets and removed several items; then pulled his gun belt from him, picked up his revolvers and walked toward Tom. He was sitting on the tongue of a nearby wagon trying to stop the bleeding on his side. He unbuttoned his shirt and held his bandana firmly against the flesh wound. She looked at the blood on his hand and bandana and asked, "Do you have a bullet in you?"

Tom said, "No, it's just a deep flesh wound."

She took his arm and said, "Come with me. I'll take care of it."

She led down the street toward the edge of town. She did not speak or walk fast. They came to the largest house on the street; she opened the door and motioned for him to enter. She worked fast and soon had the wound cleaned and bandaged. Tom said, "Thanks, I'll pay you for your help if you don't mind."

"I don't need your money. You killed Quirt, that's all the pay I want."

"Why do you say that?" Tom asked.

"He lied and cheated all the time. He planned to kill me and steal my money. He was no good."

Tom inquired, "I don't know your name?"

"I'm Silvia. Now I can go home to Portugal."

She told of her attempts to leave Quirt and go back to Portugal. Quirt always had someone watching her. Tom thanked her for the help, wished her luck and left to take care of Cisco's body.

With a sad heart, Tom rode north leading Cisco's horse with him tied in the saddle. Cisco would be buried north of the Rio Grande. He'd have to face justice, but not on this earth.

Tom decided to take Cisco to Tubby's place to bury him. On the way he purchased items that Tubby had requested Cisco bring him. It had been a long night and day, Tom was tired, and the horses had just about reached heir endurance. When Tom dismounted, Tubby came out of the dugout and said, "I guess that is Cisco you have there on the saddle? I didn't expect to see you or him again. What happened?"

"We had a little set-to with Quirt and his gang. They lost and so did Cisco. He accounted for a high share of the bodies before he cashed in."

"I notice you are not walking so spry? You get gut shot?"

"No, just a flesh wound; still sore but healing." Tom replied.

Tubby helped bury Cisco and invited Tom to eat supper with him. It was surprising good. Tom asked, "Tubby the stew is very good; you didn't have time to use the salt and pepper I brought, where did you get the seasonings?"

Tubby replied, "One of the women brought things to eat with her. She is a good cook."

After finishing the meal, Tom walked out in the yard and Tubby followed; Tom turned and said, "I can agree to that. Thank you for helping with Cisco, I know he considered you a friend. He died fighting evil."

"He's buried here and I will join him some day. Thanks for bringing him; I know he would want to be here." Tubby replied.

Tom said, "I see that my horses have been moved to better grass. They need rest and grass; if you do not mind I will spread my roll in the barn. I too need rest."

Tubby laughed and replied, "Suit yourself, but one of the girls would be happy to put you to sleep."

"Thanks, Tubby but I want to leave early in the morning and I do need some sleep."

Early the next morning Tubby and one of the girls came out to the barn just as Tom was putting the saddle on his horse. They brought hot coffee, bread, fried eggs and ham.

While eating Tom said to Tubby, "I'm leaving Cisco's horse and gear for you. I know you will take good care of the horse."

"I'll keep the horse for own. He will be well treated." Tubby replied.

Tom thanked him and then set out for Bat Cave. Jake's letter indicated that he departed from the cave on his way to Tincup. According to the clues, Jake hid the gold near some odd shaped cactuses. He was still alive when he reached Tincup, so it would be reasonable to assume the gold must be somewhere between Bat Cave and Tincup. When Tom got to Bat Cave, he took time to rest his horse and study the ground out to the horizon; it was almost flat and desert like. Tom guessed that Jake was well acquainted with the desert and knew how to survive its perils. Seriously hurt and weak he would have taken the most direct route to Tincup hoping to find help for his wounds.

Tom rode out toward Tincup late that afternoon; taking what he considered the most direct route. Tom was sure Jake had also took what he thought was the most direct route to Tincup. Tom was determined to find the gold on this trip; he did not want to come back to the desert for another search.

He purposely kept a slow pace and scanned the desert on all sides looking for Jake's clues. He spent that night in the desert. Early the next morning he looked off to his left and saw a clump of cactuses. He saddled his horse and led him toward the cactuses; the closer he got to the clump, the higher his spirits soared. Could this be the answer to Jake's plea for forgiveness?

The description of the cactuses was almost exactly like the fictitious cactuses Jake wrote about in his letter. Tom stopped and removed Jake's letter from his saddlebag. He read once more what Jake had written: '*He wanted me to wait in his cave. My wounds will kill me. I wanted you to know.* There was a little more about his remorse and then he asked, *Tommy you remember the guessing games we played; one of us would say we hid something worth a lot of money, and then give some clues where it's hid. Do you remember you once said it was hid near large twin cactus which twisted together at the top? You said it was southwest of our place . . . I was dumb and went to find it. I never found anything I walked all way to the cave we played in and it was not there. I hope you remember, it important to not forget such things.*'

He placed the letter back in his saddlebag and urged his horse toward the clump of cactuses. He had mixed feelings when he dismounted and walked toward the cactuses. It took just a few minutes to uncover the blanket and saddlebag with the gold coins. Tom asked no one in particular, "Jake why in hell did you have to turn bad in the first place. This gold will not absolve your crimes. Now it's between you and the Lord."

Tom shook his head to clear his thoughts, placed the gold on his horse, and rode toward Abilene, as there was no longer a reason to pass through Tincup.

EPILOGUE

Ten-year-old Susan sat down on the porch swing near her father. She asked, "Daddy why can't I go see Aunt Tess in California? I'd like to see something more than corrals and cattle."

Her father replied, "Susie, that's a long way out there. You'd have to go by stage some of the way. You know it's a far piece out there; and much too rough and dangerous for you to travel alone. If your mother was here she'd tell you the same thing."

"Was my mother pretty?" Susan inquired.

"Susie I'll told you many times that she was the prettiest and happiest mother any child could imagine. She'd be very happy to know that you are just like her; she called you her beautiful darling."

Susan made a sad face and said, "It's my fault she died. I hate it that I was born." Tears streamed down her cheeks.

Tom Leach drew his daughter to his chest and said, "Susie don't talk like that. Your mother was proud of you. We've been over this before and I tell you again my lovely daughter; your coming into this world had nothing whatever to do with your mother leaving us."

Susan tried to brush her tears away, "Aunt Tess said Momma never recovered from my birth. I don't know who to believe."

"Your Aunt Tess often says things she does not believe herself. Now I want you to quit blaming yourself; your mother died from a heart condition, there's no treatment yet for such an ailment. It happened months after you were born. She loved you something furious. That's better, dry your eyes. After round up we'll go to

California and see Aunt Tess and she'll now tell you what I am saying is right." He hugged his daughter and left the porch.

Tom Leach went to the corral and saddled his favorite palomino and as he mounted, he could feel the pain from his old battle wounds. Those pains were the least of his concern these days. He rode to the top of the hill and stopped under a large majestic tree; he dismounted and stood at the foot of Blanche's grave; He said, "Sweetheart, our daughter is just like you, she speaks of you often. I'll take her to visit Aunt Tess after round up. She is growing up fast. She is beautiful and looks just like you. My darling, you will always be close to our hearts."

He stayed a few minutes more trying to regain his emotion, then mounted and rode to the crest of a nearby hill. His thoughts continued to dwell on Blanche and the long ago events that still burned in his mind.

He could see the valley below; the ranch house, barns, corrals and cattle grazing on the green grass. His mind flashed back to his ride out of the desert with the government's gold and the events that brought him to this hill. All that seemed light years in the past, but a turning point in his life; one he had never regretted. The hard blow came when he learned that Blanche had an irregular heart condition; Susan was thirteen months old, a happy beautiful baby that Blanche spent all her energy, which was declining everyday, to care for baby Susan. Tom's mind often revisited those early years with mixed feelings.

When he rode in to Abilene, carrying the government's gold he soon learned that Blair had recovered Helen Parks' tin box with her valuables. That Helen and Sissy were still staying with Blanche and Tess. Then a bombshell; the biggest surprise was the pending resignation of Marshal Andrew Decker. Somehow Tom got the idea that Marshal Decker was the U. S. Marshals Service. Tom showed his surprise and asked why.

He said, "My life has been on hold all these years, now I intend to spend the rest of my days raising a family and caring for others."

Marshal Decker went on to say that the Texas Rangers are ready to take the lead in quelling lawlessness in the state. The new governor of Texas signed a proclamation giving the Texas Rangers wide latitude to rid the state of rustlers, killers and outlaw gangs. He also announced that every county in the state would be encouraged to elect a sheriff whose independence would be a continuing force to establish and maintain law and order throughout the state. Decker said that the role of the U. S. Marshal Service in Texas would now be shifted to the western frontier all the way to the Pacific Ocean. He had recommended that Tom replace him in charge of the western district.

Tom had asked, "Did you get my letter of resignation."

Marshal Decker smiled, "It would be unthinkable for me to learn that one of our best Marshals violated International Boundaries without authority; I'd be sad and hard put to read such a thing. You are appreciated and still on the rolls." He smiled and winked.

Tom said, "I'm obliged for your sentiments, but my resignation is final. Like you, I intend to pursue a new life. Hopefully it will be with Blanche Longmire if she hasn't changed her mind. Tell me what pushed you to find a new trail?"

"Well, I guess you need to know; Helen Parks has agreed to consider my proposal but asked for a year or so to find her way without the man she loved so much. She is honest in sharing her feelings and I understand exactly what she is going through. Sissy is on my side and encourages her mother to marry me. I couldn't have a better advocate for my side; she's a wonderful child."

Tom asked, "Is Sissy in school yet?"

"Yes, Blanche has one of the ranch hands bring her to school each day. Rain or shine, she sends the buggy every morning, and then again in the afternoon to bring Sissy back to the Ranch. Helen is quite happy out there; so I'll wait as long as she needs to make up her mind. She talks about going back to their farm and ranch; rebuilding the house and starting a herd of cattle. Sissy is not sure she wants to return to their home destroyed by the outlaws; then sometimes she says she can hardly wait to get there, so many things she wants to do. It's great being able to change your mind without any consequences; I suppose we did the same when we were young." Marshal Decker laughed as if he had hit on a funny joke.

Tom asked, "Where is Blair? I'll like to talk with him."

Decker replied, "I sent him with a prisoner to Fort Worth, he should be back in a day or so. He tells me he will also resign and head west with Tess. They'll be married next month. Tom, things are changing out here; it's a new life for all of us."

The following month Tom learned that Tim McCall had joined the Texas Rangers and that Steve Sutton had announced for sheriff and with no competition he would be elected that month. Clay Longmire's killer and other members of Quirt Evans' gang, held in Tincup and Abilene, all walked up the thirteen steps to the waiting nooses. Oddly, there was no coordination between the separate trials or dates set for hanging, but all happened on the same Friday at high noon.

Then after less than a year of wedded bliss, he received the happy news that Blanche was with child; those were the happiest days of their lives. The ranch was prospering and lawlessness in the area had disappeared, but then later Blanche steadily became weaker and could not do all the things she wanted to do. Tom spent all his time with her.

Then at the end, she woke him up on that last night and asked, "Darling will you promise me something?"

He remembered his reply, "Blanche go back to sleep, you know that I'll do anything you ask me to do. You need your rest."

She'd said, "I'm not sure you will that's why you have to make me a promise."

"Tell me what's on your mind, you know I love you."

"I have no doubt about your love; that's really the problem. I want you to promise me that when I'm gone you will not waste your life away. You promise me here and now that you will find a lovable, honest girl to help raise our daughter. I want her to have a mother; not go through what I did."

He had said, "Blanche that's a terrible thing to say, you going to be here a long time, perhaps even longer than my time; we never know what the next day will bring."

She replied, "What you just said makes my concern for Susan's future even more important. I want your promise Tom. You know that Tess and I never knew much about our mother as she died when we were so young. That must not happen to Susan; she'll need a mother. Promise me now."

Tom had thought about trying once again to evade her persistent urging a promise that he did not want to make. He hesitated and then said, "Blanche I'll do what you asked, God knows it would be against everything I hold dear. One other thing I'll promise, you'll never leave me as long as I live."

She had simply said, "I'll rest now. I have your promise."

That was long ago. He walked to his horse, mounted and looked out over the valley again; he could feel Blanche everywhere he went. He rode down the slope toward the ranch house. He whispered to Blanche, "I know this is weak, but I have found no one that Susan and I could love, you're still with us. Susan is doing real good and will be a beautiful young lady just like you. Don't think harshly of me, I just have not kept that promise yet." He rode on trying to shift his mind back to the present. Susan's future meant everything to him; he would dedicate his life to her and his memory of Blanche.